Praise for Katerina Di

'Diamond is the master of gripping literature'
Evening Standard

'All hail the new Queen of Crime!'   *Heat*

'A web of a plot that twists and turns and keeps
the reader on their seat . . . don't read it before
bed if you're easily spooked!'   *Sun*

'A page-turner with a keep-you-guessing plot'
Sunday Times Crime Club

'Packed with twists until the last page'
Closer

Also by Katerina Diamond

KATERINA DIAMOND burst onto the crime scene with her debut *The Teacher*, which became a *Sunday Times* bestseller and a number one Kindle bestseller. It was longlisted for the CWA John Creasey Debut Dagger Award and the Hotel Chocolat Award for 'darkest moment'. *The Teacher* was followed by sequels *The Secret*, *The Angel*, *The Promise*, *Truth or Die*, *Woman in the Water* and *Trick or* Treat, which featured detectives Adrian Miles and Imogen Grey. *The Heatwave* was her first standalone thriller and became a *Sunday Times* bestseller. *The Silence* is her second standalone thriller.

Katerina has lived in various glamorous locations such as Weston-Super-Mare, Thessaloniki, Larnaca, Exeter, Derby and Forest Gate. Katerina now resides in East Kent with her husband and children. She was born on Friday 13th.

Katerina Diamond

THE Silence

avon.

Published by AVON
A division of HarperCollins*Publishers*
1 London Bridge Street
London SE1 9GF

www.harpercollins.co.uk

HarperCollins*Publishers*
Macken House
39/40 Mayor Street Upper
Dublin 1
D01 C9W8
Ireland

A Paperback Original 2023

1

First published in Great Britain by HarperCollins*Publishers* 2023

ISBN: 978-0-00-836182-2

Typeset in Sabon LT Std by Palimpsest Book Production Limited,
Falkirk, Stirlingshire

Printed and Bound in the UK using
100% Renewable Electricity at CPI Group (UK) Ltd

For Nikki – who emotionally blackmailed me into dedicating this book to her.

Part One

Chapter 1

June 11th – Three years ago

Within twenty minutes of walking through the front door, I am showered and sitting in pyjamas on my sofa, hair knotted in a towel on my head, my work uniform in the washing machine already and a cup of tea warming my hands. I switch on the television and leave it on, settling in to watch the second half of a film I have seen before, knowing I will probably fall asleep here. Exhausted and more than aware that there are less than ten hours until I have to be back at work, I drift in and out of sleep, the period drama making less sense as I nod off through chunks of it. At one point I wonder why one of the aristocracy is holding a machine gun but then realise I have missed the end and am now watching a late-night Steven Seagal movie. The kind they only show at two in the morning. I turn the volume down on the TV as a threat emerges that it will switch itself off in five minutes unless I press a button. With only just enough energy to reach behind me, I pull the sherpa blanket I have folded over the back of the sofa onto me, my limbs too heavy to move, too tired to go to bed.

When I open my eyes, the light in the room is strange, moving somehow. The television is off, so it isn't that. Another night terror maybe? It has been a while, but this feels different. I feel awake but somehow blind. I'm unable to move, the heaviness I felt in my legs earlier amplified tenfold. No matter how hard I try to lift my legs there is no movement; they feel as if they are nailed down. Although the shadows keep moving, I still can't see anything. It dawns on me that there is something on my face, around my head. As I breathe, a perfumed fabric clings to my mouth each time I suck in air. I try to reach up and remove whatever is on my face, but my hands don't belong to me, I have no agency over them, they just lie on the ground. I don't know how I got down here. The tips of my fingers are cold, icy, I want to ball them into a fist to warm them but as much as I try, I fail. The reality of my situation becomes apparent as I feel the elastic of my pyjama bottoms pulling on my ankles. I feel at peace, an artificial calm. Somewhere in the back of my mind I am screaming but it's so far away that I can't access it. I have been drugged. My mind feels like a hall of mirrors, everything distorted and shining back at me as I barely recognise my own reflection. Words like 'intruder' and 'trespass' amble through my mind with no urgency. I realise with a dull clarity that I am not alone as I hear the sound of breathing close to my head, too warm to be my imagination. He kisses me through whatever is on my face, that sweet-scented fabric. I feel his hot sour breath go into my mouth, snaking its way inside me. His words echo and rattle inside my mind. I know them, but I can't remember what they mean. Lying like a poseable doll, I hear the crinkle of a plastic sheet beneath me as he moves my legs into an arrangement that makes things easier for him to do what he came here for. The only warmth I can feel is the one ankle that my pyjama bottoms cling to, and his naked body as he climbs into position. *Please, not again.*

Chapter 2

DS Shona White ate her third KitKat of the day before ten in the morning, making a promise to herself to eat something green and leafy at dinner time and not just order from the takeout app. This was a promise she made almost every day and a promise she was often unable to keep. That sugar hit was the only thing that kept her awake on slow days like this. The mounting pile of overdue paperwork on her desk wasn't going to complete itself. She stared at her phone, willing it to ring, hoping for a last-minute reprieve from the day of form-filling and report-filing she had in front of her. Leaving things until the eleventh hour was something Shona excelled at – if only it were a useful skill. The shiny black surface of the phone remained unchanged. It just sat there, doing nothing.

She sucked in a breath before pulling a folder from the top of the pile that she had perched in the only corner of her work surface without anything on it, slightly hanging over the edge. One good knock of the desk and it would be all over the floor. The air conditioning in the station hadn't worked for several weeks, she remembered as she inhaled the stifling smell of stale coffee and the lingering odour of tobacco on the smokers' coats. To top it all off, she wished she hadn't worn woollen trousers, but they were the only clean thing left. Tiny needles from the fabric pricked at the sweaty skin on her thighs and at the base of her spine. At lunch she would venture into town and buy something a little less itchy and tonight she would put a wash on. Every new year her resolution was to get her shit together and every year she failed before February. Maybe it was time to accept this was who she was. It was June now and she was well and truly back in the throes of her bad habits.

'Busy then?' DS Aaron Langford came and perched on the desk opposite her, watching her stuff the last of the KitKat into her mouth. The expectant look on his face jogged her memory. No lunchtime shopping trip for her, she had a prior engagement.

'I'll still be hungry at lunchtime. Where you taking me?' she said after she remembered he had woken her up this morning with a bunch of lilies and a box of chocolates to celebrate their one-year anniversary.

'I can't tell you. That would ruin the surprise,' he said with a smile. Oh, that smile, those perfect teeth.

Everything about Aaron was well thought out and tidy, unlike herself. She could only imagine he was drawn to the chaos, because things were good between them, more than good. He was her forever man, the best man she had ever met. He was always joking with her that she was out of his league but if anything, the opposite was true. She had been waiting for a year for him to realise the same, but he never seemed to. In fact, she had already seen the red velvet box with the engagement ring in it. He was going to propose, and she would be lying if she said she knew what she was going to say when he asked. There was a wall between them and she knew it was her doing, trying to keep a part of herself separate, self-preservation or self-sabotage, she didn't know which.

'I missed you,' she said. Their shifts hadn't lined up for a few days now and she really had missed him, although he could clearly see straight through her.

'You're not getting it out of me that way.' He smiled.

'I hate surprises, just tell me where you're taking me.'

'There's a new restaurant on the marina, Darcy's. It has a glass floor and overhangs the sea, have you seen it?'

'You know I'm afraid of heights though, right?'

'It's about five inches off the water at high tide. . . You can swim, can't you?'

'How on earth did you get a reservation?'

'My sister knows someone who knows someone,'

he said, leaning over the piles of papers and stealing a kiss while no one was looking. 'Our table is at one.'

'Blimey. I'm surprised Anna lowered herself enough to do you a favour.'

'I can be very persuasive. I've got to dash now, DI Post needs me to check out some surveillance tapes or something,' he said, flashing those pearly whites before leaving her staring at the pile of brown folders again.

'Shona?' Gavin, the duty sergeant, called to her. She got up.

'What's up?' Shona said, eager for an excuse to get away from the dreaded admin.

'There's a lady out front who wants to speak to a female officer. She looks pretty shaken up. Are you busy?'

She didn't need telling twice. An escape. She threw the folder she had barely been holding for ten seconds back onto the precarious pile, watching tensely as it slid across the surface, hoping it would stop before it slid off completely onto the floor. Shona walked through the security doors to see a young woman with wet hair and skin so pale she barely looked human.

'Miss? You wanted to speak to someone?' Shona said softly, the haunted look on the woman's face informing her to tread carefully. Shona had seen that look before, almost hollowed out, both empty and scared at the same time.

'I've been attacked,' the woman said, her voice barely audible.

'Come through, let's get you a cup of tea. What's your name?'

Shona took the woman through to the interrogation room and pulled out the chair for her. Under the bright strip light, her polished skin reminded Shona of a glass of milk after the milk had been drunk, colour barely clinging to it. The woman's fingers were delicate and frail, everything about her looked fragile. There was an overwhelming smell of bleach coming from her.

'I'm Gail, Gail Reynolds.'

'I'm DS Shona White. How do you like your tea?'

'White, no sugar, thanks.'

Shona went to the vending machine in the hall and got a tea. She looked around the room for someone more senior to observe her interrogation. On one side of the room DI Graham Post was showing the pretty new DC how the filing system worked and Shona decided she'd rather not deal with him right now. Instead she gestured across the room to her colleague DI Nicola Coleridge and pointed to the interrogation room and then the observation room next door. Shona liked to have a more experienced observer when it came to complex witness statements. She still didn't completely trust her instincts and was trying to impress her superiors into choosing her for more complex assignments. DI Coleridge walked over. Her hair was a crisp blonde bob, never out of place, her suit always pressed to perfection and tailored to her frame.

'What have you got?'

'Woman says she's been attacked. I'm thinking sexual assault. Would you observe?'

'Go on then. Does she have a name?' DI Coleridge said.

'Gail Reynolds,' Shona said.

'OK. You sure you don't want me to sit in?'

'Only if you think I can't handle this.'

'You'll do great. Just be yourself, you're a natural,' Coleridge said before walking into obs. Shona took a deep breath before re-entering the interrogation room.

Back in the interrogation room, the woman was hunched forward, biting her nails and staring into the distance. Shona knew what kind of attack this had been without asking. She put the tea on the table in front of her. Shona felt bad that she couldn't take her to a less intimidating room. The strip light flickered once every few minutes, which was surprisingly hard on the nerves.

'Sorry about the light in here, try to ignore it if you can. There was a flood in our other room and it smells terrible. Trust me, this is the lesser of two evils. Why don't you tell me what happened, Gail?'

Shona watched as Gail took a few shallow breaths, her eyes fixed on the floor. Finally, she looked up.

'I got home from work yesterday and had a shower and fell asleep in front of the TV. I woke up with

11

something over my face, some sort of cloth, a pillow-case maybe. I think it was taped around my neck, not tight, but I wanted to shake it off. I was on some kind of plastic sheet on the floor, my PJs were gone. There was someone with me. I couldn't really move. Like, I could feel things but I couldn't move, does that make sense? After he had finished, he made me shower with bleach, I felt sick and my eyes stung but he made me put it everywhere. He told me to keep my eyes closed or he would stick a knife in them. I believed him. I felt the knife against my skin.'

'Do you live alone?'

'I do.'

'Where do you live?'

'Blossom Hill. Like the wine.'

'I need you to be specific about what he actually did.'

'He raped me. More than once.'

'Did you recognise his voice? You say he spoke to you.'

Gail paused for a moment, picking at the skin around her fingernails. 'No, I didn't.'

'Where do you work?'

'Dawson's chip shop.'

'Did you walk home alone?' Shona hated these questions, the ones that felt accusatory, as though the victim could somehow be complicit in the crime just by doing completely normal things that people should be able to do without fear of being attacked.

'Yes, but it's not that far and it's mostly main road. I do it all the time.'

'What time did you finish work?'

'Eleven.'

'So, Gail, do you think someone followed you?'

'No. Possibly. I don't know. The attack happened a while after I got home.'

'How did he get in, do you know?'

'Maybe through the kitchen window, I might have left it open – the latch is a bit sticky and it's warm at the moment.'

'We will get a forensic team around to check your house.'

'He took everything: the plastic sheet, my pyjamas, whatever was on my head. He even took the towel he let me use to dry myself.'

'Well, he might have missed something. We will also take you to get a rape kit done. Do you know if he used protection?'

'I think so. I don't know. I can't be sure. I couldn't see anything until he cut the tape around my neck and forced me to get into the shower.'

'You didn't look at him then?'

'I was too scared to open my eyes,' Gail said, closing her eyes tight as though she was back there again.

'Do you think you were altered? Had you had a drink of anything?'

'What do you mean altered?'

'Like, do you think you had been drugged?'

'Yes, I do. I felt sick and dizzy and was paralysed. He paralysed me with something, is that what you mean?'

'Oh I'm sorry, I misunderstood, I thought you meant that you were unable to move because of what was happening. Fight or flight. He administered a drug to you that made you unable to move?'

'Yes,' Gail Reynolds said, visibly annoyed.

'And did you have anything alcoholic to drink when you got home? Or take any drugs.'

'No, I had a cup of tea. I don't usually drink alone. What are you implying?'

'Sorry. I have to ask that's all. Are you on any prescription medication at the moment?'

'Nothing. I don't even take paracetamol when I have a headache.'

'But then he made you shower? How did you shower if you couldn't move?'

'It wore off after a while, I guess. I don't know. I know I couldn't move then a while later I could. Is that possible? There must be a drug that does that?'

'We can get a doctor to do a toxicology report and see if there is any trace left in your system.'

'You can do that? I feel fine now though, maybe it's all gone.'

There was a tap on the door.

'Excuse me,' Shona said.

Outside the room DI Coleridge was holding a file. She handed it to Shona.

'What's this?'

'Looks like your girl has made a false report before.'

'I really don't think she's making this up,' Shona said.

'She accused a man she was at college with of sexual assault, but all evidence pointed to buyer's remorse. Including witness reports and flirty texts from her to the man she accused after the alleged attack. It's all in there.'

'Wow. "Buyer's remorse", that's a horrible expression in this context.'

'Well, you know what I mean.'

'This seems like a completely different situation to that one though,' Shona said as she thumbed through the file.

'Well, maybe that didn't get her enough attention so she's trying something new. You have to ask her about it. At least let her know that we know. If you're not up to it, I can come in. She's already made excuses for why we wouldn't find any forensic evidence at her house or on her body, a little too convenient, if you ask me. Plus, she was drugged so she couldn't move but then she took a shower, I'm not buying it.'

'What could she possibly have to gain from doing this though?'

'It may not make sense to us, but some people like this kind of attention. You also have to ask yourself what we have to gain by spending time and resources on a claim made by someone with her history. This is just going to get stuck in our unsolved pile and our stats are in the toilet.'

Shona knew the department was already under scrutiny for the volume of unsolved crimes and rising drug-related violence in the town thanks to the use of teenagers in moving the drugs around. Teenagers with less impulse control, all desperate to be in some kind of gang, feel some sense of belonging. With poverty on the rise, these kids were all an easy target for the dealers who recruited them, used them up and then threw them away.

'Can't we get the hospital to do a toxicology report at least? She thinks she was drugged.'

'Drugs might well show up in her system, that doesn't mean she didn't take them herself. We know from her file that she has taken banned substances before.'

'A little pot at a party. . . really?'

'I can take this case over if you want, DS White. I'll make a note in your file that you felt unable to continue.'

Shona didn't miss the pointed tone in DI Coleridge's voice. Rumours about Shona making accusations against a senior officer had been floating around the office for months now. Of course, no one really knew what had happened between her and Graham Post, what he had done to her. Coleridge was insinuating that Shona was taking this personally, which she wasn't. Shona had heard all kinds of things whispered about her in the corridors, including that she wasn't up to being police. She had never even made an official report about his conduct because she knew it would be more damaging for her than him, but she had confided in one of the other officers on her training course about the assault. You couldn't trust anyone.

'I can't just tell her we aren't going to investigate,' Shona said, choosing her own comfort over rocking the proverbial boat in her station house. She felt the twinge of self-loathing as she accepted that she was going to do what she was told.

'That is absolutely not what I am suggesting. I'm suggesting you try and ascertain whether this is a false report or not. The woman has form. My guess is it won't take long for her to drop the whole thing once she knows we are onto her. Now are you going to talk to her, or do you want me to?'

'I'll do it,' Shona said, knowing what was being asked of her. She didn't want to be a DS forever and so she had to take her superior's advice.

'I'll send a uniform in with you in case it gets ugly,' DI Coleridge said before sashaying back across the room to her desk and picking up the phone.

Shona walked back into the interrogation room, dreading this next conversation. Seconds later, PC David Jenkins was in the room, standing by the door.

Shona put the file on the table.

'What's that?' Gail said defensively.

'Gail. What can you tell me about Stuart Potts?' Shona asked, hating herself for asking the question.

Gail Reynolds' face immediately hardened and she folded her arms. Shona pulled out a chair, but Gail turned away from her ever so slightly. She was trying to look stoic, but Shona could see her jaw clench and unclench, her eyes darting from side to side, anger building inside her. Was she annoyed she had been found out? Any rapport or trust that Shona thought they had built up was now gone. Who could blame her? Shona immediately felt like shit for suggesting she was making it up. Even though she hadn't said it they both knew that's what mentioning this previous report implied. She was calling the victim's character into question, there weren't many other crimes where you could get away with that. Still, she couldn't ignore the previous report either. She was stuck between a rock and a hard place. Shona didn't like feeling like the bad guy. Was this the kind of officer she wanted to be? Hard and cold like Coleridge? The fact remained that Shona felt like she had a lot of making up to do to regain her credibility after the rumours of her being a troublemaker. *Just toe the line for a little longer.*

Chapter 3

I clench my fists at the mention of Stuart Potts'
name. I haven't heard it said aloud in a few years
and it jars as much as it always did. Someone I had
once trusted, someone who violated that trust.
Someone who wouldn't take no for an answer. For
the most part I manage to avoid thinking about him.
Occasionally when I am walking along the seafront,
I will hear a voice on the wind that sets my teeth
on edge, and my eyes scour the beach until I see
who it has come from, satisfying myself that it's just
my mind playing tricks on me again. He lied and
lied and lied about what happened between us. He
convinced everyone that I had misunderstood the
situation, that I had consented, that I was untrust-
worthy. For this policewoman to mention him here
and now makes me realise exactly where this is
going. Nowhere.

'I know what that file says and that's not true. He did rape me. I literally had finger marks on my neck where he tried to choke me.'

'That was not the conclusion the police came to at the time of that attack.'

'And the police are always right? I thought there was some kind of protocol about believing the victim? He told them it was rough sex, that I was into it, that I had asked him to choke me. You lot made me feel like shit, like you didn't believe a word I said,' I say, the vibration of rage breaking through the fear in my voice.

'We need evidence, not just belief. Look, what you are saying about tonight sounds truly horrific. I can send the forensic techs round, we can go to the hospital and do a full examination, take any photos of you or your flat. We can do all that if you want. The problem then is what happens next. What if we find no evidence? Which, from what you've told me, we're unlikely to. What happens then? If you make this report now and no evidence comes back, they are going to find this file and you may get prosecuted for wasting police time. Or worse. Are you sure this is what you want?'

This can't be happening. Did you know this would happen? Did you know about Stuart? Or maybe not him specifically but just that there was something in my eyes that only you can see, you and people like you.

Since Stuart I have always felt I was given a special kind of superpower, a connection between us, all of us, the ones who exist on this other plane. The plane where no one else can go. Predators and victims with a special ability to sniff each other out. Is that what happened? Did you sniff me out?

'*They* are going to prosecute me? Do you mean you?' I say. I can't believe what I am hearing. I feel like I am being threatened, being silenced all over again.

'I don't know the exact circumstances of what happened before, but I know that this is going to be very hard to prove. Are you sure you want to put yourself through that?' DS White said.

'Stuart was my friend, I would go to his house and we would watch movies together. He got the wrong idea about us and then things happened that I didn't want to happen. I tried to push him off me but he kept telling me that he knew what I wanted, that he knew why I kept hanging round with him. He was gaslighting me *while* it was happening, telling me I had wanted it all along. But I still said no, again and again but he didn't listen, my voice didn't matter. He put his hand over my mouth and didn't stop until he was done. Whether he actually convinced himself that he was right I don't know but I can tell you this one thing: I didn't consent, not once, I repeatedly and emphatically said no. But even my friends told the police that I would flirt with him, that I led him

21

on. I was just being friendly, nice. . . I thought we were friends. There wasn't enough to move forward with a charge and so the case was dropped. I left and moved here to get away from everyone who looked at me like I was lying. And now this has happened. This is a nightmare.'

The things they said about me, people I knew, friends, family even. All happier to accept the fact that I was lying, that I had misunderstood the situation, that I had given him the come-on. The whispers and sideways glances pushed me to the edge. You know all about that though, don't you? You probably knew I wouldn't make a fuss, or maybe you just knew they wouldn't believe me? People don't, do they?

For the months following Stuart's attack I doubted myself. I replayed that night over and over in my mind wondering if they were right about me, had I made a mistake? Was it even really rape? But then I remember his hand over my mouth as I protested. He knew I didn't want it. He knew what he was doing was wrong. You must know, too. Reporting the crime at the time had been almost as traumatic as the crime itself, or at least an extension of the trauma, all balled up together as one complete nightmare I can't bear to go through again. At least this time I can spare myself the indignation of an examination.

'Look, let's just take a breath. I believe you. But you have to think about how this is going to come across to a jury, if we even make it that far. There are no guarantees,' DS White said.

'I don't think you do believe me. I don't think any woman would encourage another woman she believed had been raped to just keep her mouth shut. What kind of shit is this?' I say, my breath getting shorter as I realise the futility of my situation. I was stupid to have come here, stupid to think anything different would happen. I've made myself vulnerable all over again by allowing them to judge me.

'Don't get upset, Gail.'

'I'm not upset, I'm fucking livid! After what just happened to me do you think it was easy coming here? Do you not think it took every fibre of my being to step out of my house and walk here to talk to you? Do you not think recounting the events was hard? Do you think I did this just for fun? Like I get some kind of kick out of people thinking I've been raped, or thinking I'm lying!'

'Sit down please, Ms Reynolds,' DS White said.

I haven't even noticed that I am standing, leaning over the table and shouting in the detective's face. The uniformed officer by the door steps forward and looks poised to lunge. The idea that I am somehow a threat is laughable. I'm barely even five foot one. Is that why you chose me? Did you think I would be easy to subdue? Easy to control? Makes sense, I suppose, to pick off the weaker ones.

'This is fucking ridiculous!' I say, slamming my hands on the table.

'Please. Just calm down,' DS White says with her hand held up as though she's instructing a dog. Is the gesture meant for me or the PC? The uniformed officer moves even nearer.

'Don't come any fucking closer,' I say, kicking the chair out behind me. The officer steps forward again and then I am not sure what happens. The rage that has been steadily building inside me is all-consuming, violent energy pulsating through every vein. I fly forwards and start to hit him. Maybe I'm pretending he is you, maybe he is you. I wouldn't know, would I? The various plastic and metal police trinkets hanging from him catch my skin. I feel the blister from the burn I got at work the day before split open but it doesn't stop me. My hands become slippery, bloody. In my mind I am telling myself to stop and take a breath, but there is another part of me that feels wild with fury, and that's that part that's in control right now. It's no use, some primal part of me has taken over. The part that isn't going to stand for any more shit. You have awoken something in me, an emotion I don't recognise. Pure unadulterated rage.

The next thing I know, I am in a holding cell banging on the door and screaming obscenities. I don't even remember getting from one place to another. How the hell has this happened? Dried blood cakes my fingertips and knuckles, trailing down my forearm in smudges. The last twelve hours have been an unimaginable nightmare. I can't remember how I felt yesterday, I can't even remember who I was. I think about the last time this happened and how it took me so long to get over it. Not even over it but away from it, distanced, by both time and proximity. That attack is a deep dark secret I keep locked inside of me, unwilling to go through the scrutiny again. Even the people I love the most asked me if I was 'sure' about what he had done. Would they say the same this time? Maybe they would say this is just something I do to get attention. Or maybe they would believe that it had happened but somehow still find a way to say I invited you into my house to do those things to me. I just can't put myself through all of that again. Self-preservation dictates I take control now or lose it forever.

Bury it. Forget it. You've done it before, you can do it again.

I moved from London down to Eastport and restarted my life after Stuart. I felt completely abandoned by everyone at the time, knowing full well they were all judging me, taking sides in their minds, wondering if they had picked the right side. I can't do all of that again. I refuse to go through the upheaval of changing my life completely. I won't let you drive me from my home. I have to fight back, for myself, for all the others like me. I won't just be erased again. Not this time.

Chapter 4

Shona was staring at Gail Reynolds' file and wondering if she had done the right thing. She knew that she hadn't, she knew she was in the wrong. She was ashamed that she had followed Coleridge's advice and basically told a potential rape victim that no one would believe her. She wasn't sure she could feel much lower.

'Why the long face?' Aaron appeared.

'We just had a walk-in, a bad one. Coleridge has put the pressure on a bit for me to get rid.'

'You want a rain check on lunch?'

'Oh, I completely forgot. I'm sorry. I don't think I should leave before I've sorted it.'

'It's OK. We can go anytime. I understand if you need to stay.'

'What did I do to deserve you?'

'Right place right time, I guess.' He beamed before leaning in for a kiss.

'Give me half an hour and I'll be ready. Will they hold our reservation? If they don't I'll make it up to you tonight.' She smiled. She was a half-decent cook when she made an effort, and he seemed to love her speciality poppyseed chicken dish – or maybe he was just being polite, she wasn't entirely sure. Sometimes she thought he was just too good to be true. If she couldn't make things work with Aaron there was no hope for her.

'Promises, promises. I'll wait for you in the car.'

She waited for him to leave before going to visit Gail Reynolds again, hoping she had calmed down although she had every right to be angry. The sad fact of the matter was that Coleridge was probably right; with no physical evidence and with the previously reported rape that went nowhere, it was really unlikely that anything would come of this. Maybe Shona was doing Gail a favour by sparing her the humiliation of going through it all again.

When Shona opened the cell door, Gail looked as despondent as she had when she first arrived. All the fire and fight had gone out of her. Maybe that was a good thing.

'Have you decided what you want to do?' Shona asked.

Gail Reynolds smiled, resigned. She looked up, straight into Shona's eyes. 'I just want to go home.'

Shona didn't think she would ever forget that look

– hatred, disappointment at the crushing inevitability of how this was going to turn out. They hadn't believed her before and they didn't believe her this time. Except Shona did believe her. So why was she content to just let her go? The answer was simple: selfishness. Shona didn't want to be associated with a rape case, she knew what the people at the station would say. That this was personal, that she was a man-hater, that she was a one-trick pony only interested in pursuing a certain kind of case. They just seemed to find her, or maybe she found them, she wasn't sure, but the fact was most of her cases had some element of sexual assault involved. Her actions were being directly affected yet again by what had happened between her and DI Post. She was too much of a coward to admit it to herself and so here she was – sacrificing this poor woman just so that she didn't have to deal with her own demons.

'You can go.'

Chapter 5

I can feel those imaginary eyes on me as I walk back up Blossom Hill towards the front door of my house and I wonder if I will ever be free of them now. Maybe they were never imaginary, maybe it was always you. It's a familiar, if unwelcome, feeling. Since moving to Eastport I have managed to push that feeling to one side, dismissing it as paranoia, confident that Stuart couldn't get to me here. I didn't know about you back then, I hadn't considered your existence. My whereabouts a secret; not even my parents or my brother know where I went. In the back of my mind there is a constant whispering, the fear that maybe Stuart has found me, that maybe it was him. Even more repugnant to me is the fact that I know for sure it wasn't him. You felt different, smelled different, hard to explain but I know you aren't him and I don't know if the fact you aren't him is better or worse. Is it me?

Do I make men do these terrible things? Why did you choose me?

Alone in my house again, I feel your presence; the faintest smell of you lingers in the air, or maybe in my imagination. I haven't really got any close friends, I haven't got close enough to anyone to ask if I can stay with them, or if they would have been able to come to the station with me. To say that I've had trust issues since what had happened with Stuart would be putting it mildly. Coming to a new town was about as much bravery as I could muster at the time, putting my faith in new people was a step too far after the way I had been treated. To have your own mother look you in the eye and ask if you were *sure* that's what really happened. She may as well have stuck a knife in me. I could never trust her again after that. I wonder what your mother was like when you were a child, was she cruel? Do you hate her? Is there a sneaking suspicion in the back of her mind that there is something very wrong with you?

I found what shocked me more than what Stuart did was the way people would rather think worse of me than him. Now here I am again in this house. My sanctuary. It used to be that as soon as I walked through that front door my anxiety would melt away, I could physically feel it leaving my body. A cocoon away from the outside world that was full of the unknown. Not this time. You've ruined all that, you've taken away my last vestige of peace. This time the anxiety multiplies as the door closes behind me. It doesn't feel like home anymore, no longer my safe haven. I stand in the hallway staring straight ahead, unsure which way to go next. I want to go upstairs and get in the shower again, maybe stay in there forever. The door to the lounge is closed. I did that deliberately before I left to go to the police station. I knew that when I got home, I wouldn't want to look in there. I take a deep breath and go into the kitchen instead.

The window is open.

That must have been how you got in. I thought it might be.

I reach under the sink and pull out my hammer. This is the first tool I bought for myself when I moved into this town. The handle is covered in the William Morris Strawberry Thief design. It reminds me of a cushion my mother used to have when I was young, before she chose not to believe me. I can only imagine the things she might say about you, all the ways she would make it my fault. I pull out a box of four-inch nails from the cutlery drawer before drawing the window shut and banging the nail straight through the frame and into the wooden windowsill. Of course if you really wanted to get in you could just smash the glass, but at least I might hear that and have a chance to hide. Better than leaving it open, an open invitation.

Now I know the police aren't coming, I can clean, remove any trace of you. I wonder what you touched.

I put on the pink rubber gloves and grab the bleach, the smell making me gag as I remember you pouring it on me in the shower, the viscous liquid burning my skin for a few seconds before the burning hot water washed it away. You obviously don't know that hot water decomposes the active ingredient in bleach and renders it ineffective. I have cleaned enough toilets in my time to know you should only use cold water with the stuff. Maybe you're not that clever after all, maybe you're just lucky. Or maybe I am just unlucky. My eyes burn and I can't stop coughing as the fumes hit the back of my throat. A part of me hopes this will kill me. For a moment I consider drinking it. How much would I need to end it all right here and now? Or maybe I could mix it with window cleaner to make some toxic chlorine gas which could also potentially kill me. I scrub away at the window frame, the counter tops, the draining board, anything any part of you might have touched. I can't move house, and I refuse to be a slave to fear, I have been there before, with Stuart. Is this my destiny? Build myself back just enough to feel human again and then someone else comes along to tear me back down. What is it about me that made this happen? Twice? How many people does this happen to more than once? It's hard not to give in to the temptation to just quit, to admit defeat, life isn't working out for me right now. I shake off the feeling and try to focus on the motion of my hand as I scrub, not wanting to entertain that darkness. It's not fair. It's not fair that I am going through this again.

I don't know how to rebuild my life, I didn't really succeed last time, I just ran away. Away from him and towards you. Running didn't work because the self-loathing came with me. Still, I felt an overwhelming need after Stuart attacked me to be near the sea, which is why I moved here. I'll be damned if I move again. The large seaside town seemed like such a peaceful place, and it's a place I remember from family caravan holidays as a child, a place I remember being happy. That's all I wanted, to feel safe and happy again. I almost made it, too. Almost got to a place where I could see the future as more than just the daily toil of being myself. Did you see that in me? That weakness? After this I'm not even back to square one, I'm so far behind that. Twice. . . The only thing I can think is how could I have let this happen again? How could I have left the kitchen window open? Why did I fall asleep on the sofa? Why did I work late? Why did I walk home alone? I blame myself when of course I should be blaming you.

The worst thing though, worse than anything else, is that I have no idea who you are. Literally not a clue. What I do remember is barely threaded together to form a cohesive thought. You could be someone I know, someone I have served in the cafe, one of the regulars maybe. Was it you, Bob, the man who is so gentle with his lovely terrier? Or maybe you're Keith, the bus driver that stops in for a bacon sarnie every morning. Maybe you are one of the faceless regulars that just sit in the corner and drink coffee in silence. The chances of that are high. How can I go back to work knowing that? How can I serve cups of takeaway coffee over the counter to any of the hundreds of men who pass through during the day? I know we have spoken, I just know it. I bet you got a kick out of that, making me say nice things to you all the while knowing you were going to get into my house and strip me down, treat me like I was nothing. Was I too nice? Maybe you got the wrong impression from the way I smiled at you or thanked you or tucked my hair behind my ear because it was getting in the way. You could be anyone, anywhere. At least with Stuart I knew who to be scared of.

My eyes are stinging too much to keep open now, whether it's the bleach or the fact that I have been crying for hours, I don't know. The exhaustion of the last twenty-four hours is starting to kick in and the reality of everything going back to normal is hitting me. I don't know if I can sleep tonight. You could be anywhere right now. I keep coming back to one thought though, something I have tried to ignore. You must have climbed through my window and then walked through into my lounge. How long did you stare at me while I was sleeping in there? Was it seconds? Minutes? Hours? How long did I sleep with you staring at me before you decided to take action? What's to stop you from doing it again? The police obviously don't care. I tried to do the right thing and tell them, tried to make sure they knew there was a rapist out there. I don't want anyone else to go through what I went through. It's important, isn't it? To report these things, to make sure these animals pay. I keep thinking about that police officer I confided in, DS White, and I want to hurt her for making me feel even worse, a feat I hadn't imagined possible.

After I have scrubbed the kitchen I will scrub it again and again, hoping to take the dirt away. Every time I close my eyes, I imagine you climbing through onto the worktop and then down and through to the lounge where I lay, oblivious. Your face changes every time; sometimes it's someone I know and other times it's someone off the telly. It occurs to me that when I woke up you had already started. That makes me feel sicker than anything else and I don't know why. With each new realisation I want to curl up and die. Will I ever be able to sleep again? Your hands, your hands on my skin, you were so gentle, which somehow makes me hate you even more. The anger I feel is directed at myself; although I know it isn't my fault, I still feel responsible, like I could have stopped it; stopped you. I felt this way for months after Stuart attacked me, even though he was so much bigger and stronger than me. Linking what happened last night to what happened with Stuart is not helping, it all feels so fresh again like a reopened wound. So familiar, so impossible to escape.

When there is nothing left to scrub, I grab another bottle of bleach and make my way into the hallway again. The door handle to the lounge is the last possible place you might have left fingerprints. I stare at it for several minutes before finally pouring the bleach on and cleaning it relentlessly. I open the door to the lounge and burst into tears again. Nothing is out of place, it looks clean and tidy, and yet I know what took place in here. The memory lingers in the air. I pour bleach where the plastic sheeting was. Nausea overcomes me as I drop to the floor and start to scrub. By the time I am finished there will be no trace of you left here. I will erase you just like you erased me.

Part Two

Chapter 6

I remember the first time I noticed a girl in that way. I was about eleven years old and my parents had taken me to a pub on the coast. It was one of those marriage-saving holidays. I can't remember the exact town, but it was near Brighton and we were on a camping holiday so every night we would find a different pub and my parents would buy me a burger and chips because that was the only thing I was guaranteed to eat without causing a scene. My older sister was always the perfect one, always the one who impressed my parents. She never complained or behaved badly. She was so silent and obedient it really annoyed me. She was only two years older than me but I knew they loved her more than me – at least, my father definitely did. I knew I was a mistake. We only ever went on camping holidays once or twice because my parents were too cheap to splash out on a decent hotel. My dad would always have a few beers, even though he was driving, and my mother would whisper at him that he needed to slow down but he never did.

On that day, I went and played in a back room at the pub that had a ball pit and climbing apparatus. There were other kids playing there but I was happy just arranging myself so that I was completely concealed under the balls in the pit and I would jump out whenever I sensed anyone was near. I managed to scare a few kids that way, I even made one of them cry, which was really thrilling. To have that much power over someone else's emotions made me feel less insignificant.

I was in that room for three hours before I noticed her. She hadn't been there the whole time and I wasn't sure what time she arrived but I did know that I couldn't take my eyes off her. I got out of the ball pit and sat in a beanbag chair watching her. She was on a Game Boy or some device like that. Her hair was like a sheet of gold and her skin was a golden white, like a really lightly toasted marshmallow, I remember wondering what she would taste like. She was slender and she wore a white dress. She was probably a bit older than me but you never could tell because girls sometimes looked a lot older than you thought they were. I didn't get to hang around much with girls because I went to a boys' school, but next year when I moved to secondary it would be mixed. I didn't get good enough grades to get into our local grammar school and so my parents were paying for me to go to the private school. They got a forty per cent discount because of our circumstances, which was humiliating but at least I would be in a mixed school with cooler kids.

The girl looked up from her Game Boy and saw me looking at her. I tried to smile but before I had a chance she pulled a face, like she had just smelled something disgusting. I had never been so embarrassed. She didn't even know me and yet I could tell she had decided I was a loser. I still think back to that moment, sitting in that beanbag chair, staring at that girl, all the possibilities of what might be still alive in my mind. Alive until she put me in my place with a look, a look that said I would never be good enough for her. I rushed out of the room and into the bathroom, I splashed water on my face and noticed a smear of ketchup on my cheek; maybe that was what disgusted her. I looked at my hair. My mother usually cut it for me, maybe that's what she didn't like about me. Or maybe it was my height, I was quite short, or maybe it was my clothes, my T-shirt snug on me because I had to wear my clothes until they didn't fit me anymore. Either way I made a promise to myself never to humiliate myself like that again. In years to come I would have girls like her begging to be with me. Just wait and see.

The strange thing about staying in the static caravan was the proximity to my parents. I didn't want to be *this close to them, or my sister. There was nowhere to go, the rooms were small and the walls were thin. I was either in the communal area or in my little boxy room that was damp and mouldy in the corner of the window. Still, the smell of that panelled cubicle was preferable to the smell of my drunk father. I stared at the window that night, I remember that much. It had started to rain and the corner of the window was glistening wet as though the water were about to burst through. The sound of the rain eventually sent me to sleep until I was woken again much later on by the sound of a thunderstorm. This time I was sure the caravan wasn't going to make it. I left my room to go and get into the spare bed in my sister's room. We had shared a room until a couple of years ago and so I didn't think she would mind. I opened the door to her room and I couldn't work out what I was looking at. When my eyes adjusted, I saw my father in my sister's bed. He was muttering apologies and her eyes were clamped shut. I watched for what felt like forever, then my mother put her hands on my shoulders and pulled me back towards my room. She must have seen what was going on and she did nothing. I didn't sleep for the rest of that night. I heard my father go back to his room much later and all I could think about was my sister lying there and what this meant about my family. In those few moments everything was blown apart. How would we all look at each other in the morning? I remember waking up and going to breakfast, terrified of the fallout from the night before, but there was none. Everyone behaved as they normally did. Life carried on.*

Chapter 7

Present day

The smell of bleach follows me wherever I go. I can't escape it. I scrub at my hands until they look raw for the third time this morning. I find comfort in the smell now, even though it reminds me of that night, of you. The joke is that everything reminds me of you. There is no forgetting you – in the brief moments that I do forget, nature finds a way to nudge me back into vigilance, back into fear. I am lucky if I get ten minutes' respite. You're always here lurking in the back of my mind, like a child hiding poorly behind a curtain, feet sticking out and a muffled giggle I have to pretend I can't hear. The worst thing is that I can't quite remember if you're real or not. The only evidence it happened is the missing towel from a set my mother gave me the Christmas before we stopped speaking.

There are times when I have emptied every cupboard in the house looking for that bloody towel, to prove it isn't here anymore because I can't trust my own mind. Each time I look I am terrified I will find it, because if it's there then it never happened, and if it didn't happen then what the hell is wrong with me? Since speaking to the police, their suggestion that I might have made the rape up has somehow become plausible to me. I remember it so vividly and yet there is nothing to show it happened. Even your whispered voice in the back of my mind could just be a figment of my imagination. There aren't any scars, bruises, no defensive marks, nothing. Doubting myself is practically a full-time job these days. I am trying to claw back some power but until I know I am not crazy, it's hard to silence that voice in my head, your voice.

I look in the mirror and force a grin with my teeth. My mouth feels so unnatural in this pose, those muscles in my cheeks almost unused for the last three years. They ache in complaint at being forced to perform. It has been a while since I have attempted to look human, but I need to get this job. In and out of jobs for the last three years, unable to stick around when I feel uncomfortable or undervalued. Worse than that is dealing with the public, because that's where you are hiding, you're one of them. I don't smile anymore. I snap at the easiest thing and I'm no longer able to put up with other people's shit. My fuse is shorter than I ever remember it being in the past. But I definitely need this job. I have worked at most of the cafeterias in town and my reputation is starting to precede me. Unreliable, unreasonable, lots of uns. Look at what you made. This time I am trying for a hotel, hoping my name hasn't made the rounds in that circuit yet.

The hotel is formal but quite bijou, small rooms and long meandering corridors. The rooms are outdated and worn-out. Wherever there isn't shiny wooden panelling the same wallpaper is used throughout, all bold geometric shapes in garish colours, obviously very expensive at the time it was installed but now completely out of fashion. The paintwork has been painted so many times it almost looks soft; like you could dig your nails into it and leave an impression. It still has a nicotine-stained yellow bleeding through the white in places and it's never entirely clean. Each item of furniture has been repaired time and time again, legs replaced, cushions reupholstered, nothing ever thrown away until there is no way to salvage it. I like the faux Victorian uniform even though it's completely out of keeping with the mid-century modern decor. A lace shirt buttoned up to the chin and a black skirt that swept the floor as I walk. A shapeless shifting mass, moving through the corridors like a ghost, which is pretty much how I have felt since the day we met.

The building itself isn't far from my house and I am applying for the night shift, fulfilling room service duties and some work on reception. The sun would still be up when I walk to work and would have risen again by the time I get home. I feel safer at home knowing that my neighbours are up and about. I hate being on my own in this house at night and my best friend Chowder, the German shepherd, will miss me less then. I suppose I have you to thank for bringing us together. Don't be fooled by his lethargic walk, he will rip your face off and I will let him.

I smooth down my shirt and grab my keys. I can't be late for this interview. I have another appointment to get to straight after. Getting jobs has never been a problem for me, it's keeping them I seem to struggle with. Leaving the house takes a little effort; each time a micro pep talk takes place in my head. A reminder that I can do anything I want to do. *I've got this*.

As I approach the hotel I am struck by its charm. It reminds me of a modern church my mother used to go to, all boxy and brown, built in the sixties. I used to think it was so ugly and now I yearn for the days when my hand was nestled inside my mother's as she kept me safe. Not anymore though, now I'm all alone with nothing but my paranoia, and you, always you.

I know full well it won't be long before someone says or does something that results in me committing some kind of sackable offence like slapping them across the face. I did that once, and I was lucky my manager at the time managed to talk them out of pressing charges by paying them five hundred quid to let it go, money I had to work off out back and out of the way of the public. He didn't want the bad reviews and I was grateful not to have to explain myself to the police. I have to keep my anger in check but it's so hard. Self-sabotage is easier than trying to make something work, trying to move forward. I feel your hand on my chest, a permanent presence, holding me down, stopping me from getting where I need to be. Today is the first day of the rest of my life, a mantra I have been repeating to myself for almost three years, well aware that the only day that doesn't apply to is the day I die.

Chapter 8

To call them a group is probably a stretch. It's rarely ever the same women who come to these 'survivors' meetings week in week out. Sometimes I'll see a face I recognise, but they always seem embarrassed to be acknowledged by me and so I stopped making eye contact months ago, keeping my head down to keep things simple. What is most staggering is how many new faces there always are, how many people I only see once. These were only the ones who had the courage to leave their homes and seek this kind of help, a fraction of the real number. It makes me so sad – sad and angry. There are five rows of battered old plastic orange school chairs facing the front in the old church hall. Now a community centre, the religious iconography covered with cork noticeboards and posters for the Royal British Legion that often meet in here. The way these gatherings work is that you can either stand where you are, by your chair, or go to the front to tell your story. So far I haven't been able to tell mine, ours. Too many times now I've been accused of lying and so now I'm just looking for some solidarity. Hearing these stories is both comforting and horrifying. I bet you would love it, you would love to be in here and see all these desperate, broken women. I bet you get hard thinking about the pain you caused. I wonder what I am looking for here and I know it's you, it's always you.

The scale, the relentlessness of it, the never-ending supply of 'survivors', a word that jars with me a little. Maybe because I don't *feel* like a survivor yet, I'm still treading water, still looking for dry land. One step forward and two steps back. There are days when I feel like I can take on the world, days when I feel like I am *over it*, like it's something a person can just *get over*. Other days I am thrust back in time to the cold living room floor three years ago, lying on a plastic sheet with the weight of you on top of me and between my legs. Swings and roundabouts.

Today is a good day; I have just been offered a new job and feel elated at the prospect of being able to pay my bills on time again. I have almost run through all of my savings, not that I have much, enough for another month without employment at most. It's not like I go out much or am particularly frivolous and so at least I can start saving for my next inevitable bout of unemployment. Did you keep tabs on me after you were finished? Was that night the end of our time together or just the beginning? Do you enjoy seeing who you turned me into or was there nothing for you once you had emptied yourself inside me? Are you watching me now or are you watching someone else, waiting to ruin their life?

Tonight's a busy night in the church hall. There's no sense of camaraderie, mostly it's just a frustrated kind of despair. Everyone is here alone. A young woman called Sindy gets up to speak first. I have seen her before, I remember her story. I wonder how many times Sindy has told the story and whether it's like a battery that needs recharging, the energy gained from expelling that demon dwindling until she needs to reclaim herself again. Is this Sindy's life now? To have to relive the worst day of her life every few months? I hate the thought of it, to be so beholden to something that was such a tiny fraction of my own life, a few hours at most and yet it's beyond significant, it's life-changing, all-consuming. Is there anything else? Is there anyone else but you? Sometimes I wonder.

Today a newcomer stands at the front of the hall at the makeshift podium. In all of the groups that I've been to, and there have been many, I've never seen this woman before. The woman is bubbling with nerves, steeling herself to tell her story, maybe for the first time. There is an unmistakable look about someone the first time they tell their story. It's like a contract: I will tell you this terrible thing if you promise to believe me. Like an exchanging of vows. I'll show you mine if you show me yours.

'My name is Martha. Last year I was attacked in my house,' she says, swaying a little from side to side as she transfers the weight from one foot to another, clenching her fists and visibly searching inside herself for the strength to carry on talking. 'I woke up naked, I couldn't move, I couldn't do anything. I haven't told anyone this before and I thought I could just move on but I didn't know my attacker. He got into my house when I was asleep and then I woke up with him inside me. Not knowing who did that to me makes me feel insane. I am suspicious of everyone I meet and instead of moving on I'm finding it really hard not to just get pissed every night. I can't go a day without at least a bottle of wine and I know if I don't sort myself out that things are going to be a whole lot worse in another year. I guess I left a window open or something, I don't know how he got in. I keep going through that night and I keep kicking myself. I feel completely responsible and I just can't move on.'

As Martha talks, I am struck by the similarity to my own attack. The words could be coming straight from the thoughts I have replayed over and over in my mind. Even things I didn't know I remember are brought to the surface, like the fact that you whispered to yourself as you were preparing me. I hadn't been able to make out the words and neither had Martha but that is such an oddly specific detail that my skin stands to attention. This isn't a coincidence. How can it be? She's met you, too. It's as though all of Martha's nervous energy has transferred itself to me. I stare at her, even after she sits down again, much calmer than she was a few moments before. It's like a relay race sometimes, passing the baton for just a few moments, transferring your pain and shame into someone else's hands. It always comes back around, but for a short space of time you have a reprieve. Could we have both been attacked by you? I know we have. I just know it. After months of coming to these meetings, I realise this is what I have been waiting for. Not solidarity, as I kept telling myself, but validation. If the exact same thing happened to someone else, I can't have imagined it. The relief is immense. You are real.

I haven't cried since that day in the police cell, instead anger fuelling my every move, but I struggle to keep my emotions in check as I wait for the meeting to end. There is finally some proof that I didn't imagine the whole thing, finally something to corroborate my memories. My imaginary friend brought to life by this woman's words. Maybe I'm not crazy after all.

Chapter 9

The meeting ended about fifteen minutes ago, but I am still sitting here, waiting for the hall to empty out. I'm still reeling from the revelation that I wasn't the only one you did this to. I don't know why that thought has never occurred to me. Wasn't I enough? You didn't get what you needed from me so you took it from someone else? Maybe you do this every week, I don't know. For the last three years I thought I knew you, but now I realise there is so much more to know. I am almost annoyed with you, on top of the rage you left me with. I thought we had something, you and me, now I find out you've been putting yourself about. Shame on you. That thing we had evaporated with every word she spoke. It wasn't me, it wasn't my fault, it was you all along, you are the one who is broken. I find a strange comfort in knowing you struck again, coupled with an exasper-ation at the police. Going by Martha's account, the attack happened after mine and so all of Martha's pain could have been avoided if they had just listened to me and looked for you. I rub the frayed edge of my coat between my fingers – not the expensive pea-green one I had been saving up to buy before the incident, before my life fell apart yet again. That dream lost with so many others when you broke into my house, my body, my soul.

Women shuffle out of the church silently, heads down, no goodbyes, no acknowledgements. That brief intermission in the pretence of daily life is over and the mask returns. Some are better at wearing a fake smile than others. It takes time and practice to be normal again, whatever that is. I keep a close eye on Martha as she speaks to Carol, the lady who hosts the group, still afraid to go over and speak to her. I'm not sure why. I wait for Martha to leave the hall and then I follow her outside. The way she walks I can tell she isn't heading back to a car. I decide to stay behind her and see what she does. We walk for fifteen minutes, me trailing behind where she can't see me. Is this what you do? Pick a random woman on the street and see if she is a viable candidate for your sick ritual? Is this how you picked me? I feel strangely empowered as I follow her, even though I know it's the wrong thing to do. Is this what gets you off, too? Watching and waiting. I am not even sure what I am waiting for but I need to know where she is going, I am invested. I think maybe I am looking for similarities between us, some commonality that would explain why you chose me. Do you even know why you make the choices you make? Sometimes I wish you could answer my questions but the rest of the time I hope you are dead. Now at least I know you exist. The woman stops and turns around as though she can feel someone following her. I quickly turn my head and look into the nearest shop to cover the fact that I am watching her. I wonder how many times you did this to me, followed me home. Was it once? Or several times? I must remind myself to ask you that one day.

She lives about five minutes' walk from my house. I have never walked up this street before. Did she live here when you attacked her or has she moved? She seems to live alone. Is this how easy it is? No one is really paying attention to me watching her. She seems a little suspicious as she unlocks her door and goes inside but she doesn't look at me once. I don't appear to be a threat, I guess. I wonder how you avoid detection so easily but it occurs to me we are all so lost in our own little worlds we aren't looking out for you. We don't notice you because we don't expect you. Even with my past experience, you came as a surprise. That's what you bank on, isn't it? I find a wall near a row of garages and sit and watch her house. I feel insane but this is what you've made me. A part of me wants to knock on her door but I know how unsettling that would be so I don't. She's our little secret for now.

Chapter 10

I have been following Martha for a day and a half. I know it's wrong, but I just can't stop myself. She makes me feel closer to you and I don't know why I would want that. Maybe it's because since the moment you came into my life I have been filled with all these questions and she is the first person I have encountered that might have any kind of answers. Knowing you exist is no longer enough, I think I want to find you and look into your eyes. I don't even know what colour your eyes are and I want to know. The alternative is never knowing who you are and therefore suspecting every man I meet for the rest of my life. That hardly seems fair, on them or me.

Martha goes into a clothing shop I have never been into before. It's all much more feminine and expensive than anything I would normally wear, another difference between us. The more I observe about Martha, the more

I wonder how we both got pulled into your orbit. I see no common ground at all. I go into the shop and keep my distance as Martha selects some clothes to take into the dressing room. I get closer and when she comes out she goes to the counter and pays for all of the items she tried on. She clearly has a bit of money. Another difference between us. I can't imagine there is anything she would look bad in. When she leaves the shop, I wait a few moments and then follow behind her.

After a few feet Martha turns quickly and stares at me. I'm not as stealthy as I thought I was.

'Why are you following me?'

'Can we talk?'

'You were at the meeting, weren't you? I remember the way you looked at me while I told my story.'

'I was.'

'Did they tell you where I lived?'

'I followed you. I'm sorry.'

'Wow. You need to take a step back and leave me alone before I call the police. Isn't this against the rules of the meeting? I did all the talking I wanted to do in there,' Martha says, her eyes shifting nervously, now unable to maintain eye contact for longer than a second. I know that feeling well.

I don't want to upset her but I can't let Martha just leave so I have to say something that only we could know, something she didn't divulge in the meeting, something that would have been part of his ritual.

'Did he make you wash yourself with bleach afterwards? Did he take the towel you dried yourself with when he left?'

Martha's eyes widen and she looks at me differently somehow. You did, didn't you?

'How could you know that?' Martha says in a confused whisper.

'Because he did the same thing to me. Whoever broke into your house broke into my house, too.'

'I don't understand,' she says with a crinkled brow.

'That story you told in there, it was like you were inside my head. I could have said those exact words. We must have been attacked by the same man. He broke into my house when I was asleep. I woke up paralysed, with something covering my head,' I say breathlessly, the words tumbling out. I haven't spoken about that night since I went to the police and they made me feel like I was going out of my mind, like I made it up for attention. I didn't make it up though, did I? You do exist.

'This is a lot. I don't know what to say,' she says, still visibly nervous of me.

'I'm sorry I followed you. Hearing you talk pushed me over the edge a bit and I haven't been myself since. I thought I was the only one.' I try to explain, knowing I must sound crazy.

Martha's gaze softens and she immediately lunges forward and pulls me into an embrace. I haven't been

59

hugged like this in a very long time, and the connection between us is instant. Whatever happens now, we have found each other, and by knowing what we know, we are bonded for life. We sob in harmony. I cling to this stranger as if we are old friends reuniting after a battle.

'Let me buy you a coffee?' Martha finally says as she pulls away. Mascara streaks down her rounded cheeks, cutting through the frosty pink blusher she wears, the same colour on her lips and big brown eyes. I nod and we walk towards the closest coffee shop, a small independent one that I have only been to once before. I don't tend to hang around in this neighbourhood for long, it makes me feel uncomfortable and scruffy because everyone is so polished. Not like the side of town I live on, full of vape shops and bookies, mobile phone repair shops and pawnbrokers. The only shops around here are antique shops, florists and designer boutiques. I don't see how mine and Martha's paths ever would have crossed naturally. This in turn leads me to the same question that has been thrumming away in the back of my mind since I first heard Martha's account of her ordeal. Why us? Thank God I went to that meeting though, thank God I heard Martha talk. I feel like everything inside of me has shifted back into place, all those missing pieces suddenly returned.

At the back of the coffee shop it's empty and more comfortable than the front, which faces the street; I've never ventured into this part before. Maybe I've prejudged it a bit harshly as it's decked out with a mix of beautiful furniture in soft velvets in rich peacock colours. We sit on a purple velvet chesterfield sofa in the corner under an oversized art deco lamp with a stained-glass shade. The composition of Martha in this setting reminds me of a portrait and I wish I could paint. The various pink hues she wears are striking against the backdrop of this uniquely eclectic space.

'I'm Gail, Gail Reynolds. Nice to meet you,' I say with a smile. Is it nice? I'm not sure if it is. Knowing what we share, knowing such intimate things about each other without ever having had a full conversation. Knowing that we share you. Does she talk to you like I do? At least this strange connection cuts out the need for small talk, which I loathe. Since that night, every conversation feels like small talk, always avoiding the only subject I can ever think about. It's partly why I barely speak to people at all, not really caring much how their day is going, not really interested in how the kids are. Everything pales into insignificance when all I really want to say is *Did you know that right now someone is probably getting raped, maybe even someone you know? Why don't you care?*

'Martha Akintola,' Martha says, holding her hand out. We shake hands. The formalities are out of the way now.

'I am so sorry about what happened to you. I can't believe he's done this more than once,' I say, but of course

I can believe it. What I really mean is that I can't believe we've found each other.

'Thank you for telling me, I didn't think anything anyone could say would make me feel better. I know that sounds strange and of course I am not happy that he hurt you, too. But it is comforting in a strange way to know that it is him with the problem and not me. Does that make sense?' Again, she's saying words that I have been thinking. Is it fated that we should all share these thoughts and reactions to such a disarming event?

'I absolutely understand what you mean. Was there anything familiar about him at all? You didn't recognise his voice?' I ask, desperate to know more. Surer than ever that we've both been your victims.

'No.'

'Did he cover your face?'

'Yes, with some fabric,' Martha says.

'Yes, I think it was a pillowcase. It was clean, I could smell the detergent, lavender,' I say. It feels so strange and sinister to be comparing notes on something like this.

'That's what I thought, too. Lavender,' Martha says, her gaze fixing on a distant target, past the walls and into another dimension entirely. She lowers her voice and speaks almost to herself. 'I thought I had imagined it, for so long, everything was gone, there was no evidence that anyone had even been inside my house. Finding you has made things so much clearer in my mind.'

'Did you go to the police?' I ask.

'No. Did you?'

'I did, but without evidence there really wasn't anything they could do,' I say, playing down how traumatic the whole process of reporting the crime to the police had been. Minimising how much it has completely derailed my life. I still shrug it off as 'one of those things'.

'No, there never seems to be much they can do. That's why I kept it to myself. I knew they wouldn't find anything. He knew what he was doing.'

You did know what you were doing, didn't you? You knew we would shrink quietly into our bottles of gin and hide what you did from the world. You knew there was a good chance we would keep your dirty little secret and if we didn't, you knew the system would be there to make sure we knew it was futile to even try to make you pay.

For the first time I have a chance to learn more about you. I want to know everything. Maybe together we can gather enough information to go to the police again. I try to remember as much as I can from what she said in the meeting. I start to tell her anything I can remember, too. I recall her saying the anniversary of the incident was approaching. Do you have a special day when you like to do this?

'You said in the meeting that he attacked you last year. When exactly did this happen?'

63

'It was early morning on June 12th.'

It's the same date. I catch my breath at this morsel of information. I was probably never meant to know this but now I do, it means I know something about you. The 12th of June means something to you for some reason, doesn't it? What happened to you that you feel the need to mark the occasion with something as heinous as rape? Did someone hurt you? Or was it the first time you hurt someone else? Are we just the surrogates for you, replaying that first moment over and over?

'That's when I was attacked too. Really early morning, almost three years ago.'

I don't mention that I have since wrapped my living room clock in a towel and stuffed it in the cupboard under the stairs. It's one of the most expensive things I own, a bright red and white retro plastic analogue wall clock with a built-in calendar that made a loud clacking noise every time the date changed. I wonder occasionally if the battery is still going. I think I hear it at night sometimes as I am falling asleep but as with most things, it's just a part of that terrible memory you left me with relentlessly trying to leak its way into my thoughts. It feels wrong to be talking about you somehow, as though you are imprisoned inside my mind and by talking about what you did, I am unlocking your cell, letting you out for some courtyard exercise.

'I wonder if we are the only ones?' Martha said.

'What do you mean? You think there might be more?'

'What are the chances that you were his first?'

'It doesn't bear thinking about,' I say, wondering how many more of us there might be. How many broken dolls do you have in your toy box?

'That's the problem though, isn't it? No one is thinking about it, he's just getting away with this unchecked. I nearly didn't go the other night; I nearly didn't talk about it. I could be at home right now stewing in my own thoughts, wondering if I am crazy or not. Instead I told my story and now I've met you.'

'Would you talk to the police with me? Maybe if we went together they would listen to us?'

'I'm sorry, I can't do that. It was difficult enough going to the meeting and speaking – not that I regret it. Meeting you is the best thing that's happened to me this year. . . since it happened,' Martha says. I can see why you chose her. She is beautiful, she glows with a kind of classiness that I have never possessed. What about the two of us made us your targets? Apart from the fact that we are women, I can see no similarities between us at all.

'Thank you. I feel the same, is that weird?' I say. I do feel the same.

'I don't think there is a right or wrong way to feel. I just hope he's not been doing this for long. I've got a horrible feeling we are not alone in this. For all we know he's going to attack someone else, maybe June 12th is an important anniversary for him or something. I don't know but that cannot be a coincidence. It must be significant in some way.'

I consider her words for a moment and then wonder why this thought never really occurred to me before, that the date might mean something, although of course it did. Speaking things out loud makes them change shape though, some thoughts are so intangible you remember thinking them but not in words; this is one of those thoughts. It seems so simple now she has said it.

'You're right, there must be others. Maybe we could look for them.'

'How would we do that?'

'I go to a different meeting at St Mary's on Thursday. We could go together. If he has raped someone else maybe they will turn up there. Maybe we could just keep telling our story until someone else comes forward.'

'I'm not sure I can go through that again.'

'Then I'll do it. I'll talk this time. But only if you come,' I say, empowered for the first time in a long time. She told her story and now my life has changed for the better. Maybe I should have been telling anyone who would listen about you, maybe then things might be different.

'It's a date.'

She shakes my hand, a pact. It feels like so long since I have felt the warmth of human touch. Her hands are soft and I smell coconut. I don't want to let her go but I do. If we can prove a connection then the police will have no choice but to listen.

'Are you around tomorrow? We could maybe go for a coffee, again.'

It's not like me to put myself out there but something about Martha makes me want to be near her, is it just the fact that we have you in common? I want to know why you chose her and maybe if I can figure that out then I can start to understand why you chose me.

She smiles, revealing perfect white teeth that make me purse my lips a little harder to try to hide mine. 'I'd love that. I'm working until two in the afternoon but after that we can meet at the new coffee place on Pine Street? I keep meaning to go in there and it's got a great view of the sea.'

'Sounds great. I'll see you at two,' I say, smiling and standing up. I leave first, not wanting to feel like the needy one, the one that gets left behind. I look around and check to see if anyone is looking at me before I start walking. Force of habit. You could be anywhere right now, you could be watching me. I decide you aren't but I wonder what you would think if you saw us together. Would it make you nervous? I think if I were you I would be very nervous about that indeed.

Chapter 11

There are moments in your life that stand out to you as being special in some way, even while they are happening. Not all special moments are special because they are positive but because they change you and take you a step closer to being your perfect self. One of those special life-defining moments for me was when my parents sat me down after breakfast and told me they were breaking up. It shouldn't have been a surprise to me but it was like a punch in the face. I couldn't believe it. My dad had met someone else apparently, someone younger and prettier and less annoying than my mum. I am not sure why they waited until my birthday to tell me but my father then went on to explain how me and my sister could come and visit every other weekend as though he would be fine not seeing me for ten days at a time. I had thought until that time that I was close with my dad. In the last year our relationship had changed and I had felt less out of place in the home. He had even said it was me and him against my sister and mother, but now when it came down to it he chose some random woman over me, his own flesh and blood. I wish I could explain how betrayed I felt in that moment and how much I hated this nameless woman that had stolen my father. It was right after he had got a huge promotion at work and so for the first time we were going to be able to afford nicer things and I wouldn't have to wear the crap football boots to practise every week. I hated my parents for turning me into a cliché, a teenage boy from a broken home.

After my twelfth birthday I didn't see my father for three months. Apparently his girlfriend was too nervous to meet me and so there I was suddenly without a father. I started to get upset when I didn't have the right clothes or the right hair. Being at a private school was hard. The kids there had a way about them that I tried to emulate but I never got accepted by them in the first year and so I knew I had to make some changes and become better, make them want to be friends with me. My constant demands for expensive items caused an even bigger rift between my parents and it became obvious that they would never get back together. My sister and mother got closer than ever and I felt as though I had been put on the sidelines again. My sister really changed and became quite gobby and selfish. I became obsessed with my appearance. I wanted the best shoes, I wanted this coat I saw, it was a ski jacket and it was a more up-to-date version of one the coolest kid in our year had. Faiyaz Laghari was the guy everyone wanted to be friends with, and the one all the girls wanted to get with. He was two years above me in school but I knew if I could get his attention and approval that I would immediately be accepted by the other kids in my school. As soon as I was accepted I would hopefully become desirable to the girls as well. The coat I wanted was almost three hundred pounds and was bright orange with black and white details on it. I knew I would look cool in it, I knew I would look better. I went on and on at my mother for weeks, she offered to buy me a cheaper coat but I wouldn't accept it. I felt like I had already accepted so much compromise in my life; why shouldn't I get the coat I wanted?

Eventually my mother managed to convince my father to buy it for me. He wanted more time away from me and so the coat was a bribe for me to keep my distance. I figured out that my father didn't want me around and getting him to buy me things to stay away became a habit. I didn't push my luck too much but every month I got something I wanted from my mother or my father. I wondered if it was the guilt from their divorce or whether it was because of what I saw that night in the caravan. I didn't really care as

long as I got the things I wanted. I deserved them.
My parents owed me. It didn't matter what I did
though, Faiyaz didn't notice me and I couldn't get the
courage together to speak to him. He was dating a
girl called Tori, the prettiest girl in the whole school
with her long brown curly hair and big eyes. I was on
the outside, always on the outside. I thought I couldn't
get any lonelier. Little did I know how much worse it
would get and how much I would come to hate myself
for the way I look. Don't get me wrong, I am not
ugly, I know I'm not. My face is really symmetrical,
I've measured it and I heard that's what constitutes
an attractive face. People tell me I look like my father
and I know people consider my father good-looking.
I thought maybe once I hit puberty and grew taller
then I would be more desirable. I was wrong.

Chapter 12

It feels strange to say that I am happy but a part of me is, a part of me suddenly sees a way out of this black hole that I am in. I wonder how you would feel about that, about me being happy again? I bet that wasn't part of the plan. Do you ever check on me to see how miserable I am? How much damage you have done? A part of me hopes you see me today with my hopeful smile. I'm not the kind of happy where I am actually happy, but at least I have a purpose now, a reason to get out of bed every morning. There are more of us out there, I know that now. Finding Martha is just the beginning. I'm going to try and find all of your dolly girls. We have exchanged phone numbers and been in contact constantly since our conversation at the shop yesterday. I was woken up with a raised eyebrow emoji and a *hi, it's exciting*, I can't remember the last time I made a new friend. I'm aware someone as gorgeous as Martha wouldn't even look at me twice before, but you brought us together. She's so much braver than I am, telling her story the way she did, telling my story, your story. It's been so long since I have felt connected to anyone at all. Life is starting to mean something again. If we can find more of your victims then maybe we can find you. Wouldn't you like that? A little reunion for us. We could hire a karaoke machine and I could sing Abba songs at you, make it a real party. My smile widens at the thought of us in a room together, me, you and Martha. I don't think you would like that at all, would you? Two against one. I didn't even dream it could be possible but why not? The police aren't planning on looking for you, they don't give a shit, so maybe it's my job. I don't know how or where or even if I can, but it's got to be better than doing nothing. Until I met Martha I felt like I had just been biding my time until some other pervert decided to attack me. I don't feel that way anymore, I feel empowered. . . strong. I want to meet the man who made me who I am today. And Martha is the key to finding you.

I still have some unfinished business though. I'm in the police station waiting to see the detective that made me feel like shit. Nothing feels better than *I told you so* sometimes. I'll tell her that I've found someone else, someone who was attacked after me. I did my bit, I went to the police before and reported it, but they did nothing, so this isn't on me – it's on her. I'm staring at the empty counter in the police station reception. There is a bell there and after a few minutes of no one showing up I finally press it. A man stumbles into view, spilling his coffee as he walks through the door before putting it down too close to the edge of the desk. I give him a second to compose himself, it only seems fair. He's not wearing a uniform so he must be one of the other detectives here. In another life where I think about that kind of thing I might consider him handsome with his tousled brown hair and bright blue eyes. Not now though; now I don't really care.

'I'd like to speak to DS Shona White, please,' I say, my voice shakier than I expected, the detective's name burned into my memory as the woman who didn't give a shit. That's how people like you get away with it: no one gives a shit, not really.

'It's DI White. Can I ask what this is in regards to?' the man behind the counter asks, still patting his coffee-stained shirt down.

'My name is Gail Reynolds,' I say, aware that isn't the answer he's looking for but I don't want to tell him. I don't want to speak to anyone but her. I'm not here to report anything to the police, if anything I am here to gloat. I was right and she was wrong. I hope that hearing my name will invoke some kind of shame in the detective. I want to add that she'll know who

I am but a part of me is terrified she won't even remember me. He half smiles and taps something into the computer.

'I'll go get her for you.'

Chapter 13

Shona stared straight through Graham Post as he explained the roster for the rest of the week. She had become quite adept at tuning him out for the most part, except when things like this cropped up and she was obligated to listen to him. Still, she didn't look at his face, she just looked through it until she had all the information she needed. She viewed his lack of issue with her frankly disrespectful behaviour towards him as confirmation that she hadn't been mistaken about what happened that night. As long as she didn't kick up a fuss he was happy to let her be frosty as hell with him. It certainly made her more careful about how much she drank these days – two glasses at most if she wasn't at home. For a time she had been impressed with herself for being able to put it behind her, that she wasn't one of those victims that let it destroy them. As time had gone on it became apparent to her that she hadn't put it behind her at all. She had suppressed it, stuffed it down inside with the hopes that it might lose its significance over time. It never did though, not really. It's a broken thing that can't be fixed, a shard that lodges itself inside you and with one wrong move a reminder of it stabs at you all over again.

Relieved the briefing was over, she smiled as Aaron approached her. He had coffee all down the front of his shirt, not for the first time either. He was clumsy and she wasn't entirely sure why she found that attractive but she did.

'You're a sight for sore eyes,' she said.

'This is the second shirt I've ruined this week.'

'Maybe you should start wearing darker shirts. Or maybe just stop wearing them altogether?' she said with a cheeky wink.

'I know if I keep buying new ones we'll never get a deposit together for our own place.'

'Shirtless it is then.'

'There's a lady out front looking for you. Asked for you by name. You expecting someone?'

'Nope, not today I'm not. Did she say who she was?'

'Gail Reynolds, I think.'

As soon as Aaron said the name her stomach dipped. Still burned in her brain as one of the lowest points in her so far pretty short career. The way she had handled that whole situation was a stain on her conscience and had led her to making some major changes in her attitude to work. So far today was shaping up to be a bit shit – first Graham and now this. Aaron nodded a goodbye and made his way to the bathroom to clean himself up.

'One moment, DI White,' Graham Post said. Her muscles tensed and she turned to him, face-to-face contact unavoidable. They were the same rank now but he was still somehow higher in the pecking order than her in the station. Professionalism dictated she talk to him, as much as she didn't want to.

'Can I help you, sir?'

'No need to be so formal with me, White.'

'OK. What do you want?'

'Straight to business. Fine. I need someone to cover for me next Friday, I have asked everyone else and they can't. You're my last option.'

'And why would I do that for you?'

'Come on, Shona, aren't you over that already? Time to grow up, don't you think?' he said, like he had borrowed a book and not returned it.

'Fine. I'll do it,' she said, aware that she was just trying to put an end to this conversation. She felt like a coward all over again because he could ask her for anything and she would say yes if it meant she could get as far away from him as possible. At least if she was covering for him it meant he wasn't going to be there.

'I'll message you the details. Thank you,' he said, but she had already walked away.

She took a moment to compose herself as she walked towards reception, bracing herself for a different kind of unpleasant conversation. Today was one of those days where she wished she had just stayed in bed.

Chapter 14

A blue door opens at the side of the plexiglass and there she is. DI White looks different to how she did three years ago. Her hair is cropped short in a pixie cut and bleached almost white. I like it, it looks powerful. I tend to hide behind my hair. I can tell the second I look at her that she remembers me and I am annoyed at myself for caring what she thinks at all.

'Miss Reynolds. How are you doing?'

'Not great. Thanks for asking.'

'What can I help you with? Do you want to come through?'

'This won't take long. I just wanted to let you know that he did it to someone else. Last year. A whole two years after I came forward.' I desperately want DI White to believe me and I hate myself for it.

'What do you mean? It happened again? To who? We've had no reports of similar attacks or I promise you I would have contacted you. Did the other victim report it?'

'No, she didn't feel safe coming to the police. I wonder why?'

'What are the chances of there being any evidence after all this time?'

'I think there's more. I don't think I was his first. I think he's going to do it again, too.'

'What do you mean?'

'I mean it's been coming back to me little by little and I have remembered more things. Most of it is hard to put into words but there was something very rehearsed and practised about the whole thing. And the fact that he did it all so effortlessly, almost ritually. I just think he had done it before me, and I know he's done it since.'

'Let me guess – your friend isn't willing to come and speak to the police.'

'No and that's her choice and who could blame her? After the way I was treated here, I wish I had never said anything either. I'm telling you though he's going to do it to someone else. God only knows how many other women he's done this to. Maybe you should warn people or something.'

'Look, for what it's worth, it wasn't my call last time not to pursue the investigation. I had a boss, she's moved on now, but she didn't think we would get anywhere with it. With the information you gave us, she was probably right. I know that's not a good enough excuse, I don't really have a defence and I'm not usually the sort to follow orders blindly, especially not since the morning you came in, but I just wasn't sure there was anything I could do. I regret not doing right by you. I'm really sorry.'

'Must be nice to be able to palm the blame off on someone else. Your choices are your own and you have to live with them. You were the one talking to me, you were the one making me feel like a liar. You mentioned a previous report I made. Made it seem like I was in the habit of making this kind of thing up.'

In my mind she is complicit in your crime. Her not doing what she is supposed to do enables you and people like you to do what you want. I can see on her face that she knows that, too.

'I'm really sorry. There is no defence for what I did.'

'Well, what's done is done. You didn't go after him and now he's ruined someone else's life. I tried to tell you, against my better judgement I came and spoke to the police. Even though I knew it was pointless and futile, I couldn't live with myself if it happened to someone else because I hadn't reported it, so that was the action I chose to take. What happened to the woman after me wasn't my fault, it was yours. So what are you going to do now? Just let it go?'

'What's the name of the other woman who was assaulted?'

'Raped. Call it what it is. It's not my place to tell you her name. If you do nothing she won't be the last.'

'Maybe if you can talk to her. Convince her to talk to me? Without more information, there isn't much I can do. Anything that helps narrow down the search criteria would be more help than you can realise.'

'Twelfth of June. That's when he did it to me. That's when he attacked the other woman. It's the 1st today. That gives you technically twelve days but more like eleven. Is that the kind of thing you want to know?'

'That's really helpful, thanks Gail. I could start a proper investigation if you want to make a statement. See if you can get your friend to come forward, too.'

'Well, she's got better sense than me. After going through something like that to then be accused of lying, it made things a whole lot worse. For a long time I thought you might be right, I thought maybe I dreamed it, maybe I was so screwed up by what happened with Stuart that my mind created an even worse scenario. Then I found her and now I feel sane again. Isn't it awful that I preferred knowing I had been raped to feeling the way you made me feel?' I say. Mic drop.

I walk out of the station without turning around. This time it's her turn to feel like shit. DI White was right about one thing though: there was no evidence. That doesn't excuse the way I was treated but it does mean you are one smart monster who could feasibly go on doing this for years. I can't let that happen.

If the police won't do anything then I will. I don't know what, but in the back of my mind I will always be wondering if somewhere out there some woman is lying on a plastic sheet and wishing she's dead. I can't allow that. I have to stop it. I have to stop you.

Chapter 15

I arrive at the coffee shop and Martha is sitting in the window already. I walked through several unnecessary streets and doubled back on myself twice just to make sure you couldn't follow me here. It's a habit I acquired after that night, not that it makes any difference. You already know where I live.

I feel out of place in here, my khaki overcoat frayed at the folds. Martha is dressed all in cerulean-blue today, and with the backdrop of the green sea behind her she looks like a goddess and I find myself wanting to apologise for not making more of an effort. Her face lights up when she sees me and my anxiety melts away. She signals the waitress and waits for me to sit down.

'Sorry I'm late,' I say. In truth I'm a little more than nervous to see her again.

'It was no hardship. It's lovely here, I could stay all day. Coffee?'

'Yes please.'

I don't even like coffee but I'm worried ordering anything else will make me look out of place. Why come to a coffee shop if you aren't going to drink coffee? How do you drink yours, I wonder.

The waitress comes over just in time for Martha to point at her cup and hold up two fingers to show she wants two more. You would think that would be rude, but it doesn't seem to be when she does it. It's her smile, I think, it's so enthralling. Everything about her makes me feel inferior. I remind myself that you chose us both, that we must have something in common for you to want us both. Or maybe she was an upgrade for you? Maybe I was a trial run.

'Have you been here before?' she asks.

'No. I don't really go out much. I work funny hours.'

'Oh, what is it you do?'

'I'm just a waitress,' I say as the waitress arrives at the table with our coffees. She gives me the tiniest scowl and I shrink back a little. I don't even know why I lied, why I don't want to tell her I work front desk at a hotel.

'I'm a software developer. I do websites and search engine optimisation and other boring stuff like that.'

I have no idea what she is talking about but it sounds like something you need to go to university for. Martha has a ring on every finger, including her thumbs. Gold and silver in different patterns and thicknesses. Around her neck, she wears a delicate gold chain with what looks like a coin on it and in her ears she wears thick gold hoops that nestle among the tight black curls of her hair, occasionally catching the light. She wouldn't look out of place with a crown on, to be honest. I can't for the life of me figure out the connection between us. We look different, we dress differently and we have very different lives and yet we both crossed your path for long enough for you to choose us and so there must be something, some invisible line between us that made you notice us.

'Have you always lived in Eastport?' I say, aware that I'm making small talk because I don't know how to broach the subject of you.

'I have, grew up here. My parents live here, too, and my brother. What about you?'

'No, I moved here a few years ago and don't really speak to my family anymore.'

'Sorry to hear that, that must be tough. I don't know what I would do without my family.'

'I find life much easier without mine,' I say as a joke, a flippant comedic jab at something I don't want to go into.

'This is so surreal. I don't even know why I went to that meeting and now I've met you.'

'I am so grateful you did.'

'It's weird, isn't it? How everyone else is just getting on with things and he's out there right now. Do you ever think about him?'

87

'I try not to,' I say, not exactly lying but we both know it's impossible not to think about you. That's what you want, isn't it? To matter to someone. To mean something. Well, I wasn't put on this earth to give your life meaning.

Chapter 16

Shona tried to unwind in the bath after a heavy evening of futile interviews with a couple of drunks who got into a pub fight that landed someone in hospital. The problem was she couldn't get the visit from Gail Reynolds out of her head. She had always regretted that first meeting. She was a fairly new DS and keen to impress, looking for a fast track to promotion. As a result she followed orders more often than she trusted her instincts. She had talked it through with her now fiancé Aaron several times over the subsequent months but then she had kind of forgotten about it, moved on. Seeing Gail Reynolds again, that same angry fire in her eyes, reminded Shona that she had the luxury of being able to put it behind her. Gail did not.

Shona got out of the bath and dried off before heading downstairs and grabbing a half-empty bottle of white from the fridge. Her phone rang and she looked at the screen, hoping it was Aaron, but it was her brother Elliott; she didn't have the energy to speak to him right now and she didn't want to anyway. She made a mental note to call him back later, something she always forgot to do. They weren't close and he only ever called when he wanted something, usually money. Aaron hadn't messaged to say he wasn't coming over tonight. His mother wasn't well enough to be left alone, her dementia getting markedly worse over the last year. There was a good chance he might turn up as he usually let her know if he couldn't. His mum's illness was the only thing stopping them from getting married, the situation too volatile to plan a wedding around, especially as his sister was next to useless and his mother was prone to wandering off at all times, day or night. Selfishly she quite enjoyed the time apart, although she knew it was hard on him. It would definitely be strange when she had him all to herself. She felt bad for not wanting things to change but she had never been good with other people. Her family were dysfunctional and she was just fine with it like that. Of course it meant she was a bit shit at being a fiancée.

The doorbell rang and she felt that jolt of excitement she always got when she was about to see Aaron. She wondered if that feeling would ever go away. Love wasn't something she thought she was capable of, not after Graham had made her feel so worthless all those years ago.

'Hey,' she said, but before she had the chance to

utter another word his lips were on hers. Not one of those friendly sterile kisses he gave her at the station where someone might see them. This was deep and urgent, propelling her backwards. He kicked the door shut behind him and within seconds she was swept along with him in the moment. His hand on the back of her neck as she pulled at his belt. Feeling close to him right now might be what she needed after the day she had had. She thought Graham had stolen the part of her that felt desire before she met Aaron, but being with him was life-affirming. She pulled back and stared into his eyes, a deep ocean blue in this muted light. They went dark like this when he wanted her, she could feel the hunger radiating from them.

'I missed you,' he said, tugging at her waist, trying to pull her even closer.

'I wasn't sure if you'd come tonight, I thought you would be at your mother's,' she whispered breathlessly.

'I called Anna and she stepped in last minute. I had to see you. I hope you don't mind.'

'Does it seem like I mind?' she said, planting her lips firmly on his and pulling him back towards the sofa; they fell onto it together. He pulled up her night dress as she lowered his trousers and they made love right there. They could barely keep their hands off each other and it was always like this, passionate and almost desperate, as though he needed her. Tonight she needed him, too.

Chapter 17

It was almost nine months before I met my father's girlfriend Sadie, and he only introduced her to me to tell me she was pregnant. I knew then I had lost my dad. His girlfriend was much younger than my mother, and much prettier, she looked closer to my sister's age than to my father's. Seeing her thrust the memory of that night in the caravan back into my mind. I was disgusted with both of them.

When I would stay at my father's house, I could hear them having sex and in the morning she would parade around the house in just a T-shirt and under-pants. I wondered how my dad had got together with her but I didn't feel close enough to ask him. Sadie had firm milky white thighs and she wore tight-fitting short black clothing most of the time which just accentuated the paleness of her skin. She had blonde hair and either wore no make-up or a lot of black make-up.

I preferred her without make-up. I watched Sadie like a hawk, I would play ninja in the house and move around without her seeing me. Sometimes she let her guard down enough to leave the bedroom door open when she got changed, and one time she even left the bathroom door open while she showered, thinking I was asleep in my room. I wanted to touch her so badly it hurt, but as nice as she was to me, I knew she only tolerated me because I was my father's son. I had a small video recorder my grandad had bought me for holidays. It was cheap and rubbish but I would try and get any footage I could of Sadie. I had taken a video of her showering and I would look at it when I was alone in bed, hoping no one would ever find the camera and know what kind of person I was. I knew it was wrong but there was something that made me wonder if Sadie had wanted me to see her in the shower. She did leave the door slightly open after all.

Chapter 18

Shona woke up on the sofa nestled into Aaron. Immediately irritated by the warmth of his arms around her, she jumped up too fast, sending her head spinning and knocking last night's discarded glass of wine across the floor. He barely stirred at the commotion and thankfully the glass didn't shatter. Dawn was breaking so she knew it was before five. She grabbed some kitchen towel and wiped the small puddle of wine before it soaked into the gaps in the laminate flooring. As soon as her thoughts had settled, the first thing that hit her was the recurring guilt Gail Reynolds had left her with. Shona had let her down badly the first time they met but now maybe she had an opportunity to put things right. Shona should look into what happened three years ago, maybe there were other victims, maybe even a pattern. Shona could do what was known as a rainbow grid search, checking against all possible variables until patterns emerged. It was time-consuming and a bit like fishing in the dark, but she had to start somewhere. She couldn't relax anyway, so she might as well head back to the station and use the database. She hadn't lied to Gail when she said she was sorry; if Shona could go back and do that day all over again she would have handled it very differently. Maybe this was her opportunity to put things right. There was no reason not to believe Gail Reynolds this time – not that there was last time either. What harm was there in taking a closer look?

When she got to her desk and accessed the system, the first thing she did was look up reports of unsolved rape cases in Eastport in the last five years. She was confronted with a sobering number she didn't even care to think about. She wondered how many didn't even make it into the system, how many men and women didn't even make it into the station. Shona filtered out the male victims first, then narrowed down the age to within five years either side of Gail's, then she narrowed it down further by adding things like face coverings, plastic sheets, all the grim details and was left with a more manageable number. She pulled up the notes on every single one and read through them, her anger growing the more she read. It was times like this Shona almost wished she had become a teacher instead, which was the only other career she had ever really had any interest in pursuing.

She started looking through her diary notes on past case files, looking for any mention of June 12th. If Gail was right, that animal was going to attack another woman in less than a week.

There was one other thing that was bothering Shona. What was the significance of the date? Why did that particularly trigger him into action? She wondered what he did for the other 364 days of the year. Cross-referencing between her own notes and the ones in the system she found a few possible cases, none with exactly the same details but close enough to take another look.

After widening her search criteria to go back another five years there was one name that stood out among the others. Seven years ago on the 12th of June, a woman named Kathy Lewis made a complaint about an attack that sounded almost identical. Seven years? What were the chances he waited seven years between attacks? There must be other victims out there. Shona took a note of the woman's address. It was too early to call her now, but she noted her phone number anyway. The case was never resolved, there didn't seem to have been much follow-up on the subject by the officer that had been in charge of that case: DI Coleridge, the same woman who had encouraged Shona to sweep Gail's case under the carpet. She was ambitious and keen to keep their open case files to a minimum. It wasn't long before Shona figured out her game; she would just convince the complainant that it was pointless, and they would back off. A master manipulator, and now a DCI in another station. That wasn't a game Shona was willing to play. How many other complainants had been encouraged not to press charges, convinced it wasn't going to go anywhere? How much more information would they have on this rapist if Coleridge had actually done her job and investigated? How many rapes could they have stopped if they had been paying attention? The whole thing made Shona sick. This wasn't why she joined the police, it wasn't about numbers and keeping the tables clean. Of course, no one wanted a load of open and unsolved cases, but pretending they weren't happening didn't help anyone, not the police, not the community, not the victims that trusted them.

Another question was at what point did he decide which woman he was going to attack? Did he watch them for weeks, months before he broke into their houses? Did he watch them after the deed was done? Did he like to see the damage he had done? What was it that got this monster off? She would have to visit Kathy Lewis and see if she could give her any information that could connect the attacks. If he had been operating for seven years, he might have even been getting away with this for much longer. Given that

Gail had no idea how old he was, he could have been doing this for decades. It was a sobering thought that a serial rapist with such a distinctive MO could have got this far without the authorities noticing. Gail was telling the truth, Shona believed that now. If she was honest, she would admit that she believed her three years ago as well but was more concerned with not upsetting her boss. Compelled to keep digging, Shona started looking at newspaper reports from around both attacks, to see if anything jumped out at her, or if there were any other clues in there as to who might be doing this. If he was a serial attacker, he must have made a mistake at some point and she was going to find it.

Chapter 19

I hold Martha's hand through the Thursday meeting at the St Mary's church hall. The thought that you have touched these hands is never too far from my mind. As each woman gets up to speak I can feel Martha holding her breath. I don't even realise at first but I am doing the same thing. It's strange to have a comrade in this now, I no longer feel completely alone. I genuinely can't remember the last time I felt part of something good. I feel my life between my fingers again, where previously it slipped away as I lost grip. Maybe there is a way out of all of this darkness, maybe Martha and I could find a way to move past all of this, past you. I haven't dared to think like this in so long, not since before that night, maybe even before Stuart Potts.

As the group leader asks if anyone else would like to talk, I remember I promised to speak. I couldn't have done this a week ago but now I have a little more strength thanks to finding Martha and so I stand up. Martha's hand slips out of mine for the first time in an hour. I walk towards the podium and take a deep breath. It's funny how you have made me feel like I can never talk about what happened between us, what you did to me. It seems odd to be ashamed of something that was done to me, something I had no choice in. How did you manage that? I am terrible at keeping secrets and yet here I am, keeping you inside so they can't touch you. This is your secret, not mine, I haven't done anything wrong. Some of the women stare glassy-eyed into the distance but some of them stare straight at me and I know I have to do this for them. I have to make them feel less alone. I'm not keeping your secret anymore.

'My name is Gail and three years ago a man broke into my house, drugged me and raped me. I think I left the window open because it was a warm summer's night and my kitchen backs on to my garden. It didn't even occur to me that someone would break in while I was inside. Isn't that weird? Anyway, I got home from work and fell asleep on the sofa and when I woke up there was a bag over my head or something. I didn't call out, I didn't fight back, I just lay there. I don't know what he looked like, how old he was, nothing. I felt strange, cloudy in my mind, unable to move, unable to resist in any way.'

'This is the first time I have spoken about it since I went to the police on that night. They said that because of the nature of the attack and the lack of evidence, I was unlikely to get a conviction and so I withdrew my statement and went home. Back to the same home where he attacked me. It took months before I got a proper night's sleep again. I still don't know who it was that did it to me, I've probably walked past him in the street at some point and I wouldn't have a clue. I didn't think I could get past this but then I met someone special who made me realise that I wasn't alone. It's been a hard few years but I believe I can move on with my life now. I won't let him take anything else from me, he's had enough.'

The people in the room start clapping and I rush back to my seat. I didn't know exactly what I would say before I said it, but the more I spoke the angrier I got. I felt a shift inside myself, a desire to make a change, to do something not to just keep waiting for things to happen. It feels good to be taking the power back from you.

The hall empties out after the meeting but I stay in my chair. A couple of the new girls nod a hello in my direction and I feel proud of myself for turning up, for speaking up, for not being invisible me anymore. I look at the other women here and try to imagine why you chose me and not them. There must be a reason. Maybe it was nothing but opportunity.

But you would have had to know that I live alone. You can't have just plucked my house at random that night. You chose me. How? My fingers are locked around Martha's again. I know I wouldn't be here without her. She pulled me out of my slumber and brought me back to life. We are waiting to speak to the group leader, Colleen. Colleen is the only name we have for her. Colleen has the feeling of someone who still lives with a parent; she's much older than me but dresses even older than that. Her trousers have a crease sewn into them and her shoes are both well worn and well loved. The cardigan Colleen wears looks hand knitted in a cheap acrylic wool, and in all the time I have been coming to these meetings I have only ever seen Colleen's hair in a loose ponytail. The most striking and important thing about Colleen though is that she looks trustworthy.

'Sorry, ladies, there's another group meeting here soon so we have to get out of the building,' Colleen calls across the room.

'We can help you pack away, if you like,' I say, standing up, my hand feeling cold as it leaves Martha's grip.

'Thank you, just stack the blue chairs in the corner, you can leave the grey ones out,' Colleen says.

'I'm sorry, I actually wanted to talk to you. This is going to sound a bit unorthodox but I was wondering if I could ask you a question?' I say, walking towards the woman. Instinctively she moves backwards as Martha stays well on the sidelines.

'It really depends what the question is.'

'Martha and I think we were raped by the same man. I wondered if you knew of anyone else with a similar story to ours.'

'I can't tell you anything you haven't heard in the meeting yourself. You've been coming here for months and never spoken yourself until today; you must know how important it is to maintain the trust and sanctity of these meetings.'

'I understand, honestly I do. But you see we don't think he is done; we think he is going to hurt someone else.'

'Probably, yes. But I don't see how me betraying someone's confidence is going to help you find what you are looking for. These are two separate things.'

'That's fine, you don't need to tell me a name or any information about the person, but just tell me if you have heard of a woman being attacked in her home on a plastic sheet, a bag or pillowcase over her head, made to wash with bleach afterwards.'

Colleen stands with her head tilted backwards, obviously trying to remember.

'Or any variation of that,' Martha adds, standing up and joining us.

'It does sound familiar, but then who knows with these sickos? I think maybe I have heard that before.

Not recently, mind. I can't actually remember who told that story anyway. I remember she said the pillowcase on her head smelled of her nan's lavender perfume. I don't remember exactly.'

'Can you remember anything else?'

'I wish I could help you but really, I hear so many things it's hard to place where or when I heard them. It all kind of blends into one.'

I pull out a receipt from my handbag and scribble my number onto the back of it. 'Please, if you do hear of anything please let me know. Like I said I don't need any personal details. I just want to know if it's happened to anyone else.'

She takes the paper and stuffs it into her pocket before turning away from us and continuing to clear away the Jammie Dodgers, laid out to soften the blow of spilling your deepest darkest secrets to a bunch of strangers. I can see that she's done talking. I respect her more for knowing she won't just flippantly tell me what I wanted to know. It never occurred to me the toll this kind of thing must take on a person. She's been running these groups a lot longer than I've been coming here and so these awful incidents have taken on a kind of mundanity in her mind, an everyday occurrence, something that happens to so many people. Is that what it's like for you? Just some mundane function you perform? Or maybe it's exciting, like a birthday treat for yourself. I can't get inside your head no matter how hard I try. I suppose I should be relieved about that.

'Thank you, you've been a great help,' I say, noting that she said lavender and I didn't mention that in my story today. She must have heard something about you before. This makes me both angry and more resolved that I am right. We aren't the only ones.

We finish putting the chairs away before leaving the hall and going outside.

'Well, that was no use,' Martha says.

'It means there's more of us. I never mentioned the lavender.'

'But how do we find them?'

'We'll think of something. This is how these bastards get away with it, everyone is too ashamed to talk, too ashamed to make a fuss, including me.'

If there are more victims they are scattered and suffering alone. Well, I'm not going to stand for that anymore. I'm going to make sure everyone in Eastport is aware of you, are you ready for that? I'm going to blow your little world apart. There are only nine more days until you strike again. I have to put the burning shame I feel to one side and take action. No more. There will be nowhere for you to hide.

Chapter 20

Shona drove out to the address on file for Kathy Lewis. The stillness on the street felt like an ominous prelude to something terrible but then Shona was an inherently gloomy person. It ran in her family, and her tumultuous childhood made it hard for her to trust, she had never learned how. From toxic parents who treated their offspring as an afterthought, to a brother who was only out for himself, she had cut and run the second she was old enough to. A few years of dodgy boyfriends then she met Aaron and everything changed; he made her feel safe, safe and special.

It was another quiet evening, hardly any cars about, most people resting after work ready for the night ahead. It was unusually hot for June and so parties and barbecues happened every night of the week, everyone desperate to make the most of it before the inevitable rain came. Wimbledon and Glastonbury at the end of the month were both virtually synonymous with rain. Everyone was so sure that this year, like every other year, summer would only last a week or two. It always lasted longer.

There was a parking space outside the house and Shona pulled in. She saw the curtains twitching from inside the house as she got out of the car. The fact that she should have been making this visit years ago played on her mind. She was worried that she might trigger the victim, thrust her back to a place where she didn't feel safe. *Oh, hi, remember that terrible thing that happened to you?* Kathy's registered address was a pretty house painted in blues and greens with small white stars painted here and there. It was completely out of keeping with the rest of the street, which looked a bit dour. This house had a bohemian chic about it, even though it was just a modest terrace. Knocking on the door Shona looked up to see the curtains rustle again. She bent down and looked through the letterbox. A woman was coming down the stairs, one step at a time, while clutching onto the banister. Shona stood up straight.

'Yes?' the woman said from behind the closed door.

'I'm looking for a Kathy Lewis, does she live here?'

'Not anymore, she don't,' the woman said as she pulled the door open. She was staring at Shona with pursed lips, angry about something.

'Do you know where she went?'

'She's dead. Who are you?'

'Oh my gosh I'm so sorry,' Shona said. She pulled out her warrant card and showed the lady. 'I'm DI Shona White. Did you know Kathy?'

'She was my niece, and I was her only family. What did you want to speak to her for?' the lady said, leaving the door open as she trudged inside, her blue kimono dressing gown trailing behind her.

Shona was speechless as she followed the lady into the living room. She felt like she had walked into a Victorian drawing room, looking at the matching walls, curtains and sofa in a gilded cobalt blue fabric. Velvet throws and cushions all in greens and blues. The windows were also adorned with carved and painted shutters where the summer light bled through in a Moroccan star pattern onto the large intricate woven rug. All the wooden furniture had been hand-painted. It was like something out of an interior design magazine. Shona desperately wanted to take a picture of the room, so she could copy it exactly and never leave. The woman picked up a pack of cigarettes and lit one, the red of her lipstick staining the tip as she dragged on it hard. Shona could see she was uncomfortable talking about her niece.

'I . . . just had some questions about a police report she made a few years ago.'

'Well, I've heard enough about that one to last a lifetime. I doubt there's much more to say on the matter.'

'Can I ask how she died?'

'Well, she killed herself a year after the attack. Your lot were fucking useless and what with all the harassment she got.'

'Harassment?'

'Some bloke, I don't know. Wouldn't leave her alone about it. Kept trying to get her to admit she lied about being raped.'

'Do you know his name?'

'Nick maybe, something beginning with N, he just wouldn't leave her alone. Nasty little shit he was. Put her picture all over social media. She got a lawyer to try and get him to stop but she couldn't. I can't remember the particulars exactly, but she used to read me stuff that they sent to her and it was hateful, vile stuff.'

'And was he the man who attacked her?'

'Oh no, he had one of them internet blog things. Used to write about her sometimes, saying she was lying about getting raped, said she had form for it. It was loads of them, not just him, it was his website though. They said such horrible things about her. How she was just a slag who liked getting men into trouble. All that kind of stuff. She just couldn't stand it anymore.'

'You said that he said she had form for it. What do you mean?'

'Well, it weren't the first time she reported a rape. Fat lot of good it did her that time either – her landlord in her old flat raped her when she couldn't afford the rent. He told the police it was an arrangement and they believed him. She moved into a studio flat in the town centre when the other attack happened. That's when she gave up and moved in here with me. Couldn't face living in a place on her own again. It was nice, having her here. She was very artistic and started doing things up for me. I've got this whole place to myself now. There was nothing I could do for her though. She didn't trust anyone, not even me really,' the woman said wistfully.

'I'm sorry for your loss. She did all this?'

'Yes, she had real talent.'

'It's stunning. You must really miss her.'

'I know this is going to sound like a weird thing to say, but she was in so much pain I think she's better off out of it. Watching her suffer the way she did was harder than anything. She got too scared to leave the house, spent all her time painting and eventually had to give up work, too. It was no life.' The woman ran her fingers along a table that had been decorated in a midnight blue with celestial art hand-painted onto it. A small smile appeared on her face. She was clearly remembering something specific, something private.

'I won't take up any more of your time,' Shona said, feeling more than intrusive right now.

'I go visit her grave sometimes, you know. Let me know if you find that bastard and I'll tell her the good news.'

With that, Shona left. The wake of what happened still hung heavy in that house, the memory of Kathy Lewis painted into the room. And when her elderly aunt was gone, what then? Did she just cease to exist altogether?

Chapter 21

I started to feel like there was a ticking clock on my virginity during my GCSEs. Everyone at school was doing it, or at least everyone cool was. Some of them were even doing it IN school. I felt so inadequate and unattractive, so unwanted. These were the darkest days I remember. I wasn't sure I would get through them. It was coming up to the summer holidays and after that I would be moving back to a basic school with basic ordinary kids who didn't have anything. My father was no longer willing to pay my private school tuition fees. I felt so disgusted with both of my parents for doing this to me. Why have children at all if you aren't going to make a decent life for them?

I decided I would try even harder to get a girlfriend. I knew there were a lot of beach parties happening in the run-up to end of term and so I made sure I knew when they were. I wanted to get with one of the girls *from this school, they were just better bred than the other girls in town. After about three parties, it became evident my plan wasn't going to work. The only girls that seemed to know who I was weren't very pretty, not like Faiyaz's girlfriend Nicola or even his ex Tori. She was still alone, still hands-off as though there were some rule that she still belonged to Faiyaz for a period of time after they broke up, like he could change his mind if he wanted to. Maybe because I was leaving, I didn't need to adhere to these rules anymore.*

I nicked a bottle of Grey Goose vodka from my mum's reserve drinks cupboard and went to a party I had heard about happening at West Bay. It was the fanciest alcohol I could find, all the other stuff was cheap but she had got this in lieu of a bonus at work. I cycled over to West Bay with the vodka in my backpack. There were loads of kids there so it was easy to stay out of sight and decide which of the girls I was going to offer my vodka to. Faiyaz was there and he had brought a guitar. Of course he could sing and there wasn't a girl in the place that didn't have her eyes on him longingly. In that second I really hated him and all of them. Nicole was in this spaghetti-strapped short dress and was practically draped over Faiyaz like a shawl – it was disgusting. I saw Tori burst out crying and stagger off into the dunes. I picked up my backpack and followed her. When I found her, she was still crying and looking at pictures on her phone.

She had a bottle of almost finished pink wine in her hand and she swigged greedily from it.

She didn't look as pretty drunk. Her eyes were all smudged and puffy and her nose was kind of wet and snotty, but I knew underneath all of that she was still one of the better-looking girls in the year. She was probably better than anyone I would find at the stupid comp I was being sent to. I did feel embarrassed for her; to have fallen so far in popularity was embarrassing. She was wearing a short skirt and she had a cropped hoodie on top. I decided I needed to play it cool so I pulled out my bottle of vodka and stepped out to where she was. I pretended to be surprised to see her and she apologised to me, though I wasn't sure what for. I asked her if she was OK, because that's what you are supposed to do when you see someone crying. Then she asked me what school I went to. I was mortified that she didn't recognise me. We had spoken before in school but I was of so little importance to her that she just threw those memories of me away. I listened to her blubbering over Faiyaz for what felt like forever until she had finished her bottle of wine which is when I offered her some vodka. Apparently, he was still fucking her on the side, and she was letting him. She'd promised not to make it public. I couldn't understand what Faiyaz had that had made her agree to that. I couldn't even get one girl to fuck me, let alone two. She snatched the bottle of vodka from me and drank.

I leaned forward and tried to kiss her and she actually gagged before bursting into laughter. I was so angry. Who did she think she was? She was nothing but a sidepiece and yet she thought she was too good for me? I was livid. I hated her and all the girls like her at that stupid school. It was their fault I was unpopular, they were too shallow to look past my shortcomings.

We had been there over an hour when she fell asleep. I had to listen to her mumbled ramblings and pretend to console her. She was so drunk and I knew I shouldn't leave her alone but I wasn't strong enough to move her. I got up to leave, the prospect of anything meaningful happening between us gone now that she was dribbling into the sand. I was worried she might throw up and so I rolled her onto her side like they had taught us in first aid class. In that moment with my hand on her thigh I realised she wasn't going to wake up. The thought popped into my head fully formed before I had even really considered what it was I was thinking. She was sparko, there was no way she would know what was going on. I could just slip my hand further up inside her pants and no one would know, not even her. I rolled her onto her back again and lay on top of her. I didn't do anything, I was too scared. One of her eyes was wide open, her pupil was fully dilated, her one blue eye looking at me in disgust as I lay there. I couldn't move, I couldn't do anything as I wondered whether she could actually see me or not.

I could smell the wine and vodka on her breath as our faces were so close together. All I would have to do was put my lips on hers, all I would have to do was reach up under her skirt and I would know what it felt like. Even feeling her breasts against me made me hard and I moved slightly, the friction exacerbating my situation. I kept moving slowly, my dick rubbing against the fabric in my pants, but knowing what was just beneath there made me come. Still that one eye stared at me.

I heard laughter as someone approached and I scrambled to get out of there. The pillowy warmth of Tori's body had made me even more angry. I hated her, I hated all of them. The fact that the most comfortable I had ever been with a girl was when she was unconscious wasn't lost on me. When I got home I climbed into bed and thought about her lying there, her one eye staring at me. I should have covered it up, I should have put my coat over her face. Just like that I had been given an opportunity that I had wished for so many times and I hadn't taken it. It would have been so easy but I was too afraid. I cursed myself for that. I knew how it would happen though, how I would finally get what it was I ultimately desired. If they wouldn't give me their bodies I would take them.

Chapter 22

I get home from my night shift just in time for the scaffolders at the neighbour's house to turn up and start a seemingly endless amount of clanging and drilling. There is no way I am going to be getting any sleep until they are done. I have spent most of the night shift thinking about how I can be proactive and take charge of my life. Finding Martha was the first step, now I need to find your other girls. I am more convinced than ever that we aren't the only ones. I wasn't your first, was I? The more I think about it, the more I can see how practised you were, how you left nothing to chance. I bet that wasn't always the case though. I bet you made some really big mistakes in the past. By the time you got to me it was old hat, wasn't it? The date can't be a coincidence either. There are other patterns too; there has to be a reason why you chose us. I just need to find the other people and find out what else we all have in common. I want to help them, I want to drag them out of the hell you've put us all in.

After my post-work shower I get dressed and go into the kitchen. The window is still nailed firmly shut, the rust gathering at the heads of the nails oddly comforting. The day before I occupied my sleeping time by making four lasagnes and freezing three of them. I took the fourth out and put it in the oven ready for later on. Everything feels different since I met Martha, like I now have a purpose. So many of the negative whispers have been silenced with the confirmation of my attack. Knowing I am not crazy is not something I will ever take for granted again.

I look at the calendar on my wall. It came free from the Chinese takeaway that I used most often. There is a picture of a street filled with red lanterns. It doesn't say where it is, and the resolution isn't that brilliant. I look at the date, it's the 7th of June. Only a few days until June 12th. I see it is marked down as red rose day on the calendar. Is that significant to you? I don't feel like it would be, but then what do I know?

At school I always loved to draw, but I haven't done it in a long time. Not since going to art school and subsequently dropping out, to my parents' horror. Maybe that was the beginning of the end of their trust in me. They practically begged me not to go, but I went anyway and then I couldn't see it through to the end. It gave me a kind of rep within my own family of being a quitter, someone who takes the easy way out, someone who is reckless with themselves. I know after that point that something was broken between us. I didn't think it would lead to this. I picked a side, myself, and they saw that as betrayal. After that point they didn't really support me in any way, a constant reminder that I had gone against their wishes. I fell out of love with drawing and painting as it had become associated with ruining my life. I dropped out and joined the local college to do a business studies BTEC which is where I met Stuart Potts. The incident between us happened in the weeks before my final exams and so I didn't attend. I failed that course, too. In some ways I think my parents saw the rape accusation against Stuart as an extension of my flaky behaviour, maybe even an excuse for not doing well in my course. The questioning look in their eyes still haunts me to this day. The moment I realised they didn't believe me was long before they voiced it out loud, but they still did voice it. Just Gail being Gail again, making excuses for her bad behaviour. I hated them so much for it. Now I feel mostly nothing. I don't miss them, I don't long to go back. Being alone here has always felt less lonely than being stuck with a family that thinks you would do something like that. Still, I can't go back. Those things are in the past and everyone has already said what they wanted to say on the issue. I have moved on.

I keep all my art materials in a trunk in the utility room. Do you like to draw? So many people don't do it because it's something we stop doing when we grow up. Isn't it? It's one of the few parts of my old life that I brought with me. The trunk itself once belonged to my grandmother. It's a metal trunk painted a matt black and decoupaged with huge red roses. There is a big dent in the lid where I stood on it to try and fit a lightbulb once. I lift the trunk and bring it into the lounge, the smell of paint and pencil shavings taking over the room as soon as I open the metal box. All I can think about is how to get people's attention, I need to make them notice what's going on around them. It feels good to be holding a paintbrush again, like I am reclaiming myself. The familiar chant of *No more* runs through my mind as I paint picture after picture until I look at them on top of my trusty old trunk to decide which I like best. I am out of practice and so they all look quite basic but I still feel good to have created something. I settle on the image I want to use. A bleeding red rose.

The doorbell rings and I pull back for the first time in hours, unshackled from my task. I open the front door and find Martha standing there holding a box of yellow paper she took from work.

'I got a phone. No contract so no way to trace it back to me,' I tell Martha as I usher her inside. She's my comrade, my partner in crime. 'I've just got to write the number on the flyers. What do you think?'

I hold up the flyers I have been working on. A picture of a bleeding red rose surrounded by text.

EVERY YEAR IN EASTPORT
A SERIAL RAPIST STRIKES
ON JUNE 12TH
ARE YOU ONE OF HIS VICTIMS?
WE CAN HELP YOU
CALL ERIS 07223 766331

'What's with the red rose?' Martha asked.

'I was trying to find out the significance of the date and the only thing I really found was that the 12th of June is red rose day. I want it to stand out, you know? I want people to notice. Maybe we can get everyone talking about it. It will be harder for him to go about his business if everyone knows about him.'

'Who is Eris?'

'We are! Eris was the Greek goddess of discord, strife and chaos. Daughter of Zeus, or Nyx depending on what mythology you read. We are going to shake things up a bit. I haven't worked out exactly how just yet, but let's start with getting information. If they don't want to help us, we can help ourselves. I won't be silenced anymore, I won't be pushed around.'

'So, what now?'

'I've got some printing to do. I'll set it running now. I made a lasagne and when we've eaten, we can go out and put these babies up. I got us a mask, gloves and some spray glue each.'

'Will we get into trouble for this?' Martha said nervously but with a hint of mischief in her expression.

'Just try not to be seen when you put them up. I would rather see where this goes before everyone finds out who I am. I've got a bit of a reputation for being a flake and I think we would get a better response if it were from an anonymous source, makes it feel more menacing, if you know what I mean? Like Batman or something like that.'

I put the paper in the printer and then rest the flyer on top, programming in one hundred copies. I will print as many as I can until the ink runs out, and if needs be I will buy more ink tomorrow. I'll make us impossible to ignore. Our actions may even force the police to act. I will keep pushing until the local press get a hold of this, I will make sure everyone knows what's been going on in this town right under their noses.

Martha sits at the table. Today she is all in black like me. I have noticed before that she picks a colour and dresses in it from head to toe. I barely even think about what I wear beyond what is clean and comfortable but tonight is different, tonight we need to be invisible. Is there any colour that doesn't look good on her? I tidied the house but I still feel self-conscious having her in here. Chowder is loving the attention of having someone new to fuss over him. I look at Martha, she is everything I am not. She's elegant, beautiful and demure. I want to know more about her. There has to be a reason for you to choose us but I can't see a connection.

'Do you ever wonder why he chose you?' I ask outright, not expecting myself to be so direct.

'It's all I think about.'

'How did he know you would be alone? That's what I wonder, how could he know?'

'Do you have an alarm fitted here? A couple of weeks before it happened, I got an alarm fitted to the house. Well, a fake alarm. It was one of those boxes that looks like an alarm. I couldn't afford the real deal. I wondered if it was someone at that company who did it. That's how it works in the movies, isn't it? It's always someone who has been at your house recently.'

'I haven't got an alarm, unless you count Chowder and I didn't have him then.'

I never thought about what job you might have, not really, but you must have one. Funny how you consume my every waking thought, but I still don't really think about you as a real person with real things going on in your life. Do you have any children? You might have, but I really hope you don't.

'I ruled them out anyway. The alarm company was small and run by a married couple and they were on holiday when it happened – I found out from my

123

friend who recommended them that they had no staff, did all the work themselves. It was a long shot. I've been wracking my brain since it happened as to how I could have met this person. I got nowhere.'

'I worked and I came home and slept. I barely had a life when it happened but he still knew how to get to me, when I would be in, that I would be alone. I can't see a pattern either. That's why we need to get our message out, put the flyers around town and hope someone gets in touch.'

'Where do we put these flyers?' Martha asked.

'Everywhere.'

Chapter 23

To Shona's horror a quick search online found several hundred mentions of Kathy Lewis in various forums, some local, some not so much. Her whole life was laid bare and scrutinised to a microscopic level. Pictures had been taken from her own social media from after the alleged attack, showing her to be smiling, people commenting that she didn't look particularly trauma-tised, as if you had to wear your trauma for every second of every day. Beyond that there were images of her face pasted onto pornography, rape fantasy fiction by an alarming number of men who wanted to show Kathy what it was really like so she would stop making false accusations. The level of vitriol aimed at Kathy had driven her to suicide. Some people seemed gleefully happy about that, as though her ending her life was even further proof that she had lied, that she felt so much guilt for what she had done that she took her own life. When you read things like this it's a wonder anyone comes forward to report their sexual assaults at all. With freedom of speech suddenly meaning say whatever the hell you want without consequence or regard to people's feelings, Shona was glad she had never got too involved in this online world. She liked to stay on top of the latest trends and apps – you never knew when someone was going to mention something in an interview and it was good to know what they were talking about – but beyond that she much preferred the real world. Maybe it was naive of her not to acknowledge all this stuff online as significant too. Crimes were being committed here. Imagine going through something as devastating as a rape and then to be publicly outed and shamed for it, on a forum that could be seen from anywhere in the world. It must feel like being assaulted all over again, as people decide what kind of person you are based on second-hand information and lies. You couldn't behave like this on the street. The law had a lot of catching up to do.

Shona started looking at the dates of the entries and traced it all back to a local Eastport website called The Sanctuary which had its own blog dedicated to Kathy, with a lot of unflattering and candid photos, details of her personal life including any previous boyfriends she had had, social media screenshots from private messages, an old CCJ from not paying an electricity bill – your bog-standard character assassination. There was even the court transcript from when she tried to prosecute her former landlord for rape, annotated and highlighted with words like LIAR and BITCH scribbled in the margins. The landlord had claimed she had offered him sex in exchange for a reduction in the rent and when he refused to lower it even more, she set out to destroy him. She told them how he used his own key to come into the house whenever he wanted and one time he wasn't satisfied with just looking. Unfortunately, she was behind on the rent and because she'd been evicted it looked like a revenge plot to the jury and they believed him over her. No stone had been left unturned, and the conversations that came from these posts within the forum were chilling. Thankfully Shona didn't know any men like this in real life, but they seemed to find each other online, each one reinforcing the others' beliefs, until they were convinced they knew the truth and no one else did. Kathy's case was reminiscent of the taxi driver who raped over seventy women before he got caught, even after a woman reported him. The police officer who questioned him had practically told him to say that she had offered to pay for a ride with sex before letting him go, because the girl was drunk and an unreliable witness. Shona would like to believe incidents like that were rare, but she had not only witnessed them first-hand, she had been party to it with Gail Reynolds.

For a moment Shona considered looking up her own name and seeing if anything about her came up anywhere but then she decided ignorance was bliss. Having your whole life dissected like that was enough to drive anyone over the edge. She imagined Kathy reading all of this stuff and how hard it must have hit her.

The comments in the forum were even worse. Peppered among the seemingly innocuous ones were some profoundly disturbing ones, detailing the best way to deal with someone who accused someone else of rape. At no point did anyone in the comments even entertain the notion that she was telling the truth. The overall feeling of this website was that women were liars and that men who didn't see that were idiots or 'cucks', as they liked to call them.

Shona took down the name of the former landlord from the court transcript and looked for the host of the site. Nathan Barker was a name that appeared more than once. In the comments section his die-hard followers all referred to him as Natemod. She looked through some of his other blog topics, many of them with just a woman's name as a title. Always the same story, trying to out women who had made rape allegations. He even had links to crowdfunding sites to raise money for the men who had been accused. When she found the admin page for the site he was listed as the lead moderator and host of the site. There was a members-only forum discussion called 'Lying Stacy whores #34' and when she looked through there were thirty-three other threads of the same nature, each one was basically open season on any woman who had ever looked at one of these guys the wrong way. From women who ran shops to wives, there was a level of bitterness that took it beyond venting and to another place, where violence was not implied but stated explicitly, both sexual and physical. A 'Stacy' seemed to refer to a certain type of woman, physically perfect and out of reach for the type of men that frequented this forum, something they took very personally. In some of the comments the men used codenames for the women, but in others they just used their full names. Within the photographs she recognised local streets, shops, houses. These women's privacy had been well and truly violated. Shona left the tab open but closed the laptop, feeling sick on Kathy's behalf and feeling guilty for even reading it.

There was a podcast, too. She wondered why Nathan was so obsessed with female rape victims and shaming women in general. His address was easy enough to find, and so she wrote it down. She wanted to see what kind of person could write such hateful things. Looking in the mirror, she made sure she looked presentable enough. She didn't relish going to speak to him but at the same time, men like that hated having to speak to women in authority. She hoped he said or did just enough for her to slap the cuffs on him and drag him to the station by his ear. These keyboard warriors had very little concept of the damage they inflicted. Rage had displaced her disgust and she wanted answers. She looked at the clock. Nathan Barker was going to have to answer some questions.

Chapter 24

Shona stood on the street in a part of town they rarely got called to. It was nice here, tidy, suburban. It certainly wasn't the kind of place she imagined the owner of The Sanctuary, Nathan Barker, living in after reading some of the content on his site. How did he look his neighbours in the eye? Each house here was uniform but unique at the same time, bungalows on large plots of land with a view across town to the sea. Obviously Shona was in the wrong job as she couldn't imagine ever being able to afford to live round here on her salary. She noted two cars in the driveway and one had a car-seat in the back, a pink car-seat. She hoped he didn't have a daughter after reading some of the things he said about women. She rang Nathan Barker's doorbell. It was one of those ones with a video screen, and his face appeared. It occurred to her that she'd had no idea what he looked like and had just assumed he was a slightly older man, but the man on the screen couldn't be past thirty.

'Who is it?'

Shona pulled out her warrant card and held it up to the screen.

'I'm Detective Inspector White. Could I speak to you a moment?'

'Wait there,' he said before the screen turned off. Moments later he appeared at the door. He opened it, shirtless and grinning. It seemed he was excited at the prospect of talking to a female police officer. She had seen some awful posts on his site with regards to women in the police and so she knew he would relay this encounter to his following. As he looked her up and down she could see the judgements and opinions forming in his mind. There was something instantly unlikable about the man and that was without thinking about all the hateful crap she had read on his blog.

'Bit early for a house call, isn't it?'

'Do you run The Sanctuary website?'

'I maintain and moderate it, that's not a crime, is it?'

'I'd like to talk to you about Kathy Lewis. I doubt you even remember the name, judging by the number of women you have named and shamed on your site,' Shona said, putting her warrant card back in her pocket.

'Rest in peace.' He smiled and kissed the silver cross around his neck.

What an obnoxious man.

'Can I come in?' Shona said, signalling towards the door. She wondered what the inside of his house looked like. You could tell a lot about a person by how they live. Although with someone like Nathan Barker who liked to spew his every thought it was less necessary. She had weeks of reading material if she really wanted to get inside his mind.

'Out here is just fine. What can I help you with?'

'How did you find out about Kathy's attacks? The rapes, I mean,' Shona corrected herself, reminded of Gail's words to just call it what it was. Did she soften it for others, or for herself?

'It was all online, I don't remember exactly. These things kind of take on a life of their own,' he said, as though he were just an innocent bystander, as though he wasn't somehow complicit in these online revelations.

'I have looked and the first mention of her online is on your site, and the first mention on that site is from you,' Shona said, not willing to let him wangle his way out of responsibility.

'There are a lot of Stacys out there who make false accusations. Men contact me about them all the time and ask me to help clear their names. When these accusations don't even have enough merit to make it through a trial you know that something is up and yet no one from the police ever apologises to these guys, no one tells their friends and neighbours that they have been cleared of any wrongdoing. Once you have that stain on you it's hard to shake. No doubt someone messaged me and asked me to talk about her, to make sure people knew she was a liar and now it's on record. I have an extensive file of men who have requested my help. I'm like a white knight to these guys.'

'I'm not sure you are using that term in the correct context.'

'I'm sorry Kathy Lewis felt so guilty she had to take the easy way out, but she shouldn't have gone around trying to ruin decent blokes' lives, should she?'

Shona looked him up and down. The veneer of feigned politeness was slipping and his hatred of women was starting to seep from his every pore.

'I don't suppose I could take a look at your extensive file, could I? Maybe see who contacted you about her in the first place?' she said, trying to stick to facts and not his opinions, which were problematic at best. At worst she wanted to smack him one.

'We take privacy on the site very seriously and I have a lawyer you can speak to if you want but I won't be giving those files up. It's called The Sanctuary for a reason.'

'I've had a look at your blog. You make a lot of statements on there that could be considered harassment or online bullying. Possibly even incitement to violence.'

'All I do is point out the truth. I don't tell anyone to do anything. I try to remove any and all comments that are illegal. I just want equal rights for men in these cases. A woman can make an accusation, and before an investigation even happens the man is considered guilty. Nine times out of ten, even if he didn't do it, he is still considered a rapist. A woman gets to keep her anonymity. How is that fair?'

'Just because a case doesn't go to trial it doesn't mean the attack didn't take place. You know rape is a notoriously hard crime to prove.' But she knew it was futile, knew he had already made his mind up and a woman certainly wasn't going to change it.

'Especially when it hasn't really happened. Do you know how many blokes' lives are ruined by these crazy vindictive bitches?'

'Do you know how many people are raped every year? It's a lot. Last year alone over fifty thousand reports and yet less than a thousand resulted in charges. Are you suggesting all of those people who made reports are lying?'

'Maybe not all, but I bet they weren't all telling the truth either.'

'I looked on your chat forum. Some of the things your members say are horrific.'

'I can't control what people say on the forum. There's a disclaimer at the top everyone has to accept before contributing. Their opinions are their own and I do not endorse them in any way, I just allow them a chance to get their truth out.'

'Do you have a list of member names?' Back to facts.

'It's all on the forum.'

'But what info do you need from them for them to be allowed to post?'

'Just an email address, most of them are probably encrypted or private emails, so not attached to real names or information. It's not my place to police people.'

'No but it is mine. Do you agree with the sentiment that women who make what you call false allegations deserve to know what it really feels like?'

'I don't think those were my exact words,' he said with a smirk. God, she wanted to hit him.

'Are there any women in your life? Mother? Sister? I hope that pink car-seat doesn't belong to a daughter or anything. I doubt you have a girlfriend anyway,' Shona said, trying to push his buttons. People were often more honest when they were angry, when they didn't think too carefully about the answers.

'Why do you doubt that?' he said, seething. She had finally pressed a button he didn't want pressed.

'I think you might be a bit more chill if you were getting laid.'

'Are you allowed to talk to me like that?'

'Sorry, did I upset you?' Shona said, pulling a fake frown. She didn't much care what he wrote about her on his hate forum.

'No. And that's my sister's car, she is visiting me. If it's all the same to you I'd like to get back inside,' he snapped, obviously upset.

'How many members does your website have?'

'Around eight thousand.'

She tried to process the magnitude of the number, knowing his was just one of many sites like this, and that it was a relatively unknown one for that matter.

'That's a lot of hate.'

'The way things are these days, I'm surprised it's not more. More and more men's rights are being eroded in order to coddle what women want. And you have the ultimate weapon. It always comes down on the woman's side. The men get made to feel like scum and then when the allegations go nowhere, the guy is just cut loose, let go, no concern for the hell he has been put through, no concern about how being accused of something like that can destroy a man's life. What happens to the women who make these false claims? Are they prosecuted for wasting police time? No. Nothing happens to them. They just get to carry on until they need to use it on some other schmuck.'

This conversation was going nowhere. Nathan Barker was probably the kind of man who would disagree with a woman on principle alone. She wondered if he would be talking to her this way if she was standing with a male officer. Maybe he wouldn't even be addressing her at all. She had met his type before, maybe not as brazen as him, but she could see him, for what he was.

'I don't know how much clearer I can explain to you that just because charges often can't be brought against a suspect in a rape allegation, it doesn't mean that the rape never happened. Sometimes it's purely down to a lack of evidence. Like I said before, a very difficult crime to prove.'

'That doesn't mean that all those women are telling the truth.' He smiled behind dead eyes.

'They aren't all lying either. What's your skin in this game exactly? Did someone accuse you?'

'No. I don't need to use force to get a woman.'

'You just seem quite invested and your hobby seems pretty time-consuming.'

'Not that it's any of your business but this is my job, not my hobby. I get a lot of ad revenue through the site. I get a lot of hits. There are a lot of angry men out there who feel like their voices aren't being heard. I have created a safe community for these people to be able to say what they want without fear of being cancelled.'

'Do your members pay a subscription fee or anything?'

'They don't have to, although there are special privileges for men who pay for extra access, it's a monthly fee. I do also have a BeneFacton account which allows content creators like me to raise a monthly income by offering perks and benefits to the people who decide to contribute.'

Shona made a mental note to try and get the information of the subscribers from BeneFacton, although from previous experience she knew they would drag their feet and try to delay if not outright refuse to supply the information.

'What kind of perks and benefits?'

'So, if they pay a hundred quid I will tell their story on the podcast.'

'And how often does the podcast go out?'

'About four times a week, depending on how busy I am.'

'Presumably they can't pay anonymously so a list of those contributors would be a great start.'

No harm in asking but she already knew he would have some kind of spiel prepared for any kind of invasive question. She couldn't imagine this was the first time he had been questioned by a police officer.

'I'll get back to you on that. I'll need to speak to my lawyer first. Members of The Sanctuary expect complete privacy. If I just out them all then I lose my livelihood. I want to help you I really do.' He smiled disingenuously.

'So, these men get anonymity but they can say these women's names and ruin their reputations?'

'Not cool, is it?' Again with the smirk.

'Is this just about money to you? Are you exploiting these men's fears by posting your controversial bile?'

'You may not agree with what I say but there are

plenty of people out there that do. Everyone has a right to express their opinions and I give them a place to do that safely, to vent, to let off steam. The world is a big place. You lefties are all the same. You wouldn't want everyone to think like you, would you?'

Finally conceding this entire interaction was a complete waste of her time, Shona decided to get the forensic techs to do a deep dive on everything Sanctuary-related and see if they could dig anything up.

'I'll be in touch, Mr Barker.'

'I look forward to it,' he said before closing the door in her face.

He was an interesting one, alright. His personality seemed unreasonable on the surface, as the things she had read before she met him suggested. She'd noticed a hint of pride when he talked about Kathy Lewis, as though he felt like he had personally achieved something by her not being alive anymore. Maybe he really was just playing to a crowd. Capitalising on an unfortunate subset of society that viewed him as some kind of Mensch. She had seen it countless times before. Some people just needed someone to follow, and he had monetised it.

She pulled out of his street and started driving towards her house. The traffic light turned amber and she slowed the car down. That's when she saw them. A boarded-up construction site with a wall of yellow flyers plastered to the side of it. She pulled over and got out of the car. It didn't take a genius to figure out who had made these flyers and she knew when she got back to the station they would have calls from the public about the flyers. Not to mention what would happen if the press got hold of the notion that there was a serial rapist operating in Eastport. Time to get her ducks in a row. It was hard not to admire Gail's fortitude and dedication to outing the man who raped her. She was taking action and not waiting for the police to take her seriously. The DCI wouldn't like this at all. What was Gail Reynolds planning?

Chapter 25

It's getting dark, the streets are empty, but the sound of revellers is never far away, although no matter which corner we turn we don't find them. I can hear people singing along as they drink with the occasional cheer after the sound of smashing glass. Are you out tonight? Are you on the hunt? Are you looking for your next victim? Or maybe you know who she is already, maybe you are sitting in her garden, watching her through the window. Is that how you get your kicks? There is always the faint smell of marijuana in the air during these summer months, it's oddly comforting. I am reminded of college days in the art room, headphones in my ears as we worked, the traces of smell on our coats from lunches on the green followed by a joint. Those are the days I barely think of in the present day, stolen and replaced with memories I wish didn't exist. Memories of you.

Every so often I get the feeling that I am being watched, and tonight is no different. I scan the beach and the path that runs alongside it. There are people around, mostly in groups but up on the verge near the edge of the cricket ground I can see a single figure, too far away for me to make out. I can't tell if he is looking at the moon or the sea. But maybe he isn't looking at either. Maybe it's you and you're watching me. My skin crawls at the thought of you but a part of me wants to get up and run towards you, hurt you in some way. As if I am even capable of that. Seconds later another figure appears from the opposite direction and they hug. It wasn't you after all.

Martha and I have put up hundreds of flyers on walls, windows, doors, lamp posts, everywhere we think people might look. We've printed off a ream of five hundred copies and stuck them in large blocks wherever there is space. I feel so rebellious and alive for a change, like I am taking control of my own destiny, instead of waiting for someone else to protect me, to avenge me. I have come to realise that no one really cares, not really. We have put the flyers anywhere we can, they are impossible to miss. That's the point. I'll go out again when the pubs are shut and stick some more up on their windows. There are a few shops that have been shut down since the shopping centre was opened outside of the town. Their windows are whitewashed with paint and so we have covered almost the entire surface of those windows with flyers. People will notice, they were sure to. I wonder how long before my phone rings. It feels wrong to be excited about this, but I am. Fuck being a victim. Fuck sitting at home and waiting for you or some other piece of shit to break into my house again and defile me. Enough is enough, I have wasted three years of my life feeling shame and guilt for your actions. No more; if I am going to be ashamed of anything it will be something I have chosen to do, not something you forced on me.

We walk down to the beach and sit on the sand. There is a group of teenagers a little further along who are stripping down to their underwear and running into the sea. I remember being like that, but it feels so intangible as a memory, as though it's trapped behind a mirror. I can barely imagine being that free again, that unburdened by fear. Somewhere out there in a parallel universe is an alternate version of me that no longer exists here. I smile as I watch them and hope that nothing ever takes that freedom away from them. I hope they never meet you. Martha is sifting through the sand and pulls out a flat white shell, perfectly smooth and satin. It glistens in the moonlight.

The fondness I feel for Martha is already so strong. Martha holds the shell out for me to take.

'I'm so glad we met,' I say.

'Me too, I think you maybe saved me, I was in a really bad place. I still am but it's different now somehow.'

'You saved me first.' I smile at her before looking back up at the full moon, his face smiling down on me. I shake you off, you aren't invited tonight. This is a private conversation. As my mother used to say: I'm talking about you, not to you.

Although we've discussed what happened to us that night, we have never really dug deeper. There are questions I have been afraid to ask, worried I might expose my own feelings by the way I phrase them. I am comfortable enough with Martha now to be a little more vulnerable.

'What do you remember about him? I remember he had really soft hands, he was quite gentle really. I think that's one of the things that upsets me the most. The fact that I even thought that,' I say almost to myself, Martha somehow an extension of consciousness.

'He was gentle because he didn't need to use force, he incapacitated us. . . drugged us.'

'I guess. Do you even know what drug he used? I remember what I was thinking more than I remember what he did and I can only think that's because of whatever drug he used. I think because I was raped once before, I just compare him to the other guy, who was definitely not as gentle. I had bruises on my arms and legs for days,' I say.

'You were raped before?'

'Yes, several years ago and in another town. Unlucky, eh? To have something so terrible happen twice.'

'I was, too. I was here though, I have always lived here. Grew up about a block away from where you live.'

'What happened to you? Did you go to the police?'

'I did. There wasn't enough evidence to go forward. I still see him around sometimes, walking through town without a care in the world.'

'Did you know him?'

'He was my boyfriend, well, my ex. We had broken up, but he couldn't accept it. Unfortunately, that made the assault harder to prove. He had an answer for everything and in the end they decided his story was more plausible than mine or something. I don't know. I know I had never felt so helpless. It didn't help that we sort of got back together for a few weeks afterwards because I was so confused about what happened.'

'I'm really sorry. That sounds shit.' I'm unsure how to respond to that. How could she get back together with him after he had done that? It makes no sense to me.

'I think I always knew he was capable of it, that's why I broke up with him. He had this way about him, you know? Like his way was the right way and everyone else was wrong. I struggle to remember what I ever saw in the man. He was such a charmer though, knew exactly what to say to the police to make me seem like the unreasonable one. I don't like to think racism played a part but he was a white man and I'm neither, hard not to think that had something to do with it.'

'Do you ever look him up? Your ex? Sometimes I look up the guy who raped me. He's married with a kid now, I saw his wedding photos. She's pretty, seems nice. Did he tell her about me? In his version of events, am I the villain? I wonder sometimes if it was me that made him do it. His life looks normal now, he looks normal.'

'He's not normal though, is he? If you know you didn't lie, you know who he is.'

It sounds so simple when she says it like that, and of course I have thought it myself but just hearing it come from someone else makes it real. He isn't normal, he's the freak and not me like I told myself so many times. Why do I still waste my time thinking about him and what he did? He gets to live his life and I cower away hidden? That hardly seems fair.

'Let's go out somewhere,' I suggest before I have even thought it through. Screw him and screw you.

'What, now?'

'Yeah, why not, I could use a drink and I haven't been out in three years. I think I am due a Friday night on the town.'

'I'm not really dressed for a night out,' Martha says, looking more polished and better than I ever could achieve. I may not be wearing make-up but I think I would at least get let in somewhere.

'You look stunning, let's just go somewhere. Anywhere. It will be fun. I have to work a little later on so I can't get wasted but a couple won't hurt.'

'I know a place.' She gets to her feet and holds her hand out to me, helping me to mine. 'It's just out by Wayland Gap, like a pop-up nightclub set in an abandoned hotel.'

When I stand up she doesn't let go of my hand and we walk together back up to the road, leaving the calmness of the beach behind. I feel braver with Martha holding my hand, like I can do anything. But I still don't know what your criteria are. Is it just circumstance? Woman living alone? How could you know that? I can't think about you right now. I am going to drink until you disappear completely.

Chapter 26

I forgot how nightclubs smell, a mixture of sweat, booze and a cocktail of perfumes. I tell myself I look chic in my black top and trousers, no patterns no jewels. I pull my ponytail out at least and let my hair hang naturally around my shoulders. Martha goes to the bar and flashes a smile. Despite the throng of people she gets served immediately. I can't imagine anyone would ever keep Martha waiting. She comes back with two blue drinks, not the beer in a bottle I usually plump for. There is something attention-seeking about the drinks we have, immature, flamboyant. I try to suppress how uncomfortable I feel and attempt to summon some of that bravery I found earlier on the beach. I can't remember the last time I was among so many people.

The club itself is set in the ballroom of an old hotel that I have been past on the bus before but never been inside. The room has large pillars that support the painted ceiling. It would feel quite fancy if it weren't for the temporary disco lights rigged up and flashing in our faces. One wall is all windows and the blackness of the sea lays just beyond, a veranda in between.

'Where did you hear about this?' I shout over the noise of the music.

'One of the girls from work was thinking about coming. It's only here for a month.'

'What is this place?' I say, looking around at the ornate sculpted cornice around the ceiling. It's far too fancy to be a nightclub.

'It's a hotel that got shut down during the pandemic. I guess the owner is trying to recoup some losses by hiring it out for private events. It's pretty cool, isn't it?'

For the first time, maybe in my life, I feel old. I'm not, of course, but I have been so out of this life, since college, that it feels completely alien to me. I thought this would be fun but it's just exhausting. So many people, so many eyes, so many risks. I watch the girls dancing on the elaborate parquet floor, short skirts and heels that would make me dizzy. So pretty, so carefree. I am not sure I was ever like that. I remember nightclubbing, it wasn't even that long ago, maybe six or seven years. The men lingering around the scantily clad women like lions watching antelopes, waiting to see which one is weakest and pick them off. Is that what you do? Look for the weak ones? I watch the guys hit on a girl and when she refuses they move onto the next, and so on. It's not about the girls, not as individuals; these men are hunting and their prey is inconsequential as long as they get to feed that beast inside them. Desperate for some reciprocation, from anyone. I guess that's the part that disgusts me the most. It could be any girl here for them, they don't care about anything but the end game, physical release. Is that so wrong? They are all adults, maybe the girls come here for the same thing, for a connection, to stave off the loneliness for a few hours. Lord knows I understand how that feels.

'Oh my God, I love this one!' Martha shouts as she grabs my arm and pulls me towards the dance floor. Of course she can dance. I bob awkwardly from side to side to a song I have heard maybe twice on the radio. I see three men just behind her watching as she dances, they may as well be snarling. Their eyes fill with hunger as they follow the curves and lines of her body. We are both dressed much more modestly than any of the other women here. Considering we're actually dressed for a covert operation there's nothing about what we're wearing that could be considered alluring or provocative and yet we're being circled just like the girls in their cheek-revealing dresses. Proof that it's not about what you wear, it's just the fact that you're a woman. It's what's under your skirt that counts.

Would you come to a place like this? Is this one of your hunting grounds? I don't think it is. I get the feeling you are much more selective than this but maybe that's

151

my ego talking. Maybe in some twisted way I want to imagine there is something special about me that brought us together. I am aware how crazy that makes me sound but it's so much more upsetting to think that it was just bad luck, that it was completely random.

I manage to slip away from Martha and head back to the bar. I'm leaning against it and waiting as everyone but me gets served. I don't mind because I like being invisible. I like going unnoticed so I can watch everyone else. Eventually the barman makes eye contact with me which feels weirdly intrusive.

'Two blue moons,' I say, now fully committed to the creamy slushy blue cocktail. I hate making decisions anyway so I'm relieved that Martha made it for me. A few seconds later the drinks are placed in front of me and I slap my card against the machine. My brief interaction with the staff over, I can go back to observing others.

Jostling out of the bar area, I stand by the side of the dancefloor and see Martha dancing with a man. If I didn't know her I would think they had come together, his hands all over her. I prop myself up against the railing and balance the drinks on the shelf. I try to look anywhere else. I'm not jealous or anything, I wouldn't want you to think I think I have any claim over Martha, but this is the second time she has confused me today. How can she stand to have his hands all over her? Maybe I am just so rigid in my feelings that I can't understand how anyone else could deal with what we went through differently. Have I rationalised my bizarre behaviour so much that anything different feels deceptive in some way? It's been three years since you came into my life, that's how long it's taken me to even attempt to come to a nightclub and mix with actual people. She's had barely a year and it feels like she comes here every week. Am I annoyed at her or myself?

There is a couple near me. She is wearing a floral dress, more suited to a summer fete than a nightclub, and he has a crisp white shirt on, starched and ironed it's so smooth. She excuses herself and goes to the bathroom at which point I see him pull a small bottle out of his pocket and hide it in his closed fist, its brown glass almost medicinal. I watch him look around and slip her glass off the table. Under the surface he pours some of the liquid into her glass and then puts everything back exactly how it was before she left. Is this how easy it is to violate someone? She returns from the bathroom and I know I can't let her drink that drink. I pick up my two blue moons and walk towards them. With very little subtlety I crash into him drinks first, the icy blue slush making him scream out as he knocks into the table and spills the drink he just spiked. The girl suppresses a chuckle at the sight of him, blue dripping down the front of that crisp white shirt.

'What the fuck are you doing?' he shouts at me, but I couldn't care less.

'I'll go get some napkins,' she says, before disappearing to the bar. Do I continue to pretend it was an accident? I don't think I should. Would you stop if someone shone a light on you? Maybe. Creeps like you operate in the shadows, through secret bottles of snake oil.

'You've ruined my fucking shirt, you bitch!'

'How about I tell your girlfriend what you just slipped in her drink,' I shout, sounding less calm than I wanted to.

'What are you talking about?' He shrinks back, trying to put physical distance between us.

'Maybe I should call one of those big bouncers over and get him to empty your pockets.'

'You're fucking crazy.'

I turn and see his girlfriend trying to get the barman's attention.

'You should leave before she gets back. Or I'll tell her what I saw.' I feel powerful as I speak, relishing the hold I have over him. It's nice to feel power when you have none. I step forward and reach my hand into his pocket. He is visibly shocked that I have the audacity to touch him, but I pull the bottle out and stuff it in my own pocket knowing full well he isn't going to say anything. He's weak, they all are. Is that what draws you to doing what you do? Are you weak and pathetic in every other waking moment? Is rape the only crack you get at power?

He glances over at the bar and then grabs his jacket

from the back of the chair before leaving. Maybe I didn't do the right thing, I don't know, but it felt like I was doing *something* for a change, not just letting things happen. I like this feeling I have. I feel like I've made a difference tonight. I stopped something bad. How many other people here have those little bottles in their pockets? Or pills? Or something else to help their prey loosen up. I feel above them, above this. I want to get out of here.

Martha is walking towards me, laughing, her face a tonic among all these predators.

'I'm knackered. I want to go home.'

'Already?' she says. We have only been here an hour.

'I've got the night shift tomorrow night, so I need to try to sleep beforehand. You don't have to leave.'

'It's fine, I'm done anyway. That bloke won't leave me alone, keeps trying to kiss me.'

'You're not interested? You seemed to be having a good time,' I say, trying not to sound bitchy or judgemental.

'I can't emphasise how much I am not interested. I just smile and play along so they don't get aggressive. Let's get out of here.'

I'm relieved to hear her say that and I'm happy to have her back by my side. Just being with her keeps me calm, stops me thinking about all the ways I wish I could hurt you.

Chapter 27

I had a secret no one knew about now. It was exhilarating, I didn't feel like the loser I had always felt like. The veil had been lifted and I knew the truth, I knew how to get the thing I desired most. I had to take it, it was that simple. The planning of it wasn't going to be easy but for the first time I didn't feel like I had to wait for someone's permission to get what I wanted. I just had to be ready when the opportunity presented itself to me again. Maybe I could even make the opportunity present itself. Starting a new school suddenly didn't feel like such a burden. I would be in a place where no one had any preconceptions of me. I would take everything I learned from the private school and put it into practice. I still had cool clothes that I hadn't grown out of, I wasn't ugly. I just had to pretend to be someone better than I was. In those last few days I studied Faiyaz like a mockingbird, trying to mimic his walk, his facial expressions, his mannerisms. That's all a person was, right? It wasn't about what was inside at this age. OK, so I knew I could never look like him, not really, but everything else I could take on. I was going to kill my present self and start all over again, I was going to be reborn.

My mum was pleased at my new attitude. I had noticed she was starting to make more of an effort too, going to the hairdressers and wearing more make-up. There were some rumours surrounding my mother but I didn't listen to them. One of the boys in my school reckoned his brother paid a pro to lose his virginity and the woman who turned up looked just like my mum. At first I thought they were just saying it to get a rise out of me but then I started noticing things about my mum and I couldn't stop noticing them. The lodgers became more frequent and stayed for less time. It must have been true. The truth of it was I didn't care. For the first time my mum was making money and buying me the things I wanted. Maybe we were going to be OK. My sister had barely visited since moving out and so I felt like I was finally the favourite child. I knew my parents felt her rejection keenly but she was always selfish, always looking after number one. She even forgot my birthday. I felt like she wanted nothing more to do with me. I phoned her once or twice but she never picked up, she never answered my texts. Message received loud and clear. Despite her not being there *anymore I felt like things were finally looking up. Maybe I wouldn't have to fake being cool for long, maybe it would be natural to me, maybe those girls at the new school would be impressed with my clothes and not ignore me the way everyone had done before now. I didn't feel as powerless as I always had done in the past and when the day finally came for me to start at the new school I was actually excited.*

Of course, I was put in my place quickly enough. It was like these bitches all had a pact to deny me what I wanted, what I deserved. It didn't matter how nice I was, it didn't matter that I held open doors or offered up my spot in the lunch queue so they could line up together. I was invisible to them at best, held in contempt at worst. I was misnamed more than once, proving to me once and for all how little esteem I held in their eyes. It wasn't just the girls either, it was the boys too. It was easy enough to see who the alphas were, and I caught their sideways glances. In almost record time I became the loser. My clothes didn't matter, nothing mattered. I didn't know how to fix this. Money was the only thing people respected and people were talking, they knew where my mother's money came from. I began to wish I had never been born.

I was eighteen and I had no prospects. My father was off caring for his other family and my mother barely spoke to me. She left me alone a lot. She would meet up with guys, sometimes a different one every night and I hated her for it. She had no self-respect and she had no respect for me or how her actions might reflect on me. People talked about her. Sometimes I would hear her having sex with whichever man she brought home and so I would put my headphones on to block out the noise. I felt completely alone. It didn't matter how much stuff my mother bought me, I still wanted more. I would give things away to impress people and then curse myself for doing it. I needed to stop being so desperate for their approval. I needed to stop caring what other people thought of me.

My mum suggested I needed my own freedom to be able to bring girls home. After several months of me not bringing anyone home she sat me down and asked me if I was interested in boys instead. She said it would make a lot of sense about me. I didn't know what she meant by that but I hit her around the face. She was so shocked but I didn't know what else she expected after what she had just implied. Getting away from my mother became a priority at that point.

I finally found a job I thought I could be good at. It was steady and reliable and the likelihood of me getting fired was quite small. I felt a part of something bigger than myself and I started to worry less about my private life. I was almost nineteen and still a virgin and I didn't know how to change that. Men that I worked with would come in and talk about their conquests and I would just have to laugh in all the right places because I had no idea how it felt.

I still couldn't afford to move out of my mother's house. I joined several dating sites and took lots of women out for dinner but nothing ever went anywhere, they always seemed in a hurry to get away from me. I decided to go and stay with my father for a while. My father's wife Sadie regarded me with that same sneer the girl in the ball pit had. There was something about me that repulsed women and I didn't know what it was. I didn't know how to fix it. Where I had hoped to maybe make a life for myself with my father, it became apparent before long that that was never going to happen. Within a week my father kept asking me how long I was planning on staying and other questions that made it obvious he didn't want me around. I knew it was Sadie's doing though. I heard them arguing at night and my father protesting that he was my father too. I hated Sadie for what she had done to my family. I wanted to kill her. I decided that's what I was going to do.

Chapter 28

I am covering on reception in the hotel and Martha's gone home to bed. From the window I can see one of my flyers and it makes me feel bigger than a night clerk in this rundown relic of a building. You must be out stalking your prey, looking for an open window or a broken gate. You will have chosen her by now, I expect. She's just going about her business without a clue that you are there, lurking in her peripheral vision, waiting for an opportunity to reveal yourself, to destroy her. You must have noticed the flyers by now. I know it hasn't been long but we put them everywhere. I have already heard people talking about them. Have they asked you what you think about them? Do they make you nervous? Or is this what you wanted all along, for someone to notice you? I haven't worked you out yet, but I will.

Night shifts feel endless when you don't sleep in the day. I'm grateful when there is a room service order to break the monotony so I don't fall asleep at my station. There are two other staff members on with me tonight, Hakim in the kitchen and John in security. John is an older man in his mid-thirties, I think. He is married with a young child. He seems perpetually exhausted and mostly quiet, which is a blessing. I try to stay out of his way but it's hard when I am stuck on reception all night. It's late now so most of the guests are back in their rooms but it's Saturday night so some are still in the clubs on the front. We have two main clubs and both shut at three in the morning so I stare at the clock and wait. It's two hours away.

John has made his rounds already and comes to sit next to me in the booth, I dread these conversations as there is nothing I want to say to him and I couldn't care less about his life. I had hoped a night shift would entirely remove me from any communication with anyone I didn't specifically choose to speak to. I have the inevitable panic of thinking he might be you for a moment, as with every man I meet, but then I look at his hands and they are coarse with thick fingers and calloused skin and I know they aren't your hands. I am disgusted that I know that, that I even think it. I shake off the thought and go back to thinking of John as irrelevant.

'You local?' he asks. He asked me the same thing the last time we spoke.

'No, I moved here a few years ago from London.'

'You one of those DFLs then?' he says with a smirk. It's a bizarre local insult for the people who moved here 'down from London', usually because there is an air of superiority about them. Us. Lots of DFLs get involved in big community projects as though they are saving this little rinkydink town, even though it's not that little and certainly not in need of saving.

'I guess,' I respond apathetically, hoping my lack of reaction puts him off speaking to me anymore.

There is an awkward silence between us. I'm not playing the game right, he wants me to ask him questions, too. I won't be doing that. I can feel him getting annoyed that I am ignoring him.

'How did a young woman like you end up in a job like this?' he finally asks.

'I applied for it,' I say, making a mental note to bring a book on my next shift.

The phone rings through the room service line and I let out a sigh of relief before I answer. It's Hakim telling me the room service order is ready for me to pick up and deliver to the guest's room. I stand up to go through to the kitchen and get it, although I don't know why Hakim can't deliver it himself – something to do with health and safety. John shuffles back a little, spreading his legs wide to give me enough space to squeeze past. He looks up at me as I start to push through and I see a look in his eye that I know too well. He thinks he has some power over

163

me in this position. He knows I have no choice but to edge past his open legs to get to where I need to go. I know if I look away he will have won and so I maintain eye contact. You don't like that, do you? You predatory sorts don't like it when we hold your gaze, when we don't display fear. Power and fear, that's what you crave. You'll get none of that from me. None of you will. The temptation to thrust my knee into John's testicles is hard to ignore but I have to remember he's not the one I want to hurt, you are.

As I am delivering a ham and mozzarella panini to a room on the fifth floor, I feel the phone in my left pocket vibrate. It's the SIM-only pay-as-you-go phone I bought specifically for the Eris project, the number that's on every flyer we put up. I rush along the corridor, hoping to get to my destination and drop the food off before the caller hangs up. I practically throw the tray at the occupant of the room before rushing into the stairwell and answering the phone. Caller ID blocked. This isn't the first time the phone has rung. Some kids had phoned up and said some violently explicit things to me on the phone, shocked when I had responded with some equally violent things. I was ready for time-wasters and sickos. Sticks and stones.

'Hello?' I say quietly. I don't want anyone in the hotel to hear me on the phone. There is a weird atmosphere between me and the rest of the night staff; not that I am particularly bothered about making friends here, but I don't want anyone to grass on me. I can't afford to lose this job. I wait for a response but there isn't one, just faint breathing on the other end. I listen to the sound of the air hitting the receiver and feel a mild panic at the idea of who might be on the other end of this call. Is it you? It could be you. Funny how that never occurred to me until now; that by giving out this number to other possible survivors I am also reaching out to you as well. You're out there, living your life, and I am shouting into the void. It makes sense that you could feasibly be the one calling me. Did the flyers make you angry? Proud? Did you feel a strange sense of accomplishment for driving me to this? Maybe a part of me wants it to be you on the other end of the phone. I don't like admitting that to myself.

'I saw your flyer,' a voice finally said, a woman. I can hear her shaking as she speaks and I'm ashamed of the instant relief I feel.

'Do you know him? Did something happen to you?' I ask.

'I think I know him, yes.'

'June 12th as well? How long ago?'

'Yes,' she says with a slight scoff. 'A long time ago, I don't recall exactly.'

I find it hard to believe she wouldn't remember the year, but I don't want to push.

'Did you see anything? Did you recognise him?' I say, trying not to sound as desperate as I feel.

'I didn't see a thing. I couldn't see anything, my eyes were covered,' she says nervously, her voice barely audible.

'I'm so sorry,' I say. The reality of this call, the knowledge that maybe I was right, that there are others like me and Martha feels like a hollow victory. Now that I am talking to this poor woman and hearing the pain in her voice, my previous self-congratulations have vanished. It's hard to accept that there are more victims of yours out there, more people who feel like I do. How many? Are they all hidden away or did they just leave the town completely? Maybe I would if I hadn't upended everything once before, knowing that pain and fear follow you means there really isn't any point in moving again. All of this is just a distraction from the rage inside me and hearing this woman talk is like igniting a fuse. You're still out there and you're going to do it again if someone doesn't stop you.

'Seeing your flyer, I knew it was him, I knew he had done it again.'

'Did you report him?'

'I didn't. I couldn't.'

'Would you be willing to talk to the police about this?' I ask, knowing the answer already.

'I'm sorry, I can't.'

'Please, the police will start looking for him properly if more of us come forward. There's at least three of us now.'

'There are others? I can't believe he would do this again.'

'What do you mean?' It sounds like she knows him, or am I reading into this?

'I have to go. I'm sorry he hurt you, too.'

I desperately want to push her for answers, but I can already tell she regrets calling me.

'Even if you just call the police anonymously, I can give you the number of a detective I know, she will listen to you.'

'No. Sorry. I can't go through that. I can't talk about any of this. I don't even know why I phoned.'

'What about a name? Do you have a name?'

There's a moment's silence 'You can call me Grace.'

'Do you have a number, Grace? So, I can call you at least?'

'I don't think that's a good idea. I'll call you.'

She hangs up. My first lead and she's gone, there is no way to contact her again. That's another thing I know about you that you didn't want me to find out. I'm getting closer. I'll go back to that policewoman to tell her I was right. Maybe this time they'll open a proper investigation instead of trying to gaslight me or fob me off. Now there's me, Martha and Grace. Whoever you are, I'll make sure you think twice before unzipping your pants again. Maybe I should enrage you enough to coax you out of the shadows. You are the weasel who needs to drug women in order to get laid and so maybe you're the one who's afraid of us. Why do you cover our faces? Is it just a blindfold so we can't identify you? Are you ugly? Is that it? Or maybe you're just full of self-loathing and can't stand being looked at, maybe a bit of both. One thing is for sure, I am not afraid of you anymore, I refuse to be. I'm not afraid of anyone anymore.

Chapter 29

My latest obsession became how to get rid of Sadie. With her gone my father would have no reason to stay away and our family would get back together. Even if he didn't want to come back he might be so grief-stricken that he would want me to stay with him. I couldn't see my plan going wrong. The biggest issue was making it look like Sadie had an accident. I monitored her routines and looked for any opportunity to get to her. On Tuesdays, I was alone in the house with her. He worked late, a bit like how he worked late before he ran off with Sadie. He had a three-day conference coming up, or so he said. I was certain he was cheating on her. Once a cheat, always a cheat, my mother said. She told me stories of the many women my father had entertained over the years and I was both in awe of his virility and disgusted with the women who fell for it. She told me he was a sex addict.

What kind of thing is that to tell your child? My mother had stopped being any kind of mother when my father left; she had changed. There was no denying how she was making money and I hated her more than ever. I blamed her for my inability to connect with women. Every time I spoke to a girl I choked up and I was getting to an age where being a virgin was more than embarrassing, it was social suicide. I was the guy with a prostitute for a mother, I heard them whisper when I walked past.

I figured out how I was going to kill Sadie. The main staircase in their house was polished wood and the floor at the bottom was some kind of granite composite or fake marble, I didn't know much about that stuff. Sadie always got up in the night to use the toilet and so I decided I would push her down the stairs while my father was away. I would make sure the children were asleep and had no chance of seeing it, I wasn't a complete monster. She was suspicious of me though, I could feel it.

My father was ready to go on his trip and leave me alone with Sadie and his other family. In all honesty, he was barely ever at home anyway, he was definitely having an affair. I felt a chill every time Sadie looked at me now, like she was looking right through me. Sometimes it felt like she was reading my mind. I knew I had to get better at being normal. I knew I had to work on being more like other people my age. I knew

Sadie wasn't happy about my father leaving me alone with her because I heard them arguing about it. She said she didn't feel safe in the house with me, that I was weird, that I looked at her funny. It made me laugh that she didn't trust me when she had my father in the house, I hadn't forgotten what I had seen him doing to my sister. I had half a mind to tell Sadie exactly what kind of man she had married. I couldn't have her whispering in my father's ear, making him hate me. In the end Sadie won the fight and I was asked to leave, to go back to my mother's house where I could listen to her fuck random men for money.

I didn't see my father again after that. I went to visit him a few months later but he had moved. No forwarding address. I guess it's easy for some people to just forget who they used to be and become someone new. It must have been hard for him to have me around, a reminder of a life where he was who he was. But could people like that change? I had to do that, too. I had to change. I had to become someone else. Something else.

Chapter 30

We all remember the first time. Us women, I mean, it wouldn't have even occurred to us that we could be seen like that. Sex was not really a part of our thought process. There we were, just going about our business, at whatever age we were at the time; it would have been before we were actively looking for that kind of attention, for your gaze. Most of the time we're still technically children when that first comment rolls in. Comments when I turned fourteen about how I would be sixteen soon enough. It seems like an innocent enough comment until you see the glint in their eye, or even a wink and a smirk. It hits you that suddenly you aren't a person, you are a collection of holes. I remember at sixteen my father's colleague casually asking me if I was still a virgin when my parents invited him over for dinner once. They had only left the room for a second. They make us feel wrong somehow – dirty. No one warns us, they don't tell us to be careful. That there is always someone like you out there lurking in the corners and waiting for us to be vulnerable, to be alone.

That's what you do, isn't it? You wait for us to be alone, so you must watch us. How sad, how pathetic that this is how you get your thrills, lurking in the dark and waiting for an opportunity to arise just so you can violate someone. I have been so blind until now. I thought you were the one with the power but it's the opposite, isn't it? You are so weak and so powerless, that's why you go after women like me, women who had been hurt before, women who had all the fight taken out of them by someone else. You're even lower than Stuart, you took no risks, you went for the easy prey. Your power over me is so distant now that I see you for what you are. Those things you did, like covering my face and drugging me, those were all so that I couldn't resist you, because you wouldn't have the power to subdue me if I did. Physically, of course, I have no doubt you are stronger than me. I felt the weight of your muscles against my naked body. No, that's not where your weakness lies. I could crush you with a look, I know that now. How funny. Is it wrong that I am looking forward to our next meeting? Am I supposed to be scared? I don't think I will ever be scared for myself again.

What I can't abide is the way you treated my Martha and even that poor girl Grace. I have to stop you for them, and for every other woman you have violated.

The doorbell rings relentlessly, I have not long fallen asleep and am tempted to just stay in bed until whoever it is goes away, but they won't stop. After a few rings they start pounding on the door. I grab a sweatshirt and pull it on as I'm running down the stairs, almost slipping onto the hardwood floor at the bottom. I open the door to see DI White there. She is holding a handful of my flyers.

'The June 12th rapist? I am guessing this was you.'

'Prove it.' I smirk, not really caring whether she can or not. At least I have her attention this time.

'What do you think this is going to achieve?'

'I just thought *someone* should be doing *something*. You lot are about as useful as a chocolate teapot.'

'Has anyone called you?'

'Yes. A girl called me last night. Same story as mine again.'

'Same date?'

'That's right. So that's three now.'

'Four. I found another one,' she says sheepishly.

I resist the urge to do a slow clap for the detective, heartened by the fact that I am finally getting through to her.

'Only three years too late but finally, you're taking this seriously. When did it happen? How long ago?' I can feel my heart rate increasing. How many of us have you violated?

'Seven years.'

'Jesus. All those women he has hurt. How long has he been doing this? He could go on forever and no one would give a shit except the people whose lives he has destroyed. That's what he's banking on. Is she willing to come forward?'

'Unfortunately, she won't be able to do that,' DI White said, her gaze flicking away.

'Is that because she's dead? She killed herself, didn't she?' I say, a level of anger I had no idea I was capable of suddenly hits me. Let's add murder to your list of crimes; without your intervention in that girl's life, she would still be alive today. I bet you get off on that idea, that someone as inconsequential as you could have such an impact on one person's life.

'I'm sorry,' she says, and even though I can tell she really is sorry, it doesn't matter as long as you are out there. Words mean nothing.

'Don't think the thought hasn't crossed my mind on more than one occasion. You have no idea how this feels. I decided I wasn't the one who needed punishing though. He's out there, probably planning his next attack right now. Some unsuspecting woman is just going about her business today with no fucking clue what's about to happen to her, but he knows, he knows who she is already, he's probably already planned it down to the millisecond.'

'What is your plan, Gail? This feels like a call to arms. What are you going to do when you find these other women?' White says, shaking the leaflets again. *How can she possibly understand what you put us through?*

'I had a theory, I wanted to find out if I was right.'

'What theory was that? Care to share?'

'I don't know if I can trust you. You certainly haven't given me a reason to. Quite the opposite in fact. I want to, I want you to be on my side but up until recently I have been completely alone in this,' I say, *knowing she wants to help, but also knowing that you're too smart for her, for all of them.*

'I know. I know it must seem that way to you. I don't feel great about what happened before. I promise you, I've regretted the way I handled that ever since. I can keep saying sorry if you want me to, or I can find this guy. Tell me what you think you know. I promise I am looking now, I wasn't before but I am now and I want to find this guy. I want to stop it. I shouldn't have treated you that way and I'm genuinely sorry.' I hear the desperation in her voice.

'I hated you for it. I blamed you for a long time, but you know what? Since going to various groups and hearing countless women tell their stories I realised it's not you, it's the system. Not just our little system in our little town, but *the* system. Women don't matter, we are expendable, replaceable, ignorable. Women get raped all the time, right? No big deal. We're just lucky if we don't get killed as well. What makes me any more special than any of the other unresolved cases out there? Nothing. Nothing at all. I was stupid to think anything could be done. We are playing on their field and they know the game better than we ever could. Well, pardon my French but fuck that. I'm not playing that way anymore.'

'You said you had a theory – what was it?' DI White says, her voice softening.

I decide that I have to trust her, that you don't want us all talking about you, putting things together, figuring things out.

'He's clever. He knew exactly who to target, exactly who wouldn't report him to the police.'

'What do you mean?'

'Me and the other women I have spoken to, we all have something else in common, besides him, of course.'

It's been here in the back of my mind this whole time, what it is that makes him choose someone like me and then someone like Martha. There is only one possible thing that links us. Not our hair colour or eye colour, not where we live or what our favourite cafe is. The only thing that links us is our past. He knows exactly who won't say a word.

'What's that?'

'We've been raped before. How would he know that? How could he possibly know? He must have access to inside information,' I say, knowing she won't want to accept the truth because it reflects badly on her, not just her but her entire profession. You know they don't care about us. Once they decide you are lying once, it's not that much of a leap to decide it again.

'What do you mean?'

'Both of them had previous attacks. Now I know it's more common than anyone realises, but that feels like too much of a coincidence. For all of us to have a previous rape that wasn't taken seriously by the police seems like a pattern to me. As far as I can tell, only a select few people would have access to that information.'

'Not necessarily,' she says defensively. I know what she is thinking because I have thought it too. What if it's someone in the police?

'That other victim you found, that girl who killed herself, I bet she had a previous complaint against someone.'

'She did but I don't think it was insider information. I don't think it came from the police.'

'How else could he find out? We went to the police the first time, that information is logged somewhere. Maybe you have a nice big file labelled "time wasters",

178

I don't know. Maybe he uses it like a shop, have a browse through and see who to pick next,' I say, starting to lose my temper again.

'I don't want to add more fuel to your fire, but I found whole websites dedicated to outing women for what they deem to be false accusations. Local ones, national ones, global ones. It's a real eye-opener. The local one is where I found the other June 12th victim. They named her on there. It's possible your information was posted somewhere online on one of the false accusation pages.'

'Except ours weren't false,' I say, aware that I am referring to us as a group, us, your victims.

'Well, in the eyes of these online communities, anything that doesn't result in a conviction means exactly that, a false accusation. If there is no proof, then no crime can have taken place. Except of course we know that's not true. The conviction rate for sexual assault is incredibly low.' She tries to explain but it all just sounds like excuses to me. Another way to shirk responsibility, to stay blind to the obvious.

'There's more than one community like this?'

'There are several.'

'That's legal, is it?'

'It's a grey area. Unfortunately, the law hasn't caught up to the internet just yet. They find ways around the law, word things carefully so they aren't culpable. We have a long way to go on some things. I've passed the name of the local site to a cyber-crime division to see if they can find any way to shut it down,' she says apologetically as though I will hold her personally responsible for this as well. Maybe I should. What good is the law if it can't protect the vulnerable?

'What's the name of this site?'

'I don't think I should tell you that. It will be gone soon enough.'

'So, they post women's names? Who posts them?'

'Usually the accused, from what I saw, sometimes a friend of the accused. Or they private message the moderator and ask him to share the story anonymously. It's all a bit nebulous really and hard to pin down the origin of some of these posts and photos, they have been shared so many times on so many sites. In their own fucked-up way, they think they are doing the right thing. I don't agree with it and I am not defending them but it's entirely possible that some of these men are telling the truth about being falsely accused, it does happen, it's rare but it does happen. People can be vulnerable in different ways.'

She reels off all this information like it's nothing, like she's not talking about real people, real women. How can she go to work every day and see the things she sees, knowing she can't stop it? Bound by the laws that are most likely written by the same men that try to hurt us. The victims aren't victims, we are problems that need to be silenced.

'Sounds like an excuse for misogyny, if you ask me. If this shit doesn't make your blood boil I don't know what to tell you. If men got raped you can bet your arse they would have fixed this by now.'

'Men do get raped.'

'You know what I mean.'

'Don't put your anger in the wrong place. It's not about men, it's about rapists. There are lots of good guys out there.'

I used to think that, too. The trouble is you never know which ones are the bad ones until it's too late. I bet you know how to make people like you, make them feel safe. I wonder again if we have met and I know the answer, I know we have. Did I do something to make you do the things you did? Or was it just my rotten luck? This conversation with DI White is going nowhere. I've got things to do.

'I see less and less evidence of that. I go to three or four groups a week and I hear at least one new story every night. Not only that but I see the same women over and over again, our lives all on pause until God knows what. Until we find some peace or God forbid, justice.'

'That's all you're looking at right now and so it seems so much bigger than it is.'

'You wouldn't say that if you had ever been through it,' I say, unable to contain my anger, unsure how I haven't exploded already.

'Who says I haven't?' DI White says. 'It's a crime that's usually committed very privately with only two witnesses. Most of the time people have to just choose which of those witnesses they believe. When push comes to shove, I think people would rather believe it happens a lot less than it does.'

'Did you report it? Did he go to prison?' I ask, tugging at the house of cards around her big secret. She's shown me a fraction of weakness and now I see it written on her like I see it on so many of those other women in the groups I attend. I shouldn't push, I know that, but it's the silence that keeps them safe, keeps *you* safe.

'My situation was complicated. It seemed smarter to just keep it to myself. At least that's what I told myself at the time.'

'And have you seen him since? Your attacker? Your rapist?'

'I have.' Her jaw is clenched.

'And do you still think you did the right thing by keeping quiet?'

'If I made a fuss I would probably have lost my job, definitely lost the respect of my colleagues, and there is no real evidence, no guarantee that anyone would believe me.'

'You're right there. I wish I had never told the police. Never told you,' I say, guilt picking at me. I feel bad for pushing her to a confession, that's not my place.

'I was the one who got it wrong with you. You did the right thing by coming to the police. It's all on me and I am so, so sorry.'

'So, what's your secret, DI White? How did you get through it? I see you're wearing a ring so you got a hell of a lot further than I think I ever will.' I try not to sound angry, but why does she get to move on? Why does anyone?

'I don't know. I don't think there is a secret.'

'Then what? You get married and take his name so that everyone knows you're *his* wife, or you can reject that name and keep your own, which is really just your father's name. Unless of course you don't love your daddy and decide to keep your mother's name, which of course is just *her* father's name. Women have no names, we are nothing but property, things to own and fuck and use. Our names show who we belong to, nothing more. I've had a couple of relationships in the distant past and men are all the same.'

'I guess I just got lucky and met one of the good ones.' She smiles reluctantly.

'Whereas I met another rapist.'

'I'm so sorry,' DI White says.

'So what happened to the guy who raped you?'

'He was a colleague, well, I was his subordinate and so I decided I had no chance of bringing him to justice. All that would have happened if I had reported Graham would have been that I got a reputation for

183

causing trouble. At least this way I get to keep an eye on him.'

I can hear the lie in her voice as she tries to convince herself that she made the right choices, that she is happy with the decisions she made. I know she's just making excuses so she can live with herself even though none of this is her burden to bear.

'Do you even hear yourself? You're telling me this man, this *rapist* is a police officer? the very people we are supposed to trust when we are wronged. And you just accept this? Doesn't this all start with personal responsibility? You do what you have to do to be able to sleep at night. I reported my rape, the first one, to stop him from hurting anyone else, and while he got away with it, at least he knew that he couldn't do it to someone else. He couldn't get away with it a second time so maybe me doing what I did to Stuart actually did stop him from raping someone else.' The thought has never occurred to me before but it's true, he would have thought twice before doing it again. To be accused once was one thing, get accused twice and some mud must surely start to stick. That's what was happening to us after all, the mud was well and truly stuck to us and you knew that, didn't you? You exploited that fact and came after us, knowing no one would believe a word we said.

'Yes, maybe you're right. I think we've already ascertained that I don't have all the answers. I do feel bad for not reporting it, but at the same time, it was an act of survival for me. I couldn't let it destroy everything I had worked for. I made a choice that I could live with,' DI White says, clearly frustrated.

'Cowering and waiting to be attacked again isn't my style. So yes, I put those flyers up, and yes, maybe it was a call to arms. He wants to play dirty? That's fine, I can do that, too.'

'Just be careful. We already know that man is capable of terrible things. If he finds out you're trying to ruin his fun then he might come after you again.'

'Let him try,' I say, hoping that you do. Because I'm ready this time.

Chapter 31

Going back to sleep is not going to happen so I text Martha. She is the only other human being on the planet I can stand being around at the moment. I wait anxiously for her to reciprocate, worried that she will have tired of our connection already and that I will be alone again, alone with only you to talk to. She texts me back and asks me to meet in half an hour by the harbour. I am almost grateful that you brought us together, even though I know that without you we would not need to be friends. I am not the sort of person someone like Martha hangs around with.

I am so tired, but sleep hasn't come easy since the night we met. I wonder what you lie awake at night thinking about. Do you ever think about me? Your memories of that night will be so different to mine and part of me wishes I could see it through your eyes. I have a hunger to know why you do what you do, what it is that drives you. And why us? Is it just so that you will get away with it? Is the only special thing about me that I was already ruined? I'm wounded. What voices lurk in your head, I wonder. All I hear is you.

As I approach the harbour I can see Martha's silhouette in the distance. She is holding onto the railings her gaze fixed on the horizon, a slight wind curling the edges of her long skirt. Today she is all in purple and she looks so regal, a long violet chiffon cardigan draped around her shoulders like a cape, billowing in the warm gentle breeze that is sweeping in from the sea. I see people glancing at her as they walk past. She has a magnetism about her, something not even you could destroy.

She turns her head and sees me. I see the moment she finds me with her eyes and the genuine look of warmth she sends my way. She is my friend. A part of me wants to embrace her, to feel her against me, longing for that closeness that I haven't felt in so long, but I just smile awkwardly and lean against the metal rail.

'I thought you would be sleeping.'

'I should be, but I couldn't. No plans today?'

'I want to go shopping tomorrow. I need to take some things back so I was just getting some work done so I could take a few hours off in the morning. Sundays are always a slow day. What an exciting life I lead.'

We both start to walk towards the beach; it's a lovely day even though the sun is hurting my tired eyes. I wish I had brought my sunglasses with me. We stop at an ice cream kiosk and I purchase a pair of neon pink ones from a rack as well as a couple of Mr Whippys for me and Martha. Breakfast of champions. We sit together on a wall and I kick my shoes off, digging my toes into the warm sand. I feel normal, like I'm doing normal stuff with a normal friend. I haven't felt normal in so long. Do you feel normal? You must know that what you are doing is wrong, not just legally but morally. You must know because you hide it from the world.

'The policewoman I originally reported him to came to see me earlier.'

'Have they got something?'

'No. But she saw our flyers, realised it was me straight away.'

'Are you in trouble?' she asks, but I suspect she really wants to know what I have told the policewoman about her. I would want to know that, too.

'No, she isn't going to say anything. I think she feels like she owes me.'

'She does owe you.'

It feels strange to have someone on my side, someone sticking up for me. I don't even stick up for me.

'Well anyway I found something out, a few things actually. She thinks another woman was attacked by him seven years ago – and there's something else.'

'What else?'

'She was attacked before, the other victim. I think that's how he chooses us. I think that's what we have in common. I have been wracking my brain since the day we met to try and figure out how he would go after you after someone like me. We have only one thing in common as far as I can tell and that's that we have been raped before.'

'So, my ex, Tristan, not only raped me once but was responsible for me getting raped a second time? I wish I had had the courage to kill him when I had the chance. Instead he continues to ruin my life.'

'A woman called on the burner and said it happened to her, too. So that's three of us now, all on the same date, all who had been assaulted before.'

'How could he know that?' Martha asks. It's a good question, a question I have been avoiding in my own mind.

'A police report, maybe? I reported my first one, you said you did, too and according to Detective White so did the woman he raped seven years ago.'

'Will she testify? Does she remember anything?'

'She's dead. She killed herself. White also told me about a forum that was harassing her. Did you have anything like that?'

'I did, a local one. Tristan posted all about me on there. The Sanctuary it was called, but it was just full of woman-hating lowlifes. It's full of stories about women who they think made false accusations, it really is bonkers. There are even videos on there, revenge porn I think they call it, none of the actual assaults but of other private things that you wouldn't want shared – or even deep fakes of pornography. If you're right about him picking women who have been raped before, then that forum would be like a mail order catalogue. I wouldn't be surprised if you found yourself on there, too. I am still amazed it's legal. I can't even talk about it, sorry. It's so upsetting.'

'I have to work tonight but then I am off tomorrow night and the next one. Come over, you shouldn't be alone this week,' I say as if I am doing her a favour. Neither one of us wants to be alone this week. You've taken that from us. You are out there and we don't know what your plans are. For all we know you might target us a second time. All we know for sure right now is that you strike on the 12th of June, which is in three days' time. This cannot keep happening. I have to draw you out. I have to find you before you hurt anyone else but I don't know how. I will though, I will find you and make you pay.

Chapter 32

Shona hadn't slept properly in days, not since Gail had turned up in her life again. It was no less than she deserved. Snatching moments here and there between reading the posts on The Sanctuary and comparing them to sexual assault reports they had received and been unable to pursue. She jotted down notes in her bedside notebook by the dim light of her laptop as Aaron slept peacefully beside her. Reading through some of the vile comments, she was glad she wasn't alone in the house for a change.

Sanctuary/Forum/Topic>lyingstaceywhores#17
User: floydmaster3000

I know so many blokes that have been falsely accused of rape and nothing ever happens to the liars. Just another example of how the system is tilted to favour women and they wonder why ninety per cent of prisoners in this country are male, it's because women get away with so much shit. I'm going through it at the moment. The problem is that these days you have to get written consent for even sneezing in their direction or it's assault. If a man is accused of raping a woman, they rarely even need proof to get him put in prison. It's one rule for us and no rules for them. I am so tired of being treated like a second-class citizen.

There were hundreds of comments like this one, and thousands that were worse, calling for violence and teaching women a lesson. Shona wanted to believe that only a small number of men felt this way, and on balance it probably was a small number, but it was more than she had imagined. For so many people to share this twisted view made her feel like they were fighting a losing battle. How could she not know this kind of thing was so prolific? Maybe she just closed her eyes to it like everyone else.

It was clear to her now that Gail Reynolds had been treated appallingly by her and she needed to make it right. Seeing how angry Gail was made her feel like she had been sleepwalking this whole time. Why wasn't she angry, too? Was it just such an accepted part of life that she had managed to consign it to the 'nothing I can do so I won't even try' pile? That wasn't good enough and frankly that wasn't who she was. She wanted to help people, to protect people.

She would follow up with these other women and let them know they hadn't been forgotten, thrown away. She was struggling not to fall into the trap of hating every single man on the planet even though it was an overwhelmingly clear statistic. Even in cases of violence and sexual assault against men, the vast majority of perpetrators were also men.

Since talking to Gail she hadn't been able to stop thinking about her own experience. She hadn't even allowed herself to think about her own rape in any depth from the moment she decided not to report it. Barely even wanting to consign that word to the incident, writing it off as a crappy experience and locking it away deep inside her. As it was happening, she'd thought about her options and resolved to just accept it and move on, let him do what he must, then get out, get safe and carry on regardless. Just making that decision at the time had allowed her to feel some control over the situation. Her control had been to surrender herself completely for a short amount of time, not giving any mental energy to the moment and just letting it go, closing her mind to it. Now that she really considered it, that was a crazy decision, and yet she would do the same again. Not wanting to rock the boat was a trait Shona knew she had to work on. It was why she had listened to Coleridge in the first place, why she had been so eager to please her superior by sidelining Gail.

This wasn't why she had joined the police, to toe the line, to further her own career. Making people's lives better, making the world a safer place, that was why and yet somehow that had been moved to the bottom of the list in favour of following orders, no matter how wrong she thought they were. An important lesson had been learned and that was that keeping her head down and being obedient were anathema to who she wanted to be. Add to that the guilt she now felt for not reporting DI Graham Post back when she should have. The time had gone now, she knew that, but every so often she saw him cosying up to a new female recruit and it sent chills down her spine. In the back of her mind she had assumed she had been in the wrong that night, that she had sent out the wrong signals, that she had invited his advances and so that was the price she had to pay. She had talked herself out of thinking of it as rape, but she knew, she always knew that was what had happened. It was easier to think of it as a misunderstanding, the label of rape somehow feeling like an exaggeration of the events. Maybe she just hadn't said no loud enough, pushed him away hard enough, cried enough afterwards. It hadn't gone away though, that feeling, that deep down feeling of unease and nausea whenever she was around him. She could lie to herself all she wanted but her body remembered. She still worked in the same building as him, for Pete's sake. She wouldn't ask that of a victim of a crime and yet she put herself through it every day. And it was every day, that sharp intake of breath every time she saw him, a jolt of discomfort that she had become an expert at pushing aside. As a result of her experience she had become hardened, colder even. Then she and Aaron got closer and things started to look better. She really thought she had put it behind her, but this was all bringing it back. She had never told Aaron what had happened and he had never asked her about it, so she assumed he hadn't heard the rumours, that he wasn't part of the right cliques at the station. Now that she had admitted out loud to Gail what he had done she was angry about it, angry with herself, with the way people just shrugged it off, with everything that made her think she should keep it to herself, as though it were her shame to bear and not his. It was possible that her own resistance in accepting what had happened to her led to her treating Gail so dismissively, as dismissively as she had treated herself. Maybe she should confront him about it, make sure he knew she knew what he was.

She picked up the phone and checked that her morning alarm was on. She noticed she had three more missed calls from her brother. They didn't really talk despite still living in the same town, she saw him once or twice a year and that was too much. Theirs wasn't a happy home growing up and he was just a reminder of that. It wasn't his fault that his very existence upset her but from the moment he was born he had been different. 'Troubled', their mother used to call him, but it was more than that. She sent him a message saying she would call him tomorrow. She knew he would just be after money anyway, that was all he ever wanted. She couldn't deal with him right now, it was late, she needed to sleep, there were only a few days left until June 12th and the chances of them finding this man before then were more than remote. Tomorrow she would go to her boss with her suspicions and she wouldn't let him tell her to let it go.

'What time is it?' Aaron said, squinting at the light of the lamp.

'Sorry, it's late, I didn't mean to stay up this long.'

'What are you reading?'

'Doesn't matter,' she said, closing her laptop and placing it on the floor before sliding under the covers. She probably shouldn't read so much of that forum, it was skewing her view of the world. She turned away from Aaron and closed her eyes, trying to forget what she had read.

Aaron slid his arms around her waist and pulled her into him. He was warm and smelled so good. She turned her head so their lips could meet. None of this was his fault and she shouldn't be giving him the cold shoulder.

'You need a break, maybe in a couple of weeks we could drive over to France, go around a little market or something, you could pick up a new table for the lounge,' he said.

'I don't know why you hate that coffee table so much, I only paid a fiver for it in a charity shop. It's retro.'

'It's the tiles with the frogs on it that really sets off the style,' he said with a cheeky smile, kissing her again. 'Seriously though, you've been working too hard. A weekend to recharge, that's all I'm suggesting.'

'Nice idea, but what about your mum? You can't leave her for a whole weekend, you wouldn't.'

'I'll see if Anna can do it, if not I'll just hire a live-in carer for the weekend. I've been neglecting you lately, I'm so sorry.'

'I know it's a difficult time.'

'We keep saying that but it's only going to get more difficult, and it could go on for years. I know I've been treating it like it's only temporary, but her condition isn't getting any better and physically Mum is in pretty decent health, it's just her mind that's the problem. In all honesty I think I might need a break, too.'

'What are the chances of your sister stepping up for three whole days?'

'We don't need her. I'll ask but if she says no, I will find another way. I can't just be locked in this situation until Mum dies, and I really don't want to put her in a home, not while she is still mostly there at least. She would never forgive me.'

'You're too good for your family, you know that, don't you?' Shona said. His mother piled the guilt on at every opportunity, which was why she saw so little of him, and his sister did next to nothing, not particularly wanting to be involved with either of them. She realised that maybe that was how her own brother felt and resolved to call him in the next couple of days, see how much he wanted this time. She kissed Aaron again, twisting her body to face his. They both needed an escape and so she slid her hand under the covers and pulled him in. They were each other's haven from the people around them. She wanted Aaron to know how much she valued him, especially after the toxic words she had spent most of the night reading. Their relationship was strange by most people's standards, with his mother so dependent on him, but that was one of the things she loved most about him. She knew if they ever had children of their own he would do anything for his family, and that was important to her. He may not be perfect but he was perfect for her.

Chapter 33

Why do they call it the dead of night? I always used to wonder that but now I know. There is no movement and everything feels out of place, kind of broken and unfixable. Is that where you're most comfortable? Do you feel out of place in the day? My thoughts stray to you and what you might be doing, a lot more than they used to. Maybe it's meeting Martha. Am I more angry with you for hurting her than I am for hurting me? It would be so typical of me to feel like that. Like I matter less somehow, remnants from the doubts my parents put in my mind about my own worth. How often do you think of me? Am I even a me to you? Did I ever have a name? Was I just a substitute for someone else, someone who made you feel small and worthless in the past? That's how it works, isn't it? Or maybe you are just broken and unfixable.

I'm alone in reception. I did remember to bring a

book in case John tries anything again. I know he will, he's that sort. There are two sorts out there. Those that think of us as human beings with the same rights and feelings as they do, and those that don't. Since meeting you I can really clock the bad ones; it doesn't take much to recognise that look on their face, like you might look at a cake, or a burger. They think women are here for their consumption, their gratification. Is that what you think? I bet it is. I bet you think women are stupid and need to be told what to think. I bet you say things like 'what about men' on the internet when someone mentions that thousands of women are killed every year in their homes by their partners. Maybe I'm not giving you enough credit, maybe you're smarter than that and pretend to be a feminist. Stuart was like that until the chips were down and he had me alone in a room. That's why I trusted him, because he had always been so considerate in the past, and that's why he got away with it, because that's who everyone knew him to be. I was just the wanton slut that regretted fucking him.

The phone in my pocket starts to buzz. No one of any consequence has called since Grace the other night. I look at the screen and see there is no caller ID again. It's her. I know it is.

'Hello?'

'Eris?' Grace says in her meek voice, barely audible above the sound of the air conditioning in this part of the hotel.

200

'Did you change your mind about coming forward to the police?'

'No. I hope you don't mind me calling again. I just needed someone to talk to.'

'You can talk to me,' I say. Maybe I can talk her round. Maybe talking to me will make her change her mind about going to the police.

'I don't even really know why I called.'

'We are connected. That connection is important. You're not alone.' I know how I felt when I realised I wasn't the only one.

She sounds so much more broken than me. I have more questions but I don't know how to broach them without scaring her away. She knows something I don't, I can feel it.

'Were you ever posted about on that forum?' I blurt out, failing to think of a subtle way to approach any of this. I would be useless in a hostage situation.

'What forum?'

'Never mind.' I don't need to add to her obvious trauma by bringing that up. I suppose the real question is whether *you* are one of the posters on that forum.

'Did he hurt you?'

'Physically? No. There was no pain, if that's what you mean.'

'When did it happen? Do you remember what he said?'

'I do. He said I was a whore, and that this is what I deserve.'

As she speaks the words I hear them from your voice, that low whisper that's always lurking in the back of my mind. Is that what you said to me, too? Or am I filling in the blanks again?

'Did you recognise his voice?' I say.

The question hangs in the air and I wonder whether I need to repeat it. Maybe she didn't hear me. Or maybe she did.

'I have to go.'

She rings off before I have a chance to say anything else. Why did that question spook her so much? Does she know who you are? I don't even have to ask that question. I know the answer. Grace is the key to everything. Was she your first? What is she to you? I hope she calls me again.

Chapter 34

I looked online and found a local sex worker that matched my needs. I resented having to pay someone but in order to move from this stage of my life to the next I had to rid myself of my virginity. Virginity was precious in women but laughed at in men, I couldn't carry this shame and humiliation around with me anymore and so I contacted a woman called Kizzy. Her pictures kind of reminded me of Sadie, she had the same hair colour and face shape, she was petite and very pale-skinned, too. We met in a hotel in London and I honestly thought I was going to pass out from the anxiety of being alone with a naked woman. A woman who had to do everything I said.

I told her I wanted her to just lie there, not to move unless I moved her, and to keep her eyes closed. She asked me if it was my first time in the most patronising voice and I had to stop myself from hitting her and running out. She seemed nervous of me but she still did what I asked. I lay on top of her and I could see her eyes weren't fully closed and so I pulled a pillow-case off the bed and put her head inside it. I couldn't risk her looking at me. I undid my trousers and finally I lost my virginity. It didn't take long and it was better than I had hoped it would be, so much easier without the fear of her looking at my face. In my mind I was picturing Sadie and it made it feel so much more intense. I was annoyed at this point that so many women had denied me this simple pleasure. I was insulted that I had to pay for it. But it was done. I paid her and I left a different person. I was now a man.

On the bus back to my mum's house I kept thinking about Kizzy the sex worker and how I never should have had to lower myself to paying for sex. I didn't regret it on one hand but on the other I felt so weak for not just taking what I wanted. I was confused about whether I had done the right thing or not. I decided I would never pay for it again.

I got back to the house and my sister was home. She had moved back in. I sat down at the table with my mother, who looked like she was ready to sleep a thousand years. All I could see when I looked at my sister was what happened on that holiday. I felt bad for thinking about it but it just crept in there.

I didn't get a chance to shower and I could still smell Kizzy on me for the duration of the conversation.

The way my sister looked at me gave me chills. There was no affection, there was no feeling there for me at all. She hated me just like every other woman hated me. I wasn't even sure that my mother wanted me there anymore either. If my mum made me leave I would have nowhere to go and so I would have to do something. I made my excuses and went up to my room. I had to be smart about this. I couldn't kill my mother or my sister, but it felt like two against one again and I couldn't have that.

After a few hours online I knew what I would do, how I would get what I wanted from women, even if I had to hurt people to get it. I couldn't do it yet though. First of all I had to make myself an upstanding member of the community. Someone to be respected, someone for people to look up to. I pulled up the website for the local constabulary and looked for a link to fill out an application form. I was going to join the police.

Chapter 35

I can't shake you off; drink and medication have little power here. We never really get over it, we may learn to live with it but we have to recognise the crossroads that took us off route. I wouldn't be this person without you, there is no denying that. You left your stain on me. I am forever marked. Even if I somehow manage to suppress my feelings enough that the memory is a vague intangible cloud, the hole is there, I feel that gaping hollow inside me with every breath. I know what occurred by its very absence. Something so painful I would rather wipe a part of myself away in order to be able to carry on. I'm as scared of what lives inside those absent memories as any monster you can conceive of. You are the monster under my bed, over my body. I have two choices: to remember everything or to live with this blankness. It's such an easy choice. Sometimes I think I have made it past you and sometimes I can still smell you on my skin as if it were yesterday. Out of fucking nowhere you're a part of me again, inside me.

Before you came along and after Stuart, I managed to have one or two relationships. Granted, they were very short and nothing to write home about, but I was getting there. If I am too into the sex I feel like a pervert but if I'm not into it enough then I just feel like the victim. Sex is another thing you took away from me. Sometimes it just hits me after, and I feel the pressure to explain why I need to go, why this isn't going to work out. I can tell them about you, which in my mind takes me off the table as something to desire, I become an object of pity. That's if they even believe me. If they say the wrong thing, that triggers me into an even darker mood. It's not easy to disclose something like that. The guilt never leaves, the guilt for making them deal with someone who is broken, for not warning them beforehand about what they were getting into. The feeling of worthlessness Stuart gave me was hard to ignore. Maybe I should avoid these situations entirely? Well, then I'm unfulfilled sexually. It's not the sex that I hate, it's myself. You're still in control, because what you did is still influencing what I do, and what I don't do, What I seek out, and avoid. Three years of my life consumed by you. Checkmate. Even not playing isn't the winning move, because every move of every piece is on a board that will *forever* have your fucking mark on it, because of what happened, because of what you did to me.

Or maybe I should just sleep around, give my body to anyone who will take it, remove the emotional toll completely. That doesn't work either. Even if I did that, you would still be driving the car. I would be doing that because of you, too. As far as sex goes, you will always loom in the background. Again, the control is still there. I still feel the hand, the weight, as it influences my decisions, pressing against my chest. There is no getting away from it. You're a part of me now and I can't accept that. I need to sever the connection between us and there is only one way I can think of to do that. One of us needs to die, and I have decided it's not going to be me.

Chapter 36

We sit in the park, me and Martha on a bench looking like normal happy women just having a chat. Every so often I glance behind me to see if anyone is watching us, but no one is. You're not watching us anymore, are you? You're watching your next victim and I hate how impotent it makes me feel. A part of me wishes it was you sitting next to me on this bench so that I could ask you questions, get to the root of what makes you who you are. Maybe I could even fix you. Do you think that's possible? Do you think you're fixable? I wish I knew your name. In the far recesses of my mind I can hear your voice as you whisper gently into my ear. The words have started to take on a form, but I can't even trust that's what you said; I know I am prone to filling in the gaps you left behind.

'What do you think he is doing right now?' Martha asks, as lost in you as I am.

'I wish I knew.' I do wish I knew, I'm not even lying.

'Do you think they'll ever catch him?'

'No. I don't.'

Credit where credit is due, you certainly seem to be one step ahead of the authorities. Of course it really helps your case that the authorities either didn't notice or didn't give a shit that you existed. Either way seems just as bad to me. It's all just semantics. Who cares why you have been getting away with it, all I know is that you have been.

'If only there was something we could do.'

'There are things we could do,' I say, closing my hand into a fist.

'Like what? The flyers? That's not going to change anything in time to stop him. We only have a few days left.'

'Then maybe we need to do something more drastic, something that will really make people pay attention.'

'I don't know, I don't want to get in trouble.'

'Aren't you angry? He's out there getting away with it. They all are and we what? Put up some pretty pictures and wait? I'm sick of waiting.'

'Of course I'm angry. Sometimes I'm not sure I'll ever feel anything but anger ever again,' Martha says.

'Can I ask you something?' I say, wondering why Martha seems OK, why she doesn't seem as fundamentally broken as me.

'You can ask me anything.'

'If you could get your hands on the guy who raped you the first time, what would you do?'

'Nothing. I'm too scared of him. I wish I had a different answer but that's the truth.' I don't believe her, I see a flash of that anger behind her eyes that she won't allow to manifest.

'Did you see him after it happened? You said he was your ex-boyfriend. You said you saw him again for a while afterwards?'

'It wasn't like that. Why would you ask me that question particularly?'

'I read something on that site after you told me about the Sanctuary, it had your name on it. His friend was on there talking about you two and he said you got back together briefly after the alleged assault. Said he saw you both on a date.'

'That's true, I guess. But I did it out of fear. He wouldn't leave me alone, I told you that. He twisted everything to his mates and made me out to be the bad guy. I was so confused about what happened, it took me a while to realise the situation, it's hard to explain. You wouldn't believe some of the things he said about me. I was scared of him, and after it happened I was even more scared than before. I wanted to leave so bad, but I just felt like he had me in a headlock. I didn't sleep with him again, and I had told him repeatedly it was over, but he just wouldn't let it go. His so-called friends were all the same, too.'

'Why didn't you ask for help?'

'After I finally plucked up the courage to move out of the house, I did bump into him, Tristan, I mean. I was sitting in a cafe. Do you remember the one on Broad Street that had that huge ornate window with all the plants hanging down on the inside. It shut down last year. I was sitting on the couch in the window and I bought a coffee. He came and plonked himself down next to me. I was petrified, I couldn't move. You would understand if you met him, he's so overbearing.'

'That must have been horrible.'

'He put his arm around me, tried reminiscing about old times, took a drink from my coffee mug as though we were sharing. I felt sick the whole time. I was frozen. One of his mates walked past and Tristan made a point of tapping on the window and waving at him. So that was that, they spread that around and from that moment on no one believed a word I said.'

I hate myself for doubting her. I just don't feel that rage from her, like when we went to the club and started dancing with those guys, I can't imagine doing that. I know she's not lying about you though, but maybe what happened to her the first time didn't destroy her life as entirely as it did mine, maybe it was just a toxic relationship that got out of hand. I know I'm wrong for judging her by my own standards. Maybe I am just upset about the fact that I can't move on, I can't get over it. You came into my life three years ago and you still have a chokehold on everything I do. She seems to be hitting those recovery milestones a lot quicker than I am. Am I that fragile? How do I exorcise my demons? How do I get you out of me?

'How did you move on? From Tristan, I mean?'

'I just decided that he wasn't allowed to win, and in that respect he made it easy for me. Just living my life made him angry and so I decided that was the only power I had. I carried on living and he carried on trying to destroy me until everyone got bored of listening or didn't care anymore. I didn't bother prosecuting in the end, I was told there was no way it would stick. You see there were text messages between us after, too. Those are probably on the forum as well. I was numb, hollowed out. I said all the things a girlfriend was supposed to say even though all I wanted to do was get away from him. Even after I moved out, he continued to text me and like an idiot I would respond, maybe to stop him from coming for me, I can't say. It all feels so foggy now in my mind. I don't know if he lost interest or what but eventually he let go. He couldn't destroy me and that upset him more than me calling him a rapist.'

'How long ago did that happen?'

'A little over three years ago, I think,' Martha says, picking at the skin around her thumb nervously. I should probably stop pushing but I can't.

'Which police officer did you speak to?' I ask, terrified that she will say DI White's name. I would hate to think

I got sucked in by a liar who told me I was special, that she remembered me and felt bad for wronging me. I'm aware that I could just be another in a long line of rape victims she fobbed off.

'A bloke. I can't remember his name. Young guy, a bit strange but non-threatening. I could tell when he told me it would be a difficult case to prove that he was just following orders. He was really apologetic. I was drinking quite heavily back then, not long after I quit for a year but then I started again. I was self-medicating to forget. It didn't work.'

'I'm sorry,' I say, more for my own judgements than what happened to her. Maybe it's not that easy to just unequivocally believe someone. We always judge people by our own standards; if I wouldn't do something that way then no one would. Which is ridiculous, we all react and behave differently. I don't know why anyone would lie about this either, what is the benefit of being called a liar by ninety per cent of the people you tell? There is none.

'What about you? You said you moved here after so your story wouldn't be on the local forum, would it? Have you looked?'

'I didn't think of that. I haven't looked for myself, no. I don't know if I want to know.'

'If you aren't on there then that can't be how he is choosing his victims.'

'It wasn't a secret though, I did tell people back in

my old neighbourhood. I did go to local police and try to get him charged. Maybe someone found out I live here and posted something.'

'Did you tell anyone where you are?'

'No, I cut all ties. I'm ex-directory. I even considered changing my name, but I reckon Reynolds is common enough for me to get lost with. There are plenty of us around.'

'It was hard enough getting past what Tristan did, but this, I don't know if I have the energy to do it all again. Anyway, this is different.'

'Different how?'

'I knew Tristan, the warning signs were there which is why I ended things with him. After it happened and I got away I kept seeing him everywhere which strangely made it easier to deal with. Like immersion therapy or something. Not knowing who this guy is makes it different, it could be anyone I know, or someone I don't know.'

'I understand.'

'What would you do about the first guy who attacked you?' she asks me, obviously expecting me to say something brave and heroic.

'I don't know,' I lie.

I know I'm all talk, that I want to avenge others and not myself. If I saw Stuart again I wouldn't do a thing and I know it. This fact above all others is the one I hate the most.

'You busy tonight?' I ask, hoping I have found someone to share the burden of what comes next. She looks at me and smiles. I am not alone.

That's why you get away with this. There is no one to confront you, no one strong enough to take you down. What am I so afraid of? You have already done your worst, maybe it's time we find out exactly what my worst is.

Chapter 37

I'm done with the status quo, done with the way things work now. I have to take action. You have forced my hand, your incessant silence. I need a reaction from you, I need something. You made yourself a part of my life then you left me all alone. I'm sick of being the person you made me. I need to do something more drastic. I need to cut away who I used to be and become this new version of myself, the woman who takes no shit from anyone.

I pull my sweater over my head and then open the bathroom cabinet to get the scissors. I scoop my hair into my closed fist and cut it off close to my head. The short strands spring out and I drop the fistful of hair in the sink. The sink fills quickly with the bulk of my mousy brown hair. It looks so much more when it's off my head. I'm glad to be rid of it. I stopped going to the hairdresser years ago. Putting myself in someone else's hands felt too unsafe, as though she might slit my throat when I had my eyes closed. Another thing to thank you for, my spiking paranoia in public situations. I hack away at the remaining hair until it is short all over, not perfect but good enough.

I don't feel like that girl anymore, I want all traces of her gone, you got rid of most of me, now it's time to reinvent myself. I feel like a cliché as I do it but I don't care. I mix the peroxide with the lightening powder and put it all over my head. I wonder if I will like being a blonde. I feel like I am getting ready for a big night out, and in a sense I am. No nightclubs for me tonight though. Tonight will be the start of no-nonsense Gail, and tonight no-nonsense Gail will finally make her mark on the world. I'm sweating already and I haven't even left the house. I imagined this would make me look less feminine but it seems to have achieved the opposite, my eyes looking bigger and more cat-like than I have ever seen them and the line of my rigid cheekbones running up past my ears. Running my head under the shower gets rid of any hair particles that might linger, although I have seen enough *CSI* episodes to know they need the root to tie anything to me, and they won't get anything on me. I put on a different clean sweater and check myself over. I look in the mirror and it almost feels like goodbye, I wonder how the detective will feel about my new look, so similar to hers. I pull a beanie on

over my newly cut white-blonde hair. I'm ready to go
and meet Martha.

Martha is standing nervously at the end of the road
by the post box, a sparkly navy-blue scarf wrapped
around her head in a top knot. She's covered, too.
Hands, arms, only the skin on her face is exposed like
mine. I feel like a spy or something and I can't wait
for what comes next.

'What now?' Martha says nervously.

'I got us these from the art shop,' I say, handing her
a papier-mâché mask. It was completely white with a
velour finish on the outside, it looked like a china doll
face without paint on it. It would stop us from being
captured effectively on any CCTV that might be on
the roads leading up to our destination.

'What are we going to do? What *can* we do?' Martha
says, following behind me as I march forwards. I have
a hammer in my belt and it's smacking against the
outside of my thigh, reminding me what I have to do,
what no one else has the courage to do.

'We are going to teach someone a lesson.'

'Who?'

'A rapist.'

'You found him?' Martha says excitedly.

'Not yet no, this is a different one.'

'How do you know this one's a rapist?'

'I just do, now keep up.'

I can't let Martha distract me. Maybe I shouldn't

have invited her but I feel stronger with her here, and I also think it would be good for her to see that we have some power, if we want it that is. Emboldened by my conversation with DI White, I need to get some kind of closure from somewhere. Too many men have been getting away with it for too long.

'Are you sure this is a good idea? You've never done anything like this before, have you?'

'No, I haven't and I've had worse ideas. Maybe.'

'What if we get caught?'

'If you don't want to be a part of this then you don't have to be here, but I am going to do this. It was wrong of me to ask you to come with me, I'm sorry.'

'No, I'm coming with you. We're in this together now,' Martha says, trying to mask the nervousness in her voice with feigned excitement.

People don't always realise how much they let slip when they aren't paying attention. Since that first attack with Stuart Potts, I've been unable to not pay attention. Hypervigilance they call it, it's a side effect of going through trauma or something. When I was talking to DI White earlier, I noticed her referring to her attacker as Graham and insinuating that she still worked with him. It didn't take me long to find out there was precisely one Graham working for the Eastport constabulary. I looked at his face online. He doesn't look like a rapist, but then I suppose they never do. No menacing eyes, no disfigurements or battle scars, just a regular-looking guy. Do you look like a rapist? Maybe he is you, wouldn't that be a stroke of luck? It would explain how he knew about the previous attacks. He looks older than you felt. That seems like a strange thing to say but your soft hands didn't seem to be those of an older gentleman. So maybe DI Graham Post isn't my rapist – isn't you – but he is a rapist nonetheless. Better safe than sorry.

'What is it you're going to do?' Martha calls out, tottering behind me.

'Justice,' I say, holding my hand up to silence Martha. She stops walking. We are there.

The house is empty, that much is obvious even from out here. I usher Martha to follow closely behind and she seems to understand my clumsy hand signals. There is an open window at the back of the property. I realise how easy this is, how all it takes is just one decision. I just have to decide to break into someone's house and I can probably do it, nowhere is that secure. I can't tell if it's guilt or excitement I feel as I climb into his dark kitchen. How careless to leave it open like that. I wonder if that's what you thought when you climbed through my window. A sudden panic kicks in as I see a dog bowl by the side of the fridge. There is a strange whimpering sound coming from the next room, that must be what that is. Add cruelty to animals to the list of things DI Post needs punishing for. I hear a key turn in the front door and I push Martha towards the open door of the downstairs toilet that adjoins the kitchen, pulling it closed to a sliver. With my hand on the hilt of my hammer I wait and watch as Post walks into the room and opens the fridge. I'm ready to attack if he sees me. I hold my breath and wait for him to go upstairs.

As soon as I hear the shower turn on, I know that's my cue.

Honey, I'm home.

Chapter 38

DI Graham Post threw his keys in the green glass bowl by the front door before kicking off his boots. He should get changed and shower but to be honest he was too fried to just yet. Work had been pretty boring, but he had done a double shift so he could get Saturday night off. He had a date. He went to his fridge and pulled out the leftover pizza from two nights ago, grateful that he didn't have to attempt to cook. Since his wife Belinda had left him he lived on takeaway when he could; twice a week he would do a big order and then live on it for as long as possible. He grabbed a can of dog food and emptied it out into his dog's bowl. He would let him out of the lounge and into the garden after his shower.

Pulling out his phone, he opened the dating app for people who liked men in uniform. He did pretty well on here, rarely going more than three days without a hook-up. His philandering was what had made Belinda leave and he thought he should be more broken up about it but it just gave him the freedom to let off a little steam when he needed to. He scrolled through the faces, skipping past the ones he had been with before. No point going back for seconds.

Not that Graham had any issues getting a date in the real world but this cut out all the small talk and the misunderstandings. Everyone involved knew what this was. Even though it wasn't expressly listed as a 'one-shot' site, it was an unspoken contract between the members that sex was more likely than anything more long-term. Every woman he had met in a more organic way had always asked for more than he was prepared to give, or got upset when they realised he wasn't interested in anything more long-term. He had had a few dramas with relationships at the station and so he decided to knock that on the head. No point shitting where you eat.

After a few minutes direct messaging with a couple of the women he agreed to meet one of them in an hour. She lived about fifteen minutes away and so there was plenty of time for him to shower. He arranged to meet the other one tomorrow night. May as well have one in the pocket for later.

He was going to meet the first woman at her place. They often wanted to meet at their own place, which made things easier for him, meant he could leave when he was finished. They usually assumed he was married, technically he supposed he was. Most of the women didn't care though, they weren't looking for anything more long-term either. Everyone's a winner.

In the shower, Graham scrubbed with speed, adept at being in and out within a few minutes. He wanted enough time to style his hair. He was grateful he was going grey rather than bald. Belinda had complained that he had just gotten better-looking with age where she got shorter and fatter. It wasn't true, of course. Belinda was still a looker and Graham wasn't completely OK with her leaving, it was embarrassing, but at the end of the day he didn't think he was made to be monogamous, he had needs that were too demanding for one woman alone.

He jumped out of the shower and threw on his cologne before he was even dry, while his pores were still open. He prided himself on his appearance and overall groomed look. His father had been in the military and so this had been drilled into him from an early age. Belinda was right about one thing though, he had got better-looking as he got older. The hollows of his cheeks and the flash of grey at the front made him look more distinguished, more intelligent even. He had always had a slightly pudgy face but now that was gone. He worked out every opportunity he got, he was committed to his lifestyle of being a single man, a player. He had some stubble but not enough to warrant shaving and so he just left it there. He found the women liked a little five o'clock shadow anyway. He looked at the bathroom clock and saw that he had already been in there fifteen minutes, he needed a good five minutes to style his hair and so he patted himself down before wrapping the towel around his waist.

The bedroom door was closed. Did he do that? He didn't remember doing that. He must have. Turning the handle, he stepped into the room. The curtains were drawn and it was dark. Immediately he knew something was wrong, but he didn't have time to react before he saw the whoosh coming for him.

He heard a scream, not a scream of fear, more a warrior cry and then he heard his own shrill voice pierce the darkness as a rolling gurgle of pain erupted from him after hearing an almighty crack. He knew he had been hurt as he dropped to the floor, the lower half of his leg buckling in two. He looked and saw his tibia bone jutting through the skin, his lower leg snapped in the centre of the bone, at an angle he couldn't work out. Barely able to process the horror, he tried to get to his bedside table where he kept an old chair leg in case of intruders. Another thwack. His other leg this time. He screamed out and flipped over, trying to grip on to the floor and pull himself out of danger. Through the fog of pain he could see two figures standing in the room. It was dark but they were close.

No features, no faces, just two black shapes with featureless white faces in the shadows.

'What do you want? You're making a huge mistake. I'm a police officer. I don't have any cash in the house,' he said. A lie, he wasn't sure why he lied, there was a jar of tens in the kitchen cupboard for emergencies. This was definitely an emergency.

'Shut your mouth, Graham.' A woman's voice came from the figure to his left. He saw now that she was holding a hammer in her hand. Who the hell was she? He felt ashamed that he had let a woman get the better of him even momentarily.

'Please!' he said, sobbing, the shock of the attack wearing off and the pain kicking in. It was too much, he had never felt anything like it before.

She dropped to the floor and kneeled on his crotch, as if he weren't in enough pain already. She pushed her knee in harder and he thought his testicles might burst under the pressure.

He saw the glint of the triangular blade of a Stanley knife as she moved closer, her face completely covered with the white mask. He tried to commit things about the way she looked to memory but there was nothing, a generic white mask, that was it. She was fairly slim, he supposed there was that, and obviously violent. Maybe she was someone he had put away before, someone who had just got out from a stint inside and was looking for revenge. It could be anyone,

He couldn't think. The sound of his own heart drumming in his ears was only interrupted by his sobs.

'Don't move, unless you want to wear an eye patch on that pretty face of yours. Be a shame to ruin those baby blues,' she said. All he could see of her face under the mask was her eyes and they looked black as a shark's in this light. There was nothing familiar about her at all, not her voice, her shape, nothing. Was she one of the countless women he had met on the app? Was she someone else? He genuinely couldn't think of anyone who might want to do this to him, but this felt personal. If he survived this he wondered how he would ever live it down. His police training kicked in and he tried to commit everything he could see to memory. He was six foot three, this woman couldn't have been much taller than five foot. The other one was silent but poised with her phone over his face, maybe recording what was going on. Who the hell were they? He already knew he wouldn't tell the truth when his colleagues asked him what happened. He would say he was jumped by someone bigger, someone stronger. A man.

He could feel the knife in his forehead as she dragged the blade across his skull. She was carving something into his face. He wanted to beg but it just felt so undignified. Why was he letting her do this? He could feel the blood running down the side of his head and into his ear, his leg still bursting with pain. She pulled the knife away to admire her handiwork, her head tilting to appreciate it from all angles. Now was his chance, he may be incapacitated but he was strong, much stronger than this slip of a woman.

With an almighty roar he used all the strength he could muster to unbalance her. She fell, her arms flailing as she smacked down on her backside. The other woman started to panic.

'G—what do we do? What should I do?!' the second woman said. He didn't recognise her voice either.

'Stop him!' the woman on the floor hissed as Graham ignored the pain in his leg and lunged forward until she was under him, arms pinned by the side of her head. He watched her chest rise and fall. Her eyes glistened at him as he searched for a spark of recognition in himself. He couldn't tell if she was scared or excited, a little of both maybe. As he tried to muster enough energy to pull the mask from her face he felt the other woman jump on his back and swing both arms around his neck, clumsily trying to choke him out. He grabbed onto her and pulled at her arms before flinging her off to the side. As he reached forward again in a desperate attempt to pull the mask from the woman on the floor's face he felt his fingernails scrape against her cheek a millisecond before he heard the loud crack of ceramic against the side of his head. Stunned, exhausted, he fell backwards again, a sharp reminder of the break in his leg jolting through him. He screamed in a mixture of pain and frustration.

'I think you got me,' the woman said breathlessly and with what he was sure was a laugh as she re-adjusted her mask and scrambled to her feet. He hadn't really had a chance to see her face but he'd seen a little blood on her cheek just before she covered up, a red smudge on the white mask. The middle and index fingernails on his right hand had blood under them, he had caught her cheek with them.

'I got you alright.' He smirked through a grimace, unable to muster a full smile.

She brought the full weight of her foot onto his broken leg and he felt himself blacking out. The room spun and he fell backwards. As his eyes started to close, he saw her reach for the knife and start hacking away at his middle finger. She wasn't going to let him keep that evidence, she was going to take those fingers with her.

Chapter 39

Wearing a uniform was almost like a cloak of invisibility, people saw you come and go but no one really noticed your face, you were just part of the system. I was struck by how easy it was to get people to trust me, to get women to trust me. I could flash my warrant card and they would let me in the house, sometimes I didn't even need to do that. Sometimes I would notice women trying to flirt with me to get out of trouble; shoplifters, traffic violations, drunk and disorderly women. None of them excited me though. If anything I was a little disgusted at how easy it was, how easy they were. It was never about me, always the uniform or what they could get from me.

One day a woman came in to report a crime. She claimed her landlord had sexually assaulted her. It wasn't the first claim we had heard that week and it probably wouldn't be the last. I knew she was telling the truth from the moment she walked in. Her name was Kathy Lewis. Everything about her screamed victim and yet there was no proof and after we had spoken to her landlord it became obvious there was nothing we could do and that was that. It went to trial and she lost.

I couldn't stop thinking about Kathy though. I went through the files and found her address. I found myself walking past her house every day, it became a compulsion. I wanted to know everything about Kathy but most of all I wanted to touch her. Kathy had moved house since the attack and was living alone in a basement studio flat just off the park. I could sit on the bench halfway up the walkway and see right into her window. At night when she had the lights on I could see the clearest. Her windows were big and her curtains were thin, if she even remembered to close them. I watched her for weeks. I recorded her on my phone. I managed to bump into her once or twice in the corner shop, she could barely maintain eye contact with me. That's when I knew I had to have her. What started out as curiosity soon became surveillance. Between shifts I would sit on that bench in the park and watch. Making note of when she went out, when she came home. She had a key to her back door hidden under a garden ornament, an ugly frog thing that stuck out like a sore thumb, I imagine even if I hadn't seen her put it there it would have been the first place I looked. People can be so careless.

Kathy didn't socialise much. Over the course of six months she went out for drinks maybe twice. The rest of the time she stayed home and read books or sometimes she would watch a movie. Kathy liked to paint, too. She was always in her garden painting bits of furniture, covering chairs in ornate patterns and then selling them online.

One day when I knew she was out I decided it was finally time to let myself into the house and look closer. Inside was more of the same hideously garish furniture in a mishmash of colours. Her kitchen was cluttered with older-looking stoneware crockery, either inherited or bought second-hand. The place was organised chaos. I ate food from her fridge, I drank from what looked like a favourite mug before putting it back in the cupboard without cleaning it, getting off on the idea of her mouth touching a surface I had dirtied with my own saliva. I went into the bathroom and used the toilet before washing my hands with her soap. In her bedroom I went through her cupboards, I found some old letters from a past boyfriend that I read through. There were photos arranged haphazardly on the wall, a shrine to friends she once had, people she once knew. I took one of her and put it in my pocket. Then came the bed. At first I just lay on top, but that wasn't enough and so I took off my clothes and got inside. The sheets didn't smell of detergent they smelled of the soap and shampoo she had in the bathroom, they smelled of her.

After spending the better part of two hours inside her house while she was at work I decided it was time to leave. I left by the back door and took the key to a local shoe shop where I had a spare cut. I returned the key to the ugly frog. There was no way she could know I had been inside her house and that made me feel powerful.

I thought that would be enough but I couldn't let it go, I couldn't let her go. She had become such a huge part of my routine that I still felt compelled to watch her until one day watching wasn't enough.

It was the anniversary of that summer holiday, the date I saw my father with my sister burned into my mind. I decided to do it that night. Before she got home from work, I mixed some powdered ketamine I had taken from evidence into her water filter she kept in the fridge. I knew she liked to drink that when she got in from work. If she didn't then I would just wait until she was asleep and inject some into her thigh. I sat on my bench and watched with bated breath as she did the things I expected her to do, the things I know she would do. An hour later I slipped into her house to find her unconscious on the sofa.

I liked them better like this, unable to look at me, unable to talk to me. Totally compliant. I tried to film myself with her. She dipped in and out of consciousness and I had to wrap her top around her face to stop her from opening her eyes. I made a mental note of all the problems I encountered, already knowing I planned to do this again. For the first time I felt alive, I felt as though I had become the person I was always meant to be. I felt like a god with the world mine to command.

Chapter 40

Adrenaline courses through me as I run home through the park with Martha. The trees block out the moonlight. There is no one around here. We jumped the park wall at the back of Graham Post's house and pelted across to the south exit, which is nearest the beach. I feel exhilarated, empowered even. We have actually done something. Finally, I can tell myself I didn't just sit back and let one of them get away with it. One of you. I wanted to tell him why I was doing it, why he was being attacked but then I knew it would lead back to me, or at least it could. I wish you could have seen me, I wonder what you would think of me then? I still haven't figured out whether DI White is on my side or not. I think she wants to be, but like so many of us she has been conned into thinking she needs to accept the status quo, that if we let the law handle it then the law will look out for us. That's what it's there for, right? I haven't felt this way since before that bastard Stuart Potts put his hands on me. You don't realise how important control is until you actually get some back after losing it for so long. I'm taking the power back, my power. I want to howl into the night, dance around a fire, paint my face with blood – *your* blood. I can run forever on the electricity buzzing through me right now. Even with the scratch on my face slightly stinging, I don't care. I want more.

'Oh my God. Wait. Stop,' Martha says, stopping to grab hold of her knees, panting.

'You OK?' I say breathlessly, wishing I was more athletic. I have the energy to run a thousand miles but not the muscles.

'I need to. . .sit.' Martha collapses on the grass and lay down, her chest heaving, possibly even less fit than me.

'We can't let anyone see us,' I say, joining Martha on the grass.

'Did we really just do that?' Martha whispers with a giggle as we lie side by side, our heads touching.

'You don't think it was too much? I never should have pulled you into this.'

'If he did what you say he did then he deserves all that and more.'

'He did it,' I say, looking up at the few stars I can see through a gap in the tree canopy, the sky is black as squid ink, the stars spattered across burning hot and bright. 'Did you see his face?'

'I thought he was going to kill you when he knocked you on the ground.'

'But he didn't, thanks to you. You got him.'

'Oh my God, you cut two of his fingers off.'

'That was the grossest thing I have ever done. A lot easier than you think it's going to be though, you've just got to commit.' I find myself smiling. His blood is still on my gloves, I will have to burn them and get new ones.

'What did you do with them? Have you still got them?'

'I gave them to the dog,' I say, and we both burst out laughing.

'I'm so glad we met,' Martha says, nuzzling into me and taking hold of my hand. 'I've never really had a close friend before.'

'Things are going to be different from now on,' I say, no longer laughing.

'What do you mean?'

'Next time a man lays a hand on me without asking my permission I will fight to the death if I have to. Tonight I realised we all have the same soft parts, there are ways of fighting back.'

'You're amazing.'

'Aren't you sick of it? No one cares, no one. That bastard is out there somewhere, in a couple of days he is going to do to someone else what he did to us and the police aren't even looking, they don't even care.'

Martha props herself up on her elbow. 'Do you really think so? Do you think he will do it again?'

'You're good with computers, aren't you?'

'Literally my job.'

'I want to go through that website forum thing, see if we can identify any more of these local rapist shitheads from the things they post.'

'You mean The Sanctuary?'

'Yes. Did you read what they said about you on it?'

'That's how I found out what Tristan had been saying about me. Wrote this complete fantasy story about how I was just trying to get back at him for cheating on me, something I didn't even know he had done until I read about it on that bloody site.'

'Did you not want to go after him for that?'

'I just wanted to hide from the world, it was so humiliating. One of the blokes on that forum found my mum on Facebook and sent her some private images of me, naked photos of me and my twat of a boyfriend that had been distributed on another revenge site. She was so upset about it. I decided to just remove myself from social media altogether after that. I don't even have any of the messaging apps.'

'That must have been tough.'

'It was, Still is really. There's actually a lot of pressure to be a part of all those online things and when you don't want to, people want to know why. I have even had jobs question why I don't have a social media presence. I am just glad those images of me aren't the first thing to pop up when you google my name anymore.'

'We should get home before someone spots us.' I stand up and pull Martha to her feet. We start to jog through the park again, still unseen. I don't remember ever being this free. I have blood on my hands and I probably look like shit but I don't care. I don't care about any of that because I know now what I am going to do. I'm going to find you. I'll keep saying it to myself until I believe it. I am getting stronger every day. Part of me wonders if you even consider this a possibility, a showdown between us – except this time I win.

With every stride I am reclaiming myself. I will show them all what an appropriate level of anger is. It's time I made a stand, not just for me or Martha or even Grace, for all of us, any of us. Someone needs to be fucking furious about all of this, and it turns out, that someone is me.

Chapter 41

When Shona got into work there was a sombre mood in the air, everyone keeping their eyes down except when they exchanged knowing glances. Something serious had happened, even Evelyn Jones the perpetually chipper constable looked puffy-eyed and miserable. Shona scanned the room for her fiancé, DS Aaron Langford, but he wasn't at his desk. She saw him standing with the duty sergeant in a huddle, speaking quietly so no one else could hear. She walked straight over.

'What's going on?'

'Hey, you,' Aaron said with a smile. He had such a lovely warm smile, it always reassured her, it was the first thing she noticed about him when they met.

'What's everyone talking about?'

'DI Post,' Aaron said, nodding goodbye to Ben the duty sergeant and pulling Shona into a huddle of their own.

'What about him?' Shona said, adept at hiding her disgust whenever she heard his name.

'He's in hospital. He was beaten up last night, attacked in his house.'

'What? Is he OK?' she said, not sure what she hoped the answer would be.

'I don't know all the details but he lost a couple of fingers and a lot of blood. They knocked his veneers out. His legs were broken too, it sounds like quite a brutal and messy attack. His neighbour called it in when she heard screaming.'

'Are there any leads?' Shona said, a feeling of dread creeping up on her. The last time she had seen Gail Reynolds there was a fire in her. She tried to think back to her last conversation with her. Had she mentioned Graham by name?

'I don't think so, not yet anyway. Apparently they put him on some strong meds straight away, he had something carved into his head but it's been bandaged up so no one knows what it says except the meds on scene and the docs. No one's had a chance to interview him. He was out of it when they got there, had to break the door down.'

'Did they take anything?'

'Don't know. I'm going up the hospital later with the DI to talk to him, they said he needs rest now. Scary though.'

'Yes, awful,' Gail said, slightly distracted by the

timing of it. 'Do you know anything else about it? Why did they take his fingers?'

'Sorry no, I don't know anything else. They reckon the assailant gave his fingers to the dog. How fucked up is that? I didn't realise you were that close with Post.'

'I'm not. Just scary, you know, what if it wasn't a random attack? What if he was targeted because he was a cop?' Shona said, trying to cover the reason for her interest. She didn't want to tell Aaron what had happened with DI Post, especially not now – what would be the point? She didn't know why she felt compelled to keep it secret from him. She didn't want him to feel sorry for her, or treat Graham any differently. She just wanted to forget it ever happened. Impossible, of course, but that's what she wanted.

'I didn't think of that. Yeah maybe. Just in case, can I come and stay at yours tonight?'

'You sure? Will your mum be alright on her own?'

'My sister's coming down to sit with her for a few days.'

'Blimey, did hell freeze over?'

'You know Anna doesn't have as much leeway as I do with work.'

'Just all seems very one-sided, you know?'

'We're going to have another chat about putting Mum in a home. She's getting too difficult. She can't get about like she used to and she needs constant supervision, last time I caught her hovering at the top of the stairs into the cellar, one more step and she would have fallen. My sister's not the maternal type and she never really got on with Mum so it's understandable that she's against looking after her now.'

'I'm sorry, I know it's hard for you. I don't mean to pile on. I would love for you to come over tonight. I'll cook something special. You've just reminded me I need to call my brother.'

'Don't cook, we can get a takeaway and watch a movie or something, make a real date of it. Call your brother tomorrow.'

'Sounds nice.' She smiled as he seemed to be distracted by someone waving at him across the bullpen. He pecked her on the cheek quickly before dashing over to DS Whitcombe.

Shona had only just told Gail about what happened to her and one day later, the man who raped her got attacked. She remembered saying Graham's first name. All Gail would have had to do was look on the constabulary website to find his whole name. She knew this was Gail, she just knew it. There was something inside Shona that she couldn't ignore, a small feeling of victory that someone had caused Graham pain. She wasn't sure why she felt guilty about that. He deserved it, and then some. Would any of this have happened if she had taken Gail's statement properly the first time? Did she push her into this? One thing Shona did know was that she was going to keep this to herself. It wasn't like she had any proof. She couldn't explain it without officially disclosing her own past experience with DI Post either, something she had vowed never to do. No, this was another secret Shona was going to keep. Every day in that office she had braced herself for an interaction with Post, having to ignore the fact that her skin was crawling whenever he was within three feet of her. He wasn't coming in today and for that she was grateful, so she would keep this one more secret for Gail. Was she crossing a line by not telling the DCI everything she knew? She picked up the file she had been collating from inside the locked bottom drawer of her desk and headed for DCI Tarvey's office.

'Come in,' he called out, and she slipped inside.

'White. Everything OK?'

'Have you seen those flyers up and around town about the June 12th rapist?'

'I have. Not really our main concern right now though. Do you know something about them?'

'Three years ago, a young woman came in to report a rape, it was when Coleridge was still here.'

'Fucking Coleridge, we're still cleaning up after her. Let me guess, she told you to bury it? What she didn't realise is that you don't get crime stats down by just pretending the crimes don't happen. I'm glad she's not in our district anymore.'

'She did tell me to bury it, and like an idiot I listened

245

to her. The woman, Gail Reynolds, who came and made the report was attacked on June 12th. I have been going through some of the open cases we have and some information I found online. There was another victim of a similar attack on the 12th of June seven years ago, four years before this woman. Unfortunately, that young woman took her own life and so I was unable to speak to her.'

'What about this Eris thing? I have been onto the cyber unit and the phone number isn't registered, it's a burner. Do you think this Reynolds woman is behind that?'

It felt wrong to drop Gail in it without absolute proof and so Shona thought it best to just keep those particular suspicions under wraps.

'I don't know anything about that. It could have been orchestrated by another victim for all I know. I can certainly look into it. There's something else, sir. Of the two potential victims of this man, both of them had been through a similar ordeal before, and one was never prosecuted.'

'Same guy?'

'No, their first attacks were by different men in their lives, but the fact that they both had reported sexual assaults in the past that did not result in convictions is maybe too much of a coincidence to overlook.'

'So, you've only actually spoken to this Reynolds woman? You haven't been able to speak to any other victims of this man? How do we know for sure they haven't mixed things up?'

'All due respect, sir, this is not the kind of thing you get wrong.'

'What are you thinking?'

'I think whoever did this had access to information. It could have come from online – God knows there are enough websites devoted to outing women who have accused men of sexual assault if you know where to look.'

'That sentence sounds like it comes with a but.'

'Well, I'm just concerned about the forensic clean-up of the June 12th assault. The guy scrubbed the place down and made the women wash with bleach to destroy evidence. What if it's someone who knows how we work?'

'You think the rapist is a police officer?'

'Or connected to one, I really don't know.'

'Do you think Post's attack was connected to that?' he said over his glasses.

'What do you mean?'

'I don't mean to be indelicate, Shona, but we all heard the rumours surrounding you and DI Post. Did you happen to mention it to Reynolds?'

'Of course not. No.'

He stared at her for a moment, looking for what. . . what? She didn't know. An eternity passed before he turned his attention back to the file.

'Keep looking into it then. Find out about the Eris thing if you can. We have four days until this guy supposedly strikes again and we will have no excuse if it ever gets out there was even the hint of suspicion we had a serial rapist on our hands. The press would rip us to shreds. Get DS Whitcombe to assist you.'

'Thank you, sir.'

'You'd better leave that file with me to get up to speed, I'll drop it back to your desk later.'

Finally, she could devote some actual resources to this, something she should have done three years ago. One assistant was better than none. The first thing she wanted to do was find out who the names behind the posts on The Sanctuary were. More than one of them were red flags. They might not be able to get a warrant but people in forums often said a lot more about themselves than they thought they did, such as information about their jobs and photographs of things outside their house, for instance. She was certain they would find at least one of them.

Chapter 42

Martha and I have put together a table of the members on The Sanctuary website, to see if we can work out where they live, how old they are, if they have been married, if their photos or email addresses are traceable back to anyone in particular. We joined the site under an assumed name and commented, trying to draw information out of the members, trying to remember to keep our composure when they said misogynistic things, which was all the time. Are these really the men in our town? I find it so hard to believe that I am interacting with these people on a daily basis. After a few hours we were rumbled as troublemakers and ejected from the forum, but not before getting some pertinent information, including screenshots and the private email of the site moderator Nathaniel Barker.

'I'll make some new flyers up that we can stick

up again, with information about this website on there this time. Try and exert some public pressure to take this down,' I say.

'Are you sure this is a good idea? These guys seem pretty angry.'

'Can they find out who we are or where we are from the information we gave them on the website?'

'No, I used a VPN and an encrypted private email to join so there is no way to track us.'

'Then we have nothing to worry about.'

'Is there anything in the news about what we did last night? I didn't look,' Martha says nervously.

'Not yet. We have no ties to that man and so they won't be able to trace it back to us. He didn't see our faces, the most he knows about us is that we are women and that I'm white. Don't worry so much. How do you feel about it today? Any regrets?'

'I almost wish I did regret it, but I enjoyed it – what does that say about me?'

There is a loud rattle as my burner phone vibrates its way across my glass console table. I pick it up and hold it to my ear. A part of me thinks they have found me, that those men on that site know who I am.

'Hello?' I say. Nothing. I can make out the faintest of breathing sounds from the other end. Is it Grace? Nathan Barker? Or is it someone else?

'Hello?'

'Hello? Eris?' a man's voice says through some kind

of filter. I don't recognise it but then I don't think I am supposed to.

'Who is this?' I say tentatively, knowing before you speak again that it's you. I snap my fingers at Martha, who comes closer to the headpiece to listen in.

'We've met, I know you remember me, it seems I left quite the mark.'

'What do you want?' I try not to sound too shaky or defensive, I am trying to sound indifferent and although I can feel the panic rising, you don't need to know that. Hearing you like this has taken some of the fear away though. I have obviously spooked you enough to make you call me. You are human after all, you don't just exist in that one moment of time, you've seen my flyers. I wonder which one of us is more scared right now, me or you? Martha grips my hand, her sharp, manicured nails digging into my knuckles.

'We should meet up again, be like old times. How long has it been?'

'No thank you,' I say. You're fishing, trying to find out which one of your victims I am. You don't know, do you? I wonder how many you have to choose from. I feel a thrill knowing I have something you want. This time it's me with the answers. Maybe you don't think I've realised why you have called me but I know, I know you want me to stop before I ruin your fun. You thought you were onto a winner with your sick little formula for finding victims. I know though, I know you're scared, scared the police will start looking for you. You know someone has noticed you, that you aren't playing solitaire anymore.

'Hiding behind a name like Eris isn't very original, is it?'

'You're one to talk about hiding,' I say, allowing myself to smile for a moment. I can almost hear the fear in your voice. You aren't used to not knowing, not being the one in control. I don't know why it never occurred to me before that you wouldn't know how to speak to a strong woman, of course you wouldn't. You wouldn't do the things you do if you had any social skills. I've met your type before, or at least milder versions of you.

'Know this, I am coming for you, Eris. I've got to you before and I can get to you again.'

'Next time you won't find me so compliant,' I say and hang up, knowing it will infuriate you, losing that control over me. Part of me hopes you will try and break into my house again so that I can show you exactly how unafraid I am. You wouldn't get into my house without being noticed next time and I sleep with my hammer under my pillow. Martha still hasn't let go of my hand.

'Hey, don't worry. He doesn't know who we are, he was terrified, you could hear it,' I say, comforting her.

'He wasn't the only one.'

'He can't get to us; he won't be able to find out who we are.'

'What if he decides to visit every single one of his victims? It would only be a matter of time before he got to us. I'm scared. This was fun but I think we should stop. We are out of our depth. You should throw that phone away. I don't think I can do this anymore.'

'OK, but there is one more thing we need to do before we quit. One more person we need to take care of like we did last time. It's important they don't get away with it. After that if you don't want to be a part of this anymore then I will let you go, no questions asked.'

'Who? Are you sure this man is. . . one of them?'

'A hundred per cent sure.'

'Is he the guy who attacked you?'

'No, he's the guy who attacked you. I want to help you get some justice for what he did to you. Do you think he deserves to go through the rest of his life unpunished while you are still afraid of your own shadow?'

'No, he doesn't,' Martha says, an oddly eager look on her face.

'This could get messy. If he reports us to the police for roughing him up, you'll probably be in the frame.'

'He won't go to the police. He hates police.'

'Are you sure you're willing to take that risk?'

'Absolutely.'

I hold my hand out for Martha to take again, the imprint of her nails still fresh on my skin. If I had the strength I would go and find Stuart Potts and make him pay, I still might. For now though I need to concentrate on here and now. I want to do this for Martha even if I can't do it for myself. I'm too much of a coward to face Stuart again, this feels easier somehow, more detached. I can feel she is excited. he needs me and she wants this, she's wanted this for so long. I know because it's what I want, too. Not revenge, but justice. Knowing that Stuart is out there doing all the things I should be doing angers me more than anything. There were no consequences to his actions and that's just not right. I will get to him eventually; in fact if I have anything to do with it they will all pay. But don't think I have forgotten about you, I haven't. Our time will come.

Chapter 43

The date on the calendar taunted Shona as she compiled all the information she had garnered so far into one easy to read file. It was *very* easy to read because there was barely any information in it at all. She felt like a failure for not being able to see some kind of nebulous conspiracy before her eyes as she collated the data from all possible sources. She should probably speak to Gail Reynolds again, but after what had happened to DI Post she thought it best to keep her distance from whatever it was that Gail was doing. She couldn't be seen to know her if the attack on Post was discovered as part of this thing. In fairness to herself, she didn't know for sure that Reynolds was behind this, but she had a pretty good idea it was her. There were only three days to go until the June 12th rapist struck again, if they were right about the date – and so far the theory was compelling. They just needed a couple more links before they could go public with it. Hopefully they wouldn't be too late.

She struggled to get her head around what had been happening right under her nose all these years. It made her so angry that she had been in any way complicit with this monster. By not investigating every single claim to exhaustion they had allowed him to find his victims by the very fact that they were already victims. Feeling personally responsible for the woman who was attacked after Gail Reynolds, and armed with even a little more knowledge this time, she had to at least try and figure this out.

The answer had to lie within The Sanctuary. She decided to look deeper into Barker himself, see what else she could find on him. She was surprised to read that he had been married and was involved in a bitter custody battle which he'd lost and appealed several times. He had a son by his wife, who had won sole custody and the right to move to another country with her new husband after citing domestic violence as the reason for their divorce. Prior to that, Barker had been arrested at some protests. There was nothing that would indicate why he had come down this particular woman-hating path, although losing your child was probably enough. She would have to ask him.

There were other names that came up in relation to Barker. He was arrested at a men's rights protest with a man called James Garfield. She looked on

Garfield's social media and found that his profile picture was the same avatar as one of the men on The Sanctuary site. Of course, they probably met up in person, or he introduced men he met at protests to his websites. Either way, Nathan Barker knew a lot more information about his members than he was letting on. If Shona could find any mention of Gail or what she went through on the site then it was possible the information had come from there, although it being a local site, what were the chances of Gail's original attacker posting on there about her? Shona hoped she could find something, because if she couldn't then the alternative was that the rapist was getting his information somewhere else and she didn't like to think about what that meant. Her phone rang. It was her brother.

'Elliott?' she said, answering; she couldn't avoid him any longer, as much as she might want to.

'Bloody hell, you've answered your phone. I thought miss big-time detective was too busy to speak to her little brother.'

'I am actually very busy. I'm sorry I didn't call you back though, work is crazy right now.'

'I was about to give up for another three years.'

'Did you need something?'

'Can't a man call his big sister once in a while to catch up?'

'Of course you can. It's good to hear from you,' she

said, bracing herself for the request that was coming next. That was how these calls worked.

'How's your boyfriend Gavin?'

'It's Aaron, he's fine thanks.' She didn't want to ask him how he was, was it bad that she didn't care? Her brother had been bad news from the moment he could talk. He was always stealing from their parents, from her. He pawned any item of jewellery she had: her gold christening bracelet, a locket she got on her eighteenth, even a pair of gold and sapphire studs she had bought with her first wage packet. All he ever did was take, he never gave back and he never showed any remorse when he was caught.

'I see you're as chatty as ever. I did call for a reason, you're right.'

'How much?'

'What makes you so sure it's money?'

'Is it not money?'

'I was just wondering if you could help me take a loan out. I don't have the credit rating and I need to get a new car, mine got totalled and my insurance are being real bitches about it. It would only be for ten grand over a few years and I could pay you back monthly.'

'You want me to take a loan out for ten grand? I'm not doing that, El.'

'You're the only person I can ask. I need a car for this job I've applied for.'

'So, you don't even have a job to pay me back the monthly instalments? I'm sorry, I can't take out a loan for you. We are saving up to buy a place right now and I don't want a ten grand loan hanging over me when we apply for a mortgage.'

'I don't know why I expected any different. Thanks a bunch. There's no way I'm going to get that job now.'

'That's not my fault.'

'Other people have family who support them, you know?'

'I can support you, just not financially. I'm sorry. You aren't my responsibility.'

'Sorry I even asked.'

'Don't be like that, El,' she said, but the line went dead. They had a variation of this conversation every time they spoke. She longed for the day when she and Aaron had a family of their own and they could do it all the right way instead of what she had for a childhood, which was four separate miserable people forced to live in the same house together until everything imploded.

She needed a stiff drink but she wanted to speak to James Garfield first and see what he could tell her about the site. She noticed he hadn't posted for months so maybe he wouldn't be as loyal to the site as Nathan Barker was. She texted DS Whitcombe and asked him to go to the computer guys and see if there was an easy way to sift through all the pictures on the site and find if there were any of Gail Reynolds. It felt crazy to want them to be there, but the implications of what it meant if they weren't was too horrible to think about.

Chapter 44

The rain has been a light drizzle for hours, a warm drizzle but the ground is wet. You can hear cars passing at the end of the road, the shimmer of their lights momentarily bleeding into this picturesque avenue. It's all so uniform, so pristine.

'Are you sure this is the right address?' I ask. I don't know where I expected him to live but this just seems so civilised. Monsters hiding in plain sight yet again.

'Absolutely. He has fixed rent so he said he would never leave. Pays next to nothing for this place. Used to be his parents' when they were alive and he got sitting tenant's rights.'

'Looks quite nice. What's the best way in?' I say, admiring the converted bungalow.

Martha pulled an old pink fluffy keyring from her pocket. 'I still have the keys. I doubt he has changed the locks. People don't, do they?'

'Are you sure you want this? I can't have you backing out once we are inside,' I say, hoping I'm not making a mistake by confronting Martha's attacker with her there. It will be good for her, I keep telling myself. It's what we all want, isn't it?

'I want this. I have thought about it before. I don't think I would be able to go through with it without you by my side. It's why I kept the keys all these years. I wanted to come back and suffocate him or something, I don't know. Made me feel like I had some power over him. Do you know what I mean?' Martha says with a distant tone as she stares at the keys. I see a look in her eyes that I haven't seen before, a kind of hunger. She wants this, she wants to confront him. I'm not pushing her into it, that's all I wanted to know.

I snatch them out of her hand. It will be fine. This will be fine. We've done this before and I know we can handle it. Maybe I'm still riding the excitement of the night before, but I don't know if I can go back to watching the soaps and period dramas after cutting a rapist's fingers off and feeding them to his dog.

'You can't speak when we are inside. He will know your voice.'

'I won't say anything.'

'Good. Now tell me all about the house,' I say as I look through the window, the light from the television flickering against the wall of the living room. How long did you wait and watch that flickering light before you came into our homes and drugged us? I think of you in this moment even though I am looking at someone else. Graham Post two nights ago and this man tonight, they aren't the real prize, but they will have to do for now. I wanted it to be you so badly, but Post smelled different, felt different, it sickens me that I know you that intimately, even without ever having seen your face. I just want someone to pay. Anyone. This man will get the same consideration he gave Martha, they all will. Here's your bill, don't forget to leave a tip, you prick.

Chapter 45

The next time was easier. I had learned from my mistakes. Each time I got better, each time I learned more. We had a woman in for shoplifting one time, and when I was processing her I noticed in her file she had tried to pursue a sexual assault charge against her brother-in-law. She was pretty, and she lived between my flat and the station so it was almost an open invitation. Her name was Meghan and she bit her nails, which was a shame but I was willing to overlook that particular flaw because she fit in every other way. It was February when I started observing her. I had a few months to get ready. Meghan had a soft voice, almost inaudible, as she explained to me that she forgot she had put the perfume in her pocket. I watched her lips move and that's when I knew she would be my next conquest.

Within a few weeks I knew every detail of her schedule. She didn't go out much except to work in a haberdashery in the town centre. She worked regular hours so I made sure my shifts allowed me to explore her house when she was out. I took things home from her house, then returned them later. I wondered if she noticed they were missing. I took photos of her room, her bed, her dirty laundry. I had free rein of her house when she wasn't there. She had no pets, got very little mail. She was essentially alone, which was perfect.

I'd been spending a lot of time online with other men who thought like me. Not exactly like me of course but they saw the world for what it was, they saw how women are, how much power they have. I read through their posts and stories and decided to show them they weren't alone. I wanted them to know the power could be theirs too if they want it, and so I selected a few and started a private conversation with them, sharing photos and videos from Meghan's house, nothing that could identify her. They praised me for my work and they wanted more.

By the time June came I had set up a VPN and a link via a proxy site, I invited them to watch me work. It felt good to have the validation and support of these other people. For the first time in my life I felt like part of a community. I started with a few teasers in the days before I made my final move, some videos of jewellery or underwear. Nothing that would show her face. Then the night came.

She had no regular night-time drink routine so I

had to get the ketamine in her some other way. I waited until I was sure she was asleep and then I went in using the downstairs bathroom window which I had already loosened the hinges on. When I got inside I went to her room and stuck the needle in her. She didn't react at all. I covered her face with the pillow-case I brought with me and taped it around her neck loosely. The case belonged to my sister. I liked to think of her when I did this. I set up the lounge with plastic sheeting I bought from a local pound shop. I set the camera up using the TV stand as it was the perfect height. Then I brought her downstairs before starting the link. I watched the names join the watch party and then I set to work.

Chapter 46

We have no power.

The only power we have is the power they allow us to have. Them. You and people like you. The social contract of not taking what you want when you want it. But I know. I know better than most how easy it is to break that contract. All they have to do is decide they want to and that's what happens. The police do nothing, not always because they don't care – I'll give them that much – but because of the very intimate nature of it. It happens in offices, in bedrooms, in the backs of cars, or private cubicles in public bathroom stalls. There are rarely any witnesses, or if there are they aren't sure what they are seeing. So it's just a case of which one of us is more convincing in our arguments. That's where they really win the battle, them and you. Us victims almost always see ourselves as culpable in some way, as guilty, as the cause of the pain and the ones to blame. Whereas they, them and you, usually feel nothing of the sort. There is an entitlement about it, as though somehow you are only taking what is being offered to you. You are giving her what she wants. What she is asking for. Wearing a short skirt? Walking alone through a park? Smiling? Making eye contact on public transport? Wearing make-up? We must want to get violated. We must want it or why would we have told you that you were allowed to take it? By secretly wearing these lacy knickers you couldn't have possibly known about? We wore them because we are dirty bitches, always up for sex, secretly we want it all the time, from absolutely anyone, anywhere. Even though those hidden secret lacy knickers are inside our jeans and under our coats it's still a message that we are dirty bitches who want some revolting stranger (if we're lucky) to put their hand over our mouth and peel away our layers, their sweaty heaving body leaning against us, pinning us against a wall or a floor until they manage to push themselves inside and force their smelly wet sticky semen inside us. And they know, they know when they touch that lace, as they tug desperately at it and rip at the elastic until it digs into our skin and makes us bleed, they know that we wanted it because we wore those knickers. We didn't wear them for ourselves, not to make us feel nice or because they are comfortable, or because they were a gift or because it was washing day and we didn't have any boring normal knickers, grey washed with a slight pink tinge knickers left. No, that's not why we wore our pretty red lace knickers hidden under three layers of clothes. We wore them because we are dirty bitches who wanted to get raped.

When they hold those lacy knickers up in the courtroom, if it even gets that far, the jury will nod with a knowing smile, they will lap up the words that tell them what kind of slut wears a pair of red lacy knickers like that under her baggy jeans and jumper. The worst kind of slut. God forbid we are wearing a dress, then we aren't just sluts, we are whores, entrapment personified. Per the rules of the social contract wearing those lacy knickers under that dress means we are contractually obligated to be pulled into a hedgerow by our hair and fucked by a stranger, hands around our throat, squeezing harder until we can only feel the tiniest sliver of air creeping through our tightly gripped neck, a neck that fits comfortably in one of your large hands. What are we complaining about? We asked for this. Just like me, leaving my window open that night for you. I must have known you would be watching. I must have known that by leaving my window open I was saying 'come in'. It was silly of me really not to think about how it would make you feel. My window, my proverbial lacy knickers tucked away in my garden that can't be seen unless you slip your hand inside my jeans uninvited. No, I must have known that leaving my window open was a clear sign that I am a dirty slut who wanted you to break inside, drug me and cover my face before unceremoniously fucking me on a plastic sheet on my living room floor. That's what I wanted when I left that kitchen window open for you in the middle of a warmer-than-usual summer night.

There is one part of the social contract no one talks about though. They don't talk about the part where we would rather go to prison or worse than take it anymore. That by taking something from us you are telling us the law doesn't matter, that it's weak and ineffectual, that there are ways around it, that it only applies in some situations. The moment you took my power away was the moment you created this version of me. This version of me won't be caught out again. You see, before I blamed myself for what happened with Stuart, but with you it was clear I was not to blame and so I have found a new strength. I no longer have to politely smile at the man who won't break eye contact with me on the bus, or the man who sits a little too close to me in the doctor's waiting room. I can tell them to fuck off, to leave me alone. And God help them if they push me too far because I have had enough and I am not the woman I once was. You broke the contract, you took too much and now you need to understand what that means. Now that we have established that this veneer of civility no longer exists between us, I don't have to play by those rules anymore. I'm coming for you, and this time it will be you that bleeds.

Chapter 47

Tristan Walker flicked through the catalogue of TV shows looking for something he hadn't seen before. He had been out of work for a few months now and had made his way through every box set he had wanted to, followed by the ones he wasn't that bothered by and then onto ones he actively didn't want to watch but had run out of options. His skin felt sticky, unpleasant, and when he scratched at the crease in his overhanging stomach, a smell emanated that he tried to ignore. He was getting sore from the lingering sweat and he knew tonight he should probably concede defeat and wash. Depression had been pulling him under for weeks now. His personal hygiene was always the first thing to suffer. He was desperate for the toilet. He hadn't moved in hours, but he had drunk several beers. It wouldn't be the first time he had got so drunk that he had fallen asleep only to wake up in a puddle of his own piss. He flicked off the TV. He was hungry again. He would eat now to give his stomach a chance to settle before he had to go to bed, not that he did have to go to bed at all. He didn't have to get up for anything, he didn't have anywhere to be, anyone to see.

Reluctantly, he stood up, the sudden burst of movement causing his cat, Skittles, to dash across the room in a panic. His bladder burst under the strain and he felt the warm trickle of urine down the inside of his thigh. Not again. The smell of his own festering body unignorable, he trudged upstairs and emptied his bladder for what felt like an eternity, the urine stinging as it left his body. He should probably see a doctor for that. Even as the thought entered his mind, he dismissed it immediately. He didn't really do doctors. As a rule he avoided looking in the mirror; he hadn't been pleased with what he could see for a long time. He had lost his job first, of course, and then everything seemed to spiral from that point onwards. With no parents to fall back on, he was just glad the house was cheap enough that he could afford to keep staying here. They had offered him several thousand to move out but he knew if he could hold out for longer they would eventually give him enough for a deposit on somewhere else, somewhere he could make a home with someone else.

He threw his now dirty clothes on the floor of what was now the spare room slash wardrobe, with the other clothes that were scattered there. This room needed a thorough clean as well. He needed to take better care of himself and his surroundings if he was ever going to pull himself out of this mental slump he was in. If he wasn't going to wash, the least he could do was put on some clothes that weren't soiled. The closest he had got to clearing out his parents' belongings when they passed away was to move all of his clothes into the wardrobes and all of their clothes onto racks, ready to be collected by someone who never showed up. He had decided against sleeping in here even though it was the largest room in the house, it just wasn't his room. He stood staring at his naked body for a moment in the mirror, a kind of punishment for not sorting himself out before now. He wanted to look away but held his gaze even longer, wondering how he had got to this. He was thankful the lights were off. He distinctly remembered liking himself at some point, not hating the very sight of himself. He'd had women chasing after him, he'd had a future and then it was all gone.

Something shifted at the back of the room in the reflection that caught his attention. He was used to seeing movement from the corner of his eye because of Skittles, but she was lovingly weaving between his feet so whatever he had seen wasn't her.

'Who's there?' he called out, fishing on the ground for his tracksuit bottoms to pull back on. The lights were out and all he could see were shadows. As he glanced down to see where the trousers were he heard the definite movement of fast footsteps hurtling towards him, followed by a smack on the back of the head with some kind of metal tray. As he fell to the ground he guessed it must have been the black enamel folk art tray his mother used to keep her perfume on.

'Quiet, Tristan, and this will all be over soon,' a woman's voice said.

'How do you know my name? How did you get in?' he said, the lump on his head growing.

'You've been a naughty boy, haven't you, Tristan?'

'What do you want? Get out of my house!' he said, trying to get up. She pushed him with her foot and he fell backwards again. Grateful that the lights were off but wishing he wasn't naked, Tristan grabbed something from the ground and held it over his private parts. He could tell from the texture of the fabric that it was a pair of his pyjama bottoms. She kicked him in the shin and he screamed out, clutching at his foot. Who was this? What did she want?

That was when he saw the second figure, a bit further back, watching from the shadows. How many of them were there?

The first woman pulled out a knife and put her foot on his chest, pushing him flat on the ground before kneeling over him and setting to work on his face. She was carving something into his forehead. He knocked the knife out of her hand and she lashed out at him. Her fist connected and pushed through his jaw. He heard it click or crack or something, the impact much more than he would have anticipated from someone so much smaller than him. She hadn't held back at all. The worst part of all of this was that he felt like he deserved this. He started to cry.

'Big guy like you, I bet you think you can take me,' the woman said as she got off him. He quickly moved to pull his bottoms on, aware that she wasn't done yet, and not wanting to be naked any longer. She laughed as he flailed on the ground and struggled to pull them on quickly, making no attempt to stop him, entertained by his clumsiness.

'Please don't hurt me, please just go. I don't have anything.' He was embarrassed by his own cowardice. He couldn't help wondering what the endgame was here. Was she just here to mess with him? Was this a burglary? What was going on?

He looked over to the other figure to see they were holding his cat, Skittles. They wouldn't hurt a cat, would they? There was a familiarity to the way Skittles nuzzled and purred with the strange figure. He knew who it was. It was Martha. With that knowledge the fear in him seemed to disappear, and with the added courage of no longer being pants-less, he clambered to his feet and stood up. The first woman stepped back a little, clearly shaken by the actual size of him. She grabbed the knife again. He was well over a foot taller than her, and at least twice as heavy. Suddenly the odds felt pretty good for him.

'Get back,' she said, thrusting the knife in front of her. He could hear the nerves in her voice.

'I know that's you Martha,' he said to the second woman. 'What do you think you're playing at?'

'Don't say a word,' the first woman said.

He smacked the knife out of her hand again and she recoiled backwards, no longer in control, no longer calling the shots. Even though his forehead stung and he could feel blood trickling down his eyelids towards his eyes, this was the best Tristan had felt in months, adrenaline coursing, no longer steeped in apathy. He was almost aroused. He swiped at the first woman and the mask came off her face. Even though it was dark he knew he didn't know her. She was an average type of pretty, petite, easy to subdue. He moved forward quickly and put his hand around her throat, sliding her up the wall until her feet were off the ground and her eyes started to roll into the back of her head. He smiled at her and kissed her as he brought her head up to his level. She bit him, hard on the lips, he could taste the blood in his mouth as he pulled back, Her legs flailed and her feet kicked at him. She was a fighter.

'Tristan, let her go!' Martha called out.

'What is this? I thought you wanted nothing more to do with me? I guess I'm still on your mind huh, Martha?'

he said, excited at the thought of her pining over him. He'd thought he was in love with Martha once, a few years ago. He remembered feeling so utterly bereft when she had finished with him and now he felt nothing for her, although the idea of her plotting revenge on him made him feel important. His life was such a mess, he was so inconsequential and insignificant that it was good to know that at least someone remembered he existed.

'You need to pay for what you did to me and you need to let her go!' Martha said with more of a spark than he ever remembered her exhibiting before.

'That old chestnut? You need to give that up, nobody cares about your stupid sob story. I've all but forgotten about you, Martha. You being here tells me you haven't forgotten about me.'

The first woman clawed at his hand, desperate for him to release her. He barely even noticed the dull thump of her boots against his shins, gradually decreasing in impact and frequency.

'I swear to God, you let her go or I will make you!' Martha screamed.

Even though Tristan had never been stabbed before he knew what it felt like the moment it was happening. It felt like a scratch at first, but then the pain grew as the knife entered him and he knew she wasn't bluffing. Martha pulled the knife out and he felt the blood glug out of him, a strange sensation, almost as if he could feel his life force leaving him. The second time the knife went into his back the blade glanced off the bone. He was sure he could feel it splinter and he squeezed the throat of the woman even harder. The third time made him release his grip and slump to the ground. Martha carried on attacking him, his back and legs getting wetter as the blood poured out in steady streams. As his world started to fade away to the sound of Martha's anguished cries, he lost count of the amount of times the knife went in. He had heard those screams before, that night that he had held her down and made sure she knew he could do whatever he wanted and she was powerless to stop it. As he held on to that memory in his final moments, all he could hear was the same mantra he often repeated in his mind. *I deserve this.*

Chapter 48

I pace the hallway in Tristan Walker's house as I have been for the last few hours. I can hear life starting again outside, people getting in their cars and going to work, walking past the house, unaware of the horror that has happened just a few feet away from them. He's dead, his blood is everywhere. It's on me, it's on Martha. This isn't the way it's supposed to go down. We weren't supposed to kill anyone, I just wanted to teach him a lesson, knock him down a peg or two, make him feel weak and powerless like I had felt. You are all the same, you and all the men who chose to cross that line. It could have been Martha, it could have been me, it could have been anyone. If they wrong one of us they wrong us all and so they all deserve to pay. I wanted to make him pay, but like this? I realise now he's just a surrogate for you, you're the one that I want.

I don't know if I ever meant for it to get this far, not because I feel bad for the man bleeding out on his own floor, but because Martha doesn't deserve to go to prison for this. The whole situation got away from us as soon as he realised who Martha was. I should never have dragged her into this. I should never have followed her or approached her after that meeting. Martha is in the bedroom still, knife on the floor next to her as she sits with her back against the wall. She hasn't moved for hours. I need time to think. Should we get rid of the body? Would that work? Should we just try and make sure all traces of us are gone? Then of course there is the problem that Tristan is tied to Martha all those years ago. She made a complaint against him; her name would come up in an investigation. How could I have been so thoughtless? I knew I wasn't ready to face my own attacker yet, but I still coerced Martha into this situation. In my impatience to play justice, I was irrevocably stupid, and now look where we are. Is this my fault? Am I responsible?

I take a deep breath before walking back into the bedroom and looking at Martha, who's still staring at Tristan's lifeless body. What a fucking nightmare I have gotten us into.

'I killed him.'

'Don't say that again, OK? We need to think. We can dig up his garden and bury him there, or we can start a fire in the house and destroy all the evidence. I'm so sorry, Martha, I never should have made you come here. I was being selfish.'

'I'm not sorry,' Martha says, looking up. 'I've wanted this for so long. You don't know how good this feels. I should feel bad, shouldn't I? But I don't. I'm happy.'

'We can fix this. People get away with this kind of thing all the time, we just have to be smart about it and use our brains.'

'What you're doing, it's too important. I think we need to be realistic here.'

'What are you saying?'

'I want you to take Skittles and get out of here. I'll call the police and tell them what I did.'

'I can't do that. I can't let you do that.'

'She's my cat, he only kept her to spite me. I don't want her to go to a cat home or anything. You take her, you look after her for me.'

'Of course I'll take your cat. But you can't just hand yourself in.'

'Think about this as well: if I say I was one of the June 12th victims it will get you even more media attention. The news will be all over it, especially after the flyers, and more people might come forward. I can say I was triggered by the approaching date and went to get revenge on my original rapist.'

'Martha, you're upset, you're confused. Let's just think about this for a minute.'

'There's really nothing to think about. I did this, not you.'

'But coming here, it was my idea.'

'Maybe you gave me the courage to step inside, but I have stood outside on that street so many times over the last few years and just prayed for the courage to come inside and finish him for what he did to me. He took everything from me, don't deprive me of the opportunity to let everyone know I took it all back. He didn't win, he lost. I'm the winner here. Look at him. Who's laughing now?' She's actually laughing.

'But you'll go to prison.'

'Better than both of us going. You can find him, you can stop him from hurting someone else, I know you can.'

'I want to believe that but. . .'

'I believe it. So you do this for us. All of us. I don't regret this for a second. Part of me knew when I walked through that front door that one of us would be dying tonight. I'm just glad it was him and not me. . . or you.'

'If this is what you really want. . .' I say uneasily, knowing I shouldn't accept this, but not seeing any other way that wouldn't land us both in prison and leave you out there to do this to someone else.

I start to cry, overwhelmed by this. Martha stands up and picks up Skittles before placing her in my arms.

'Don't. You need to get out of here. I'm going to call the police now. Please. Take my cat. Go home.'

'This doesn't feel right. I was supposed to be making things better for you, not worse.'

'Funny you should say that. This is the first time I have felt right in a long time.' Martha leans over Skittles and kisses me on the cheek. 'I'm so glad you found me. Now go.'

'When you call the police, ask to speak to a DS Shona White. She will be fair; I am sure of it.'

As I walk away from the bedroom with the calico cat in my arms, I hear Martha dialling the police on speakerphone. It seems crazy, but I understand why she is doing it: it's all about control and this is something she can control. I envy that right now because I feel like I'm heading down a path I'm losing control of. It's not my place to force Martha to deal with this in the way I want her to. Or maybe I am making convenient excuses for myself, but I have to respect Martha's choice no matter how wrong it feels. In the back of my mind I always knew this could end this way, the other night, too. It was a game to me then but this has been the costly reality check that I needed.

I'm not like you, I can't just do in a week what you have spent years perfecting. I need to stop trying to think like you. I don't need to understand what you do, I need to understand why. Not the why that comes from the instant gratification of subduing, overpowering and violating someone, but the why behind that. Why do you do this? You subdue us because you are a coward, you cover our faces because you don't want us to see you. . . because you're ugly? No, I don't think that's it. Is it because you can't perform with us looking at you? You feel inferior to us, to me. I am sure you try to tell yourself otherwise, just like all those other men on that website, but the reality is that you need to keep proving it and so you clearly still don't believe it. I have that power over you, the knowledge that you are nothing, you're just a loser who can only make yourself feel powerful by squashing other people, not just any people of course: women. My guess is the men you look up to all have the same sense of false bravado and general disdain for women, especially beautiful ones. Their fragile egos ready to snap in an instant if you push the right buttons. Well, I'm going to push your buttons, I hope you're ready.

Chapter 49

James Garfield lived in a flat in one of the only three tower blocks in the town of Eastport. It was definitely the nicest one as the council had only recently painted the cladding a nice sea-blue colour to replace the mouldy peach that had been an eyesore for years. Shona showed him her warrant card and he let her in, rubbing his forehead in a kind of confusion as she walked in.

'Do you know why I'm here, Mr Garfield?'

'I've got an idea, yes.'

'You do?'

'I don't want to say it out loud,' he said, going and pouring himself a Scotch and necking it in front of her even though the day had barely started.

This wasn't the response Shona was expecting anyway and so now she was even more intrigued. He seemed to be more confused about what took her so long rather than what she was doing there in the first place.

'I think you need to tell me what you know. You can do it here or at the station.' Or maybe both, depending what exactly he was going to come out with. She didn't want to lead him in any way, she wanted to see what he was so afraid of saying.

'It's about that film, isn't it? That video. It's started again, hasn't it?'

'Why don't you elaborate for me, Mr Garfield?'

'I don't even go on that site anymore. I want nothing more to do with it after seeing that film.'

'Is this video on The Sanctuary website?' she said, dreading to think what film he was talking about.

'I stopped posting on there a year ago. I don't want anything to do with them sickos. I wasn't on there for that.'

'Then what were you on there for?' Shona asked, wondering exactly what 'that' he was talking about. She would get to it, she didn't want to push him too hard, she could see he was shaking.

'I kept waiting for you lot to show up and arrest me, I didn't even watch the whole thing. I'm not about that. I was just on there to moan about the ex and my custody issues.'

'What was on the film? And where did you get it?' Shona said, still unsure what he was talking about but knowing this was going nowhere good.

'It was a link, a special one, invitation only, with a password, through a VPN and all that so no one could be traced. Once you left you couldn't get back in without a new password, and you couldn't watch it again or anything. You had to be there and then at that exact time.'

'You mean it was a livestream? A livestream of what?'

'Of a rape. I kept telling myself it was staged and it was fake, but it didn't feel fake. It didn't look like no porno I've ever seen. It's not like they can act really well or anything, but this girl, she was very convincing.'

'And you saw that on The Sanctuary website, did you?'

'Not exactly, it was somewhere else, but I got the link through a direct message on there.'

'How many other people were watching?'

'A lot, I don't remember. Maybe a hundred, maybe more. Some were talking on it, like, giving him instructions.'

'And the girl? Did he hurt her? Did you recognise her?' Shona said, feeling sick at this unexpected turn of events. The Sanctuary was worse than she had even imagined.

'She had something over her face, like a pillowcase or something. Some of the men were talking like it was something that happened regular. Then I saw those flyers up in the town and I knew I was in trouble. I got blocked from posting on the forum anyway, or removing my posts. When Nathan realised that I was thinking of going to the police about the video he—'

'Nathan Barker knew about the video?' she interrupted.

'Yes, he was there when it was happening, he was talking.'

'So he wasn't the one in the room with the girl?'

'No, it weren't him. That guy didn't have a name or handle or anything and I never saw his face, before you ask. The camera was set up on a table pointed at her when he wasn't holding it over her.'

'Did you recognise the girl?'

'No. But whoever the guy was, he posted teasers for a week beforehand.'

'What do you mean, teasers?'

'Like him in her house, how he was going to get in, going through her underwear drawer when she wasn't home. There was a few minutes every night. I didn't know what it was, I thought it was all staged at first until I saw the actual footage.'

'I don't suppose you screenshotted any of it did you?'

'I did catch some of the teasers and put them on a drive. I was going to drop them to the police but Nathan was onto me and I'm ashamed to say I chickened out. Some of the frequent flyers on that site are ex-military with criminal records for violence. I only caught them by accident because I often have screen recording software going. I make instructional videos to show people how to use photo manipulation apps and stuff like that.'

'Was there anything in the teasers that would indicate where the attack was taking place? Who the victim was?'

'Not to me, but I don't know, maybe someone would recognise it.'

'I'm afraid I am going to have to ask you to come in so we can get this all on tape. That's a lot of information. If only you had come forward sooner.'

'Nathan told me if I did he would send all my messages to my wife's lawyer and I would never see my kids again. It's not like I said anything really awful, but it would be enough to make someone think I wasn't a fit father. I'm not proud of myself.'

'Then why did you say those things?'

'You get sucked into it a bit on there, pulled into the brotherhood. It's like a competition to see who hates women the most, or who can talk about them the worst. I don't know how to explain it but that's how they bond, how we bonded. It made us feel important and maybe it had been a while since I felt that way.'

'You don't mean the things you said then?'

'I thought I did but now, when I look back on it, I'm really ashamed. It's really hard to see when you're in it though. I've really struggled to live with some of the things I said.'

'I don't suppose you remember the date of the live-stream?'

'Last summer. June, I think,'

She felt a knot tighten in her stomach. Could he have witnessed one of the June 12th rapes?

'Will you come with me to the station to give a statement?' Shona said gently. She needed all of this on the record.

'Anything I can do to help. I'll get the drive for you,' he said, clearly relieved to finally have it out of him.

Confession was a strange thing that way, how something secret could eat its way through you until you felt like you had to get it out. The only people who didn't seem to experience that were people who didn't feel guilt. She had met criminals like that before, the ones who only confessed to brag, not because of any kind of remorse. She could see Garfield wasn't faking it and so she was willing to give him the benefit of the doubt. At least he had realised he was wrong.

A video though, a livestream, that changed things. Was there any record of it? Did it still exist? How would they even find it? How could she even tell Gail that a video of that night might exist, might have been watched by a hundred people? It might tip her over the edge.

Chapter 50

I heard about her before I met her. Whispers in the station about a troublemaker. Questions around her character. Was she the type of woman to lie about something as serious as sexual assault? The number of times I heard those questions after a rape was reported. I knew though, I knew from the way she talked to me that she wasn't a liar. There was something different about Shona White, something that made me want to get to know her. It was the first time I had really been interested in someone like that, to know more of their character. She kept her mouth shut about the assault. I'm not sure she knew how much people talked about her or the awful things they said. That she was trying to sleep her way to the top and, when that didn't work, that she cried rape. That she was an attention seeker who was looking for sympathy. That she was on the cusp of being fired so she was trying to make it impossible for them to fire her. Post was a skilled manipulator who had everyone in his pocket, she didn't stand a chance. I saw through him though, I could see what he was. I watched her for a while, went into her house, looked at her things. I tried to work out enough of her likes and dislikes to start and maintain conversations with her, make her think we liked the same things. People love coincidences, so tell them you like all the same bands they do, that you buy the same coffee as them, anything, and they cling to those connections. I was going to make Shona White think I was her destiny.

Chapter 51

Shona got the call on her way back to the station with Garfield. There had been a murder, a man, stabbed to death. Aaron was waiting for her, he looked agitated.

'What's going on?' she asked.

'Tarvey wants you to take the lead on the interview in one. He told me to take your guy here and do the interview.'

'Who is in there?'

'You heard about the stabbing? The murderer's in there, she's asked for you by name. Why would she be asking for you by name?' he asked. Maybe he wanted to do the interview himself, it was a big deal after all.

Shona felt her heart dip. It had to be Gail, no one else would know to ask for her. What had Gail done? Had she found him? Who had been killed? She ignored Aaron's question.

'OK, that's James Garfield, he used to be a member on that Sanctuary website until he saw a livestream video of a sexual assault, a rape. They all but kicked him off the forum because he complained about it. From his description it could be the June 12th one.'

'Grim. Does he have any proof? Did he record it?'

'He has a drive of something but it doesn't sound like it was the actual assault. But we need as many details as he can remember. Maybe tech can find something online through the screen recording he has. I'll bet one of those other scumbags on the site recorded it. See if Whitcombe has got anywhere with a list of members from the site. I reckon Garfield will agree to a search, maybe even hand over his computers so we don't have to go through the rigmarole of getting a warrant. He seems quite eager to help and I bet he met some of the other members at one of these protest marches they used to attend.'

'I'll see what I can get out of him. Good luck with Akintola.'

'Who?'

'The woman who confessed to the murder, her name is Martha Akintola. The victim was her ex-boyfriend who she had previously accused of rape,' he said.

Shona hoped the look of relief wasn't too obvious when he said the woman's name. She had expected it to be Gail, and she found it hard to believe this wasn't connected to Gail in some way. Maybe the flyers had just inspired this attack. Shona was inspired by Gail's tenacity but it was bordering on obsession and, judging by the escalation in attacks against a certain type of man, it was contagious.

'OK. You'll need to send someone to pick up Nathan Barker and bring him in for questioning, too. According to Garfield, he knew about the video recordings. I am betting he knows a hell of a lot more.'

'Will do.'

'You around tonight?' Shona asked, needing to spend some time with a good man after everything she had read and heard over the last few days.

'I'm working until about eight but after that I can be. Let's get takeaway and watch old movies. I'll speak to you after,' he said just before walking over to Garfield, who was sitting in the waiting area.

Shona took a deep breath and went to get the file before walking into the interview. Just by looking at the photos she could see this was personal. There was blood everywhere. She could see that Akintola had alleged a charge of rape against him more than four years ago that ultimately resulted in no further action like so many others.

Shona noticed a strange sense of calm surrounding their murderer, Martha Akintola. She had calmly called the police and told them she had killed Tristan Walker. They had the murder weapon because when they arrived she had showed them where the knife was and explained what had happened and why. If only it was always this easy. Murder wasn't something that happened often in Eastport. Burglary was top of the list and theft in general, followed by low-level but widespread drug dealing. Murder was that much more serious though and the police station was buzzing with the nervous excitement that came with it. The fact that the killer had asked for Shona by name had not gone unnoticed either. As she had walked to the interview she spotted the stares from colleagues, not all of them congratulatory. This was a big deal for the station, not to mention the fact that it was a slam dunk due to the confession. Akintola herself was defiant in a way, chin raised, unapologetic, unflinching in her responses.

'You asked for me by name. Why was that? I don't remember meeting you before.'

'I heard you were fair,' Akintola said.

Shona noted that was a strange word to use. 'Who told you that?'

'Does it matter? Do I need to sign something now or what?'

'Can we just run through what happened.'

'I killed him, that's what happened. I explained back at the house.'

'We need it on tape for the trial. How did you know Tristan Walker?'

'We used to date. A few years ago now. Do you not have a file on him? Or me at least?'

'I just want to hear things in your own words. Just tell me about your relationship with Tristan Walker.'

'I went out with him for a few months, about five years ago I think roughly. Things were OK, then they weren't. He was a bit clingy, possessive, you know the type? He was trying to rush me into marriage and children, like his life depended on it. I felt like everything was moving too fast when he asked me to move in with him. I say asked but he practically ordered me to do it. He contacted my landlord and gave notice on my behalf. He was so controlling. I told him I needed some space and we broke up.'

This was the first hint of emotion Shona had seen from Martha. Even though she was trying to retain her cool demeanour, there was a slight vibration to her voice, emotion she was trying to suppress.

'Was that the last time you saw him before last night?'

'You know it wasn't.'

'So, what happened?'

'He didn't take rejection very well. He kept calling me, he would turn up at my work and he would follow me sometimes, it was insane. He just couldn't accept that I didn't want him. One day he came over to my new place to talk, I wouldn't let him in and he lost it, pushed me inside and he raped me.'

'I'm sorry.'

'Are you?' Akintola said, staring straight at Shona.

'You reported the rape to the police?' Shona said, ignoring the tone of Akintola's voice.

'Not at first. I was confused about what had happened, he kind of gaslit me back into a relationship with him but I was like a zombie for those few weeks, I wasn't even there, I was trapped and afraid. It doesn't even make sense when I say it out loud now. I really felt like I had no options. He told me it wasn't rape and I don't know why but I believed him. When I did eventually come to my senses I went to the police, for all the good it did. It went nowhere, not enough evidence. The icing on the cake was when he went online and told a load of lies about me and apparently that was fine with you guys, too.'

'Online? Can you remember where online?' Shona said.

'Some incel woman-hating website called The Sanctuary.'

'I'm sorry those things happened to you,' Shona said, trying to remember if she had seen Martha's story on the site. There were so many.

'Yeah well. That doesn't really mean anything.'

'So out of the blue last night you decided to go to his house and what?'

'Not really out of the blue. I have thought of little else since it happened. That is until I was raped again.'

'He raped you again?'

'Not him, no. Someone else. I don't know who.'

'We don't have a report of that.'

'Damn right you don't.'

'Do you want to tell me about that?' Shona said, but she knew before Martha even opened her mouth again what she was going to say.

'Last year, on the 12th of June. I guess with the anniversary in a couple of days I was feeling extra stabby,' Akintola said, almost smiling at the end there. There was no remorse here.

Shona was hit instantly by the date. This must have been the woman Gail Reynolds told her about, the one who was attacked by the same man who raped her. This also might be the sexual assault James Garfield saw livestreamed. At least this explained why she'd asked for Shona by name. Shona wondered if Gail hadn't picked her to punish her. It wasn't like Gail had any reason to trust her after the way she handled Gail the first time she came to report the rape. An over-whelming sense of responsibility came over Shona in a wave of shame. If she had been more diligent in dealing with Gail Reynolds maybe they would have stopped the rapist before he even got to Martha Akintola and then maybe Tristan Walker wouldn't be dead. Shona couldn't help wondering if this was Gail trying to twist the proverbial knife.

'Why didn't you report that to the police? The attack last year? We don't have any record of it,' Shona said when she finally composed herself.

'Ha!' Akintola yelped almost involuntarily. 'Why? So you could ignore me again? So my name could get dragged through the mud? So I could lose what remaining friends I have left? No thank you. I didn't see the point. There wouldn't be any evidence. He took it all with him.'

'Did he break into your home?' Shona said, realising she shouldn't be leading her in this way, but she just had to know if it was the same man.

'He did.'

'Walk me through what happened.'

'I went out with some mates after work, had a few, got home and turned in for the night. Then when I woke up someone had laid out plastic sheeting, I couldn't see anything and I couldn't move, everything felt like lead. I hadn't been that drunk when I got home so I knew it wasn't that. By the time my brain caught up with what was going on it was too late to do anything. He raped me on the floor. Covered me in bleach and made me scrub myself raw. I could taste bleach in the back of my throat for days afterwards. The smell of it disgusts me now.'

'How much had you had to drink? Was it possible you were still drunk? I mean, do you think it was him that made you unable to move? Did he give you something?'

'Yes. It wore off after a while. I was unable to move temporarily, long enough for him to take what he wanted without any resistance at all. I felt like a Barbie.'

'Do you know what he drugged you with?'

Martha looked guiltily at the floor. It was clear she had an idea what he had given her.

'It's OK to tell me. If you think you know what he gave you, we can investigate that and see if we can trace the source. No judgement.'

'I think it was ketamine. It was a big dose though, or maybe it was mixed in with something else. I only ever tried it in small quantities before. This felt like that much deeper. The comedown was particularly brutal.'

'Thank you, I will investigate that. Did he take the plastic sheet with him when he left?'

'He did. He took my towel, too. It was a Quiksilver towel, my favourite one. Is it weird to have a favourite towel? I bought it with my first ever wage packet. It's blue and red and orange with stripes that sort of fade into each other. A beach towel. I wanted to try surfing. I wasn't any good at it though, so I sold the rest of the kit I bought. But I always liked that towel. . .'
She trailed off, maybe remembering that she wasn't having a catch-up with a mate over a coffee. She composed herself again. Crossing her arms and leaning back in the chair.

'So last night. You went to see Mr Walker. He let you in, did he?'

'I still had keys. I went inside and waited for him to go upstairs, then when I got the chance, I attacked him.'

'Did you speak to him at all?'

'A little.'

'And it was just you there?'

'Of course. Well, apart from him. Why are you asking me that?'

'Because you stabbed him in the back. Seventeen times.'

'I wanted to make sure he was dead.'

'But in the back? Why would he turn his back on you?'

Martha Akintola leaned forward, palms face down on the table and with a concentrated look of anger that made Shona lean back. 'Because he wasn't afraid of me, not even a little bit. Even with a knife in my hand I was nothing but an insect to him. A fly to squash. He was a big man.'

'He was.'

'He isn't anymore though. He's nothing.' Akintola smiled.

It wasn't hard for Shona to understand why she had done it, it was hard not to take her side. She had a sneaking suspicion that Gail was involved in this somehow, whether she just revved her up and set her loose or whether she was actually present for it. Shona wondered if Martha Akintola had been present when

DI Post had been attacked, but she didn't want to ask her on tape. What Akintola had done had well and truly opened the door to a full investigation into the June 12th rapes. When the press inevitably got wind of what had been going on at least they could say they were in an active investigation and were dealing with it. She was surprised they hadn't been in touch already, it wasn't like Gail had been subtle with the flyers. Shona would make sure she could pull a decent team together to pursue the case now. She had already amassed a fair bit of information. Maybe she could find this guy. It was a case of finding out where he had heard about the women's previous assaults and, without knowing who else had been visited by this monster, that was going to be difficult. The chances of her finding anything significant before the deadline in two days was almost nil but she had to try. She had to go through any previous rape claims that went nowhere and ask these women if they had been targeted again. She couldn't risk Gail Reynolds finding another woman and taking revenge on her behalf, or worse, killing someone else.

No matter Shona's personal feelings about the perpetrators of this particular crime she had to respect the law, even when it didn't work in her favour. She knew that was a simplistic view but there it was. If you started allowing your own opinions to colour the way you implemented the law then that's where things went awry. So why had she kept silent about Gail and her suspicions that she was involved? Why hadn't she brought her in? It was no different to DI Coleridge deciding that Gail was wasting their time because of the previous report. You investigate, you present the evidence and then it's up to CPS and court what happens next. Even though she knew all of that to be true, she still didn't want to question Akintola over DI Post's attack. He had all but said he didn't see anything and she knew if she came forward with her suspicion then people would want to know why and then her secret would be well and truly out. Sure, there had been plenty of rumours but they were short-lived and she had never even told Aaron about what happened with her and Post – there was no need. The fact that the word 'pig' had been carved into Post's head had raised all kinds of speculation but she didn't want to entertain it. Luckily most people thought it was a crime motivated by someone Post had put away in the past and he wasn't refuting that in any way. There was nothing to link the two attacks now that Martha had explicitly said her motivation was personal. In the photo, Shona could see that maybe they had tried to write a word on Walker's head but obviously everything had gone south before they got the chance. It wasn't the smartest move but she guessed it was because they never intended to kill Walker. Shona didn't want to be caught in that web even though she knew what happened to Post was the exact same crime as the one perpetrated against Walker. Post had made out it was something else and even if he remembered what happened, which she suspected he did, he wouldn't want anyone else to know he had been overpowered by two women so he was unlikely to point the finger at Martha. No, Shona thought it better to keep Post out of this lest she entangle herself in a he said/she said scenario that she would inevitably lose. The statistics on convictions proved that much. Some people would believe her and some people wouldn't. Graham was a popular man and so she didn't fancy her chances. She had heard of more than one case where a female officer who made such allegations was ostracised by her colleagues during an investigation and then summarily dismissed for discreditable conduct a few months down the line. She would just be happy every time she saw the faint outline of the word pig on his forehead. He was marked now, just like he had marked her.

Chapter 52

All I can think about is what Martha is probably going through and how I was the architect of this mess. In my enthusiasm to get retribution for all the injustices against victims of rape I didn't really think things through. What a shit show. Nervous energy pulses through me as I wonder what I can do next. I wonder if you will recognise her on the news when the story breaks? I open my laptop and start looking through The Sanctuary forum. I look at all the pictures and all the stories and opinions and it makes me livid. I find a story about a Kathy Lewis and confirm she is one of your victims too from the way they talk about her, the fact that she killed herself and the fact they were gloating about it. I wonder again why everyone isn't more angry about this, about all of it. Do we just resign ourselves to the fact that there is nothing we can do about it? There is no way it's not happening to someone right now, right this second and here were these dickheads making fun of the victims to make themselves feel better. No. I have no remorse for what we did to Tristan Walker. He crossed that line once, he would have done it again, that much was almost certain. It's not something you do once, is it? Once you get a taste for it? Once you've crossed that line I imagine boring old vanilla sex with consent doesn't quite cut it for you anymore.

The rage builds inside me until I can no longer look at these words. For all the good I tried to do the only thing I have effectively changed is that Martha is now going to prison and there's one less rapist on the planet, and that part wasn't even my idea. Not quite the slam-dunk win I was hoping for. I look at the calendar. It's the 10th of June. I have to do something.

I look up the number for the local newspaper which I know comes out tomorrow morning. I find the reporter I want to speak to, Duncan Weston. He handles all the biggest stories for the Eastport area. He has his own radio show, too, likes the sound of his own voice a bit, a local celebrity of sorts. He will want to hear my story, probably because it will give him plenty of attention and that's what he loves. I call through to his line and he picks the phone up straight away. I recognise his voice and find myself bizarrely starstruck, which I wasn't expecting.

'Duncan Weston. How can I help you?'

'I assumed you'd have a secretary,' I say, not sure why he would care what I assume about anything.

'She's off with the flu. Who is this?'

'Who I am isn't important, but I have a story for you.'

'I'll decide if you've got a story for me or not.'

'Have you seen those flyers around town? The ones with the red rose on them.'

'They are hard to miss. Are you the crackpot who put them up?'

'Yes, but you can call me Eris.'

'I'm afraid that's yesterday's news, we've got a murder case now so—'

'Let me tell you something about those flyers, Mr Weston. I was raped by the same man who raped the other women on the 12th of June. I went to the police and they told me to drop it, and I am not the only one they did that with. The woman who murdered that man last night was also a victim of the June 12th rapist.'

'How can you know that?'

'Trust me, I just know.'

'What do you know about the woman, or the victim for that matter?'

'I can fill in the blanks for you, all of them.'

'So give me names. The police haven't released them yet.'

'The victim's name was Tristan Walker. The killer's name was Martha Akintola. Tristan raped Martha several years ago and she went to the police. They didn't proceed with the prosecution. Then last year a man broke into Martha's house on June 12th and raped her.'

'The same man, Tristan Walker?'

'No, a different man. But, get this, the man knew about her previous attack, that's why he chose her.'

'How do you know this?'

'Because the same thing happened to me. I was assaulted, I went to the police and they did nothing. Then a few years ago on June 12th, I was raped by the same man that attacked Martha Akintola. He breaks into a different woman's house in the early hours of the morning on the 12th of June.'

'Do you know who he was? What did he look like?'

'He drugged us, put a cover over our faces and then made us shower after he was done. We aren't the only ones either. Seven years ago he raped a woman called Kathy Lewis, she had also been attacked before. Then she was hounded online on this website called The Sanctuary and she couldn't take it anymore, she killed herself.'

'And the police did nothing?'

'No, they kept burying cases that were too difficult to put forward and so for at least the last seven years, he has been getting away with this. The police are only paying attention now because of the murder of Tristan Walker.'

'I don't suppose you know the name of the detective handling the case?'

'I'm sorry, I can't help you there,' I say. Not technically lying. I just don't want to drop Shona White in it. I feel our relationship is precarious, but for now she is on my side or I would have had a visit from the police already today.

'Thank you, Eris, you have been most helpful. I'm guessing you wouldn't agree to a photo to put with the article.'

'You're going to write it then?'

'It's going to be front-page news, don't you worry.'

'Brilliant, no picture though, sorry. I have to go now,' I say, hanging up the phone. It makes me nervous that he might try and work out who I am, even though I have no idea how he would be able to do that over the phone. But my work here is done. I've given the local paper what the police have managed to keep under wraps. No more secrets, the people need to know. I bet you get all hard reading the effects of your handiwork in the local rag.

As for my own mission, what happened to Martha has made me realise that, as much as I might want to play the long game, I could get caught at any moment; and if I get put away then no one will be around to put the pressure on. Martha was right, this is so much bigger than both of us. I need to stay out of prison long enough to make a difference. So, no more jaunts outside to exact justice, no more trial by combat in the dead of night. I'm not strong enough to keep control of a situation like that on my own, I've learned that the hard way. I can still feel Tristan Walker's hand around my throat, pushing me up the wall. I felt completely helpless against him. If Martha hadn't stabbed him I would probably be dead, we both might be. Martha is paying for my arrogance. The screen of the Eris project phone lights up: private number calling. I pick up the phone and press the green button.

'Duncan, I told you that's all I have to say.'

'You are certainly living up to your name. Look at the mess you've made.' A man's voice, not Duncan's. It's you again. For the last three years it's the voice I hear in my nightmares, whispering into my ears, telling me where to wash, how to wash, how to clean myself thoroughly enough to ensure there is no trace of you left on my body. So clear this time. It's exactly as I remember it, calm, cold, devoid of humanity. Somewhere in the back of my mind you only exist as a bogeyman, not someone with a life outside that one night in the summer. Not someone I might bump into on the street or speak to outside of my own subconscious. You are real.

'What do you want?' I say, determined not to let you know you have rattled me. I rush to my back door and make sure it's locked. Skittles the cat is sitting there ready to be let out. I press my index finger to my lips for her to be quiet as though the cat might understand. Skittles blinks and settles patiently.

'You're playing a dangerous game. You need to stop with the stupid posters and trolling that website.' You've found out about that already? That was quick. I try to listen for anything in the background that might indicate who you are or where you are. There is no outside noise though.

'I'm not the only one. You've gone too far. People are starting to put the pieces together. Enjoy your freedom while you can.'

'Listen to me, you bitch, when I find you, I'm going to make our last meeting feel like a day at the park,' you say, the frustration in your voice giving you away.

'You don't know who I am, do you?' I hope you can hear that I'm smiling, a wide-eyed, full-beam excited smile.

'It's only a matter of time, then I am coming for you.' I am not buying it. You're nervous, you're human after all.

'Let's just wait and see who gets who first, you sick bastard. One of your victims is with the police right now telling them all about you. They are looking for you now, you can't stay hidden forever.'

'They won't find me. I've been getting away with this for years.'

'No one was looking for you before. Now I'm looking, and you'd better pray the police find you before I do.'

'They won't find me. But I'll find you.'

'Tell you what, I'll give you a clue. I live on Blossom Hill, blue house. I'll leave the back door open this time. Make it nice and easy for you.' I hang up again. I enjoyed that. Come if you want to, I'm done being scared. I could hear the fear in your voice when you were talking, you're more afraid of me than I am of you.

Again, my overriding feeling is anger, not fear. Accepting that you are a human being was the first step to finding out who you are, and the second step is to make you bleed like humans do. Maybe I can't do it, but I'm sure I can rattle you enough to provoke you. Is there even enough time to make a difference? I hope that by telling you my address you might think better of going after someone else. The temptation of silencing me might be too much. I've shone a light on you, you're going to be the talk of the town now. There's no way any woman living alone will be leaving their windows unlocked at night. I have to think carefully about my next move. Do I booby-trap my house like some kind of eighties John Hughes hijinks movie? I can't have another mistake like Martha on my conscience. I can't pull anyone else into it. Only a man filled with an enormous amount of self-loathing would commit such a heinous crime in such a way. You're not the bogeyman. Confronting both Graham Post and Tristan Walker has cemented in my mind exactly how cowardly and weak these bastards are. I have proven that I can walk away from men like that, men like you, even if there is blood on my hands. I am not the incapable, weak and submissive damsel that everyone thinks I am, including myself. Violence wasn't the path I wanted to take when I started all this, but now, I'm not sure there can be justice without violence. I look through The Sanctuary website, certain now that you are on here somewhere. I'm determined to find you. You will have given something away to your pathetic comrades and I will figure out who you are. Those other men, Walker and Post, they were a diversion. You're the one that I want. Get ready because I will find you.

Chapter 53

Shona knocked on the door of DCI Tarvey's office and he beckoned her inside. She had put together a portfolio of everything she had so far and was going to broach the subject of broadening her investigation even more. She hoped there wouldn't be another victim to add to their list in the coming days. There was so much information to get through and if they wanted to get through it by tonight then she needed manpower to go and interview some of the contributors to The Sanctuary website.

'Did she sign the confession?'

'Yes, that's done.'

'Great. This is going to look great for you when you apply for that promotion.'

'You might change your mind about that in a minute. Can I show you something?' she said, putting the file she had compiled on his desk. He picked it up.

'What's all this?' Tarvey said as he thumbed through the pages.

'It's all the stuff I have on the June 12th rapist. Reynolds, who made the previous complaint, said the guy who came into her house took everything with him, made her shower et cetera. I squashed the case before I even filed it. Well, Martha Akintola has the exact same story. Last year a man broke into her house, raped her and made her shower, took all the evidence. On the same date as well, on the 12th of June. She had also filed a previous rape report with us against Walker that went nowhere. If this comes out it could be implied that we are responsible for the death of Tristan Walker, for not stopping the attacker before he got to Martha Akintola.'

Shona watched Tarvey for a response. God knows they had enough open crimes on their plate right now but she was certain Gail was right about this predator and if she had only followed her instincts instead of orders when Gail first made the report then none of this would be happening.

'Hold on, you think we have a serial rapist in town?'

'Not only that but I think he is deliberately choosing women who have previously reported a rape that has been swept under the carpet. That's at least three now as far as I can tell.'

'And how would he know that?'

'At first, I thought the obvious, that he is a police

officer, but then I found out that there is a local website called The Sanctuary, guys go on there and share information about what they see to be false rape accusations. They post the women's names and so maybe he's got the information from there. We've managed to ascertain the names of a couple of the site contributors. The site moderator has been blocking us as much as possible.'

'What's the significance of The Sanctuary, is it part of a larger movement?'

'From what I can gather, these men believe they are under threat from feminism or something, like they can see the real world and everyone else is living in some kind of enforced reality where women are oppressing men by withholding sex and using the system against them. There are so many sites like this, often with *Alice in Wonderland* themes or *The Matrix*, things that allude to a hidden "real" world. According to some of these guys there is no such thing as rape because sex is a natural urge that needs sating. I could go on but honestly some of the stuff I read on there is both terrifying and bonkers. Akintola mentioned the site during questioning and I have been looking into it. DS Whitcombe managed to work out a few identities from The Sanctuary website and I've sent him to speak to them.'

She realised this was a lot of information all in one go, stuff she had been holding on to, stuff she probably should have updated him on before.

'You also need to get an official statement from the Reynolds woman again. There is no point avoiding that even though it makes us look bad. It makes us look worse if it comes out and we did nothing. You can ask Langford for help with these Sanctuary blokes. Keep it fairly informal for now; if anything makes you suspicious, bring them in for a formal interview. This seems like more than a couple of days' work – how long have you been working on this?'

'Not long, a week maybe. As well as the victim I found from seven years ago who took her own life, there may be others that never came forward. A lot of the guys are smart and talk in a type of code – there are a few things we haven't worked out yet. As for the rapist, I don't know how long he has been doing this, but I do believe there are more victims.'

Tarvey stood up and walked to the window. He sighed as he removed his glasses and pinched the bridge of his nose. As hard as this case was for Shona to investigate, she knew the buck stopped with Tarvey and he knew it, too.

'There must be a catalyst for all of this, that first sloppy attack. These sickos learn on the job as it were. Maybe it's time we made this public. The Eris flyers are already getting a lot of questions from the brass, we take them down and they go back up, it's not gone unnoticed and it's only a matter of time before the press say anything. If we can come out and say we have been looking into it, then that might help. I'll organise a press conference and just hope it's not too late,' Tarvey said, always thinking about the district's reputation.

'I think that's a good idea, sir,' Shona said, knowing that even if a handful of women were more on guard than usual that could make the difference between an assault happening or not.

'Well. Let's backdate the investigation to when you first spoke to Reynolds – this time around, I mean. See if you can get anything from the men from that website. I want cyber to go through that site with a fine-tooth comb and check for any legal infractions. I find it hard to believe they aren't breaking the law. Any other similar cases in our files?'

'The woman I spoke to said she was paralysed at the start of the attack, like he injected her with something. Akintola said the same thing, she thinks it might have been ketamine or some kind of K-mix. I checked through all the June records I could.'

'Assuming Akintola is right about the drug, see if any of the names you have gathered from the website work in a hospital or a veterinary surgery and have access to ketamine. Speak to the lab and see if they know what kind of drug causes temporary paralysis and where one might get hold of some. Also check neighbouring districts, and don't just check for June – who knows why he chose that date, but we can't bank on the fact

319

that he doesn't have other significant dates he also likes to use.'

'Is there any way we can get the names of the members of the Sanctuary website? DS Whitcombe has managed to get a few together because of their lack of internet savvy but there are thousands more members. They have all seen the false accusations. It could be where our rapist is shopping for victims. The website keeps popping up.'

'Who runs it, do you know?'

'Nathan Barker, I spoke to him once already, informally.'

'Well, bring him in. We can question him about Akintola's case first and then see what else he knows. Nathan Barker seems like an obvious suspect to me.'

'I suppose he could be. He has access to all the information his members do, and his own posts don't shy away from the misogyny although he knows the law well enough to keep on the right side of it. There's one problem with him as a suspect though, sir.'

'What's that?'

'I spoke to one of the members who said he was invited to a livestream of an assault on the 12th of June last year – it was dark web invitation only stuff.'

'You're saying there is a video of Akintola's assault out there?'

'If he's right about the date and what he saw then yes.'

'Does Akintola know that?'

'I didn't think it was wise to mention it until we had our hands on the video and knew what we were dealing with.'

'And I'm guessing he didn't record the video,' Tarvey said, exasperated.

'No, it freaked him out and he stopped using the forum soon after.'

'Well, that's something, I suppose. Why does this negate suspicion on Barker?'

'According to the witness, Garfield, Barker was talking on the livestream, several people were, they were giving the rapist instructions or something. If Barker was talking on it, he wasn't the perpetrator. Doesn't mean he doesn't know who is.'

'Talk to him, see what he says. Try to shake him up. Getting hold of that footage has to be a priority now, if it even exists – and you can bet at least one of those sickos screen-recorded it. If we can identify anyone who spoke on there, whether verbally or in message form, I want them all prosecuted as co-conspirators to commit rape.'

'Yes, sir.'

'Good job on this so far, White. Remember though, hush hush for now. I've seen those flyers in town, no doubt the media have too, would be good if we got ahead of this before they come at us. I'll set up a press conference for the morning. Go home and grab a shower, take an hour or so then come back in to speak to Barker. I'll get someone to pick him up. It's going to be a long night. We need to break this story before someone else does. I want everyone ready for action.'

He held out the file and she took it from him. She was unsure now why she had been so nervous to talk to him about it. Granted, no one liked to be handed a load of open cases with almost no chance of closing them. Shona felt like she owed it to these women, to Gail Reynolds and now Martha Akintola. She had to find out who was doing this.

Chapter 54

I have spent hours looking through this website and trying to figure out if you're here. There is so much hate and resentment I find it hard to comprehend, it's a world I didn't know existed. Of course, I have come across the occasional chauvinist, but this makes it all feel so much bigger, as if the ones who aren't saying these things are still thinking them but just holding it all inside. I know that's not true; I know there are good men out there, and I know they outnumber the bad ones but it's just so hard with this imbalance of power. I have it all in a large, gridded table, each section ready to be filled with any snippets of personal information they divulged about themselves. I search for each user. People often use the same username across platforms and when that yields no results, I try a reverse image search on each photo as well.

After just two hours I have gathered fifteen names,

twelve email addresses, eight places of employment, kids' schools, what garage they take their cars to, where they get their hair cut, what their favourite restaurants are. I find them on Facebook, and any other social media I can, then I find their wives or partners, or sometimes even parents and then send through screenshots of the crap they have been spouting. If the police can't do anything, then I am more than happy to throw a grenade into their personal lives. I may not have the chance later on, or tomorrow, if he comes for me. I am exhausted; between night shifts, my night-time jaunts with Martha and then my total of maybe seven hours of sleep over the last week is making me agitated and feeling a little hollow. Still, it's better than being scared. The doorbell rings. I look through the living room window before I go and answer it. It's the usual delivery man holding a parcel for me. I remember I ordered Wi-fi enabled security cameras that can be viewed through an app. My afternoon is mapped out now as I fit them to every doorway in my house, leaving no corner out of shot. I don't know what I want the outcome to be as I do this. Maybe I'll get a shot of your face. I have imagined you with so many faces over the last three years I may have set myself up for disappointment. I take sharp knives that I have borrowed from the hotel and screwdrivers, razors, hammers, anything that I can hurt someone with and hide them in various places all over the house, one in every drawer, under the sofa, under rugs. There are at least three things in every room, completely concealed from view. I am ready if you show up here. I don't think you will though, I don't think you've got the guts.

The welcome feeling of the small throwaway phone in my pocket disrupts my thoughts. Is it you? Is it Grace? Is it another one of your victims?

'Hello,' I answer cautiously, ready to steel myself for a conversation with you.

'Eris?' Grace's voice, a relief.

'You rang off when I asked if you recognised his voice. Do you?'

'Yes. I know who he is.'

'You've got to tell the police, you could stop this from happening to anyone else.'

'It's more complicated than that. I'm sorry.'

'More complicated how?'

'He's my brother,' she says,

The words hit me like a bullet. My empathy swells and I am overcome for the first time in days. I can't imagine what she must have been through, must still be going through. I need a name though.

'I'm so sorry.'

'I knew as soon as I saw the flyer that it was him. We always knew he was wrong, but he got so good at pretending to be normal I guess we just forgot. Like what he did to me was just a one-off, a mistake.'

'We?'

'The family. He was always strange. He idolised our father and when he left for another woman and started a new family it broke him.'

'What's the significance of the 12th of June?'

A timid laugh comes from her mouth, but I know she isn't smiling. 'It's my birthday. I was abused by our dad and my little brother saw. I think it must have messed with his mind because he did exactly the same thing to me a few years later.'

'I'm so sorry. Please. Tell me his name.'

'No, I'm sorry, I can't do this,' she says before ringing off again.

I know more about you now, but I'm still no closer to getting to you. But with every passing moment I am convinced that we will meet again, and I look forward to that moment.

Chapter 55

Shona was grateful for the two hours' respite, every part of her ached and she had a thumping headache. She had been lying in the bath for ten minutes now. Sure, a shower was quicker, but she just didn't feel as clean with one and she needed a brain vacation. The radio played hits from the eighties, slow ones she remembered her mother listening to like Mr Mister and Cutting Crew. She dunked her head under the water and listened to the muffled noise for as long as she could before resurfacing. She couldn't shake the fact that no matter how hard she looked on The Sanctuary website she had seen no mention of Gail Reynolds, no photos, no nothing. As much as she wanted to hang the whole case on the site, she had a horrible feeling it was just an unfortunate side effect of a larger epidemic. She drank her coffee, wishing it was something stronger, but at the moment it was the only thing keeping her awake. The water was starting to chill, and it was a mind over matter decision to stay warm. She didn't want to get out of the water any time soon. Her lids were getting heavy, and this was the most relaxed she had been since Gail Reynolds had turned up at the station last week. Nothing like relentless gnawing guilt to bring on insomnia. With a slight shiver she lowered herself further into the water, trying to keep her knees and hands out of the chilled air surrounding the bath, her wet skin only amplifying the cold. She would get out soon. Just ten more minutes then back on the treadmill.

The Weston radio show started, and it only took a few moments to realise what Duncan Weston was talking about.

'Have you seen those flyers dotted around the town of Eastport? Well, I spoke to the mysterious Eris and asked her what it was all about. Here in our very own little safe haven of Eastport there has been a serial rapist operating for years. Unchecked by the police or maybe even protected by the police. We want to know what is being done about this menace, if anything. According to Eris, the man targets women who have already been victims of this heinous crime because he knows they won't be believed if they report a second rape that goes nowhere. Eris also told me about websites spreading hate speech against women. I have since checked out the website, which I am not allowed to name for legal reasons as it's currently under investigation, but I wonder *how* this is even legal? I'll be taking calls from anyone who may have been affected by this story. Whether you are one of the victims of this vicious perpetrator, someone who knows about these woman-hating blogs or even a police officer willing to talk to us about the case. The town of Eastport wants to hear from you.'

So much for relaxing. Time to get back to the real world. She jumped out of the bath, the cold instantly confirming how tired she was. She desperately wanted to crawl into a warm bed and go to sleep. She threw on some clean clothes, which in itself felt like a new lease of life. She grabbed her laptop and went downstairs, not wanting to wake Aaron, who was napping on the bed. She didn't have long before she had to get back into work. The landline rang and she grabbed it quickly.

'Hello?'

'It's Whitcombe. Sorry, I tried your mobile but there was no answer.'

'I was in the bath, what's wrong?'

'I got those videos. One of the men we spoke to, an Ian Corman, screen-grabbed them and kept them.'

'And he just gave them up?'

'He has a record and so we leaned on him a bit, told him it would go in his favour if he cooperated with us.'

'Good work, Ben. Did you watch them?'

'Not fully, no, they are all dated and go back a few years. I watched enough to confirm it was Martha Akintola in the most recent one. I just wanted to let you know.'

'We need to try and identify these women. How many are there?'

'There are six videos. Corman said they weren't all livestreamed, some of the older ones were pre-recorded and uploaded at a later date – looks like he's only been showing them live for the last four years.'

'We're going to have to let the victims know.'

'Do you want me to do that? Should I tell Akintola?' DS Whitcombe asked with a tone of voice that suggested he really didn't want to do it.

'No, I'll be back in soon, we can do it then,' she said with a heavy sigh. She couldn't imagine how distressing it would be to find out he filmed the whole thing. 'What's the DCI saying?'

'As you can imagine, he is doing his nut as that radio guy pipped him to alerting the public. The phones are going bananas and the higher-ups are on his case already.'

'Does he want me back sooner?'

'No, you're alright, I think it's going to be a long night.'

'Yeah, that's not good. Look, I need to eat something, then I'll be back,' Shona said. She needed to check those tapes, they would almost certainly give them something new to go on, and hopefully provide a decent lead. She immediately felt obligated to tell Gail what they had found, but she knew how much that would compound her anger if not her trauma. She knew Gail would want to see the tape.

Chapter 56

I need a contingency plan and so I pick up my phone and look for Shona White's number. I send her the link to my home surveillance system where everything will be saved so that if anything does happen to me, she will have something to go on. I can't think what else to do but it's getting late now, and I should probably eat. I go to my fridge. I have put a knife in the salad crisper already, so I know there is no food except for cottage cheese that's one day away from being inedible. I grab a fork and eat it anyway. When I am done eating, I look at the prongs on the fork and wonder how much damage it could inflict. To be on the safe side I slide the fork into my boot and conceal it under my jeans. I still don't know if I am nervous or excited, maybe both. I just know I don't want to be caught out. I know so little about you, about what you're capable of. The phone beeps and I get a text back from DI White. She tells me she has some information for me, but she's tied up with work and they have a press conference going out in an hour but if I can meet her at her house at 7pm she has something important to tell me. She gives me the address and tells me to make sure no one sees me, that she wants to keep me out of this like she has done so far. It's true that after Martha was arrested, I was sure DI White would bring me in, but she hasn't. I knew she was on my side. God knows it's taken long enough for her to accept it. It's still light out, so I have a couple of hours until sunset anyway. I'll go to see what she can tell me. I don't think you would come in broad daylight, that's not how you operate, is it?

Her house is about a ten-minute walk from mine if I walk fast enough. I can feel the fork scraping against my ankle as I walk along, I should have faced it the other way around but whatever, too late now, a part of me welcomes the pain. I get to her street and her house is set a little back from the road. There is a car parked in the drive and I can see the upstairs room light is on even though it's still light out. The windows have thick net curtains so I can't see inside. I ring the bell.

'I'll get it,' I hear called out as the door opens, a young man is standing there with his coat on. 'I was just on my way out, Shona's in the kitchen eating dinner, go on through.'

He grabs his keys and presses the button on his car lock as he steps past me and out onto the drive, getting in his white Toyota Yaris. He doesn't look like the kind of man I imagined DI White with. He's pretty in that messy surfer boy way but he looks younger than her. I remember him from the station, spilling coffee all over himself when he walked through the door. I walk through to the kitchen. I can see it at the end of the hallway, there is a radio on and I hear Duncan Weston talking to listeners about what I told him earlier. I feel a pang of pride at the ruckus I have caused. As I walk through the hallway, I feel time stop, everything slows in my mind as I remember something about that night. It's a smell, lavender detergent fills my nostrils as though the pillowcase is over my head again and I instinctively grab at my own throat to check that I can breathe properly. As my senses come back, I realise this isn't a memory of a smell but the smell itself. It's here. As I turn to leave the house, I feel someone thrust me into a doorway and suddenly I'm falling and a door slams as I hit the floor. I am in total darkness, and I know I am in a lot of danger. You found me.

Chapter 57

Shona threw her bag on the desk in the station and headed for the private room they used to view sensitive material. There was nothing she wanted less than to watch these videos, but at the same time there was nothing she wanted more than to catch this man. DS Whitcombe was already in there waiting for her. He gave her a furtive look and then pulled out the chair next to him for her to sit down.

'How bad is it?' she said, knowing it was never not bad.

'I've not seen anything like this. I've only watched two – the first two. You can see him learning from one to the next, things he does differently to make sure he isn't caught.'

'I don't suppose you see his face?'

'That's about the only thing you don't see. The video slash lighting on the ones I watched was quite poor quality, you can see a marked difference in Martha Akintola's assault.'

'Where's DCI Tarvey?'

'After the Weston exclusive on the radio he's had to move the press briefing up. As you can imagine he's delighted.'

'Right well, you go grab us both a coffee and have a little break while I catch up and watch these.'

'Thank you, ma'am,' he said, looking a little green around the gills.

She was alone in the room, and she pressed play on the first video. The video itself was a square inside a webpage. She didn't recognise the domain name, but she jotted the name down anyway. Next to the square where the film was showing was a chat box and she saw a string of user numbers, no names but each one was a different spectator. The view count box showed that seventy-three people were watching this. The box showed a living room in someone's house. He adjusted the camera and positioned it facing the ground and then he meticulously moved any furniture out of the way and laid some plastic sheeting down. Shona could see he was of medium build but beyond that there was nothing. He was a black figure moving in a darkened room. He pulled some tape out of his pocket and laid it on the ground, then he pulled a pillowcase out of his pocket, too. It was plain so there was no lead there. In his hand she saw a vial of liquid, like the ones from a doctor's and he plunged a needle into it before leaving the room. The camera was still rolling on the living room floor.

Shona knew what was coming next but still didn't feel prepared for what she was about to see. What if she knew the woman? It didn't bear thinking about. He placed his victim on the ground carefully, there was no malice in his action, he moves slowly and with care, but she was like a rag doll, lifeless and limp. He brushed her hair out of her face and looked at her, really considered her face and features for several moments before reaching for the pillowcase and placing it over her head and taping it with duct tape around the neck, checking that it was loose enough for her to breathe. There she was: a faceless body. The guilt of being relieved at not recognising the woman hit Shona. Where was she now? Was she even still alive?

Returning to the camera and adjusting the angles so that she was the star of the show, he zoomed in a little, focusing on her torso, as though her limbs were an afterthought and unimportant to the frame. When he was finally happy with the direction of his film, he started to undress her slowly and carefully. She didn't move, she still didn't know he was there, she was asleep. Was she dreaming? Shona continued to watch, feeling sicker with every passing moment as he removed all of his clothing except for his mask and climbed on top of his victim. Not by any means the worst part of this video but definitely an added layer of disgusting were the comments rolling by the side of the film. People encouraging him, calling her names, positively gleeful about what was happening. This part of the job never got easier, but someone had to watch these. She could take it. The urge to turn it off was immense but she hadn't learned anything she could use from this, she had to keep going. She watched to the end, the video cutting after he was finished. DS Whitcombe was right about the resolution, there was nothing useful here. Maybe she should start with Akintola and work backwards. She clicked on the most recent file as DS Whitcombe walked into the room with two coffees.

'Grim, isn't it?'

'That poor woman. We have to find her.' As Shona spoke, she realised she had been crying. She wiped her cheek and took the hot drink, sipping it, the scalding liquid distracting her momentarily from the images that persisted in her mind.

'I can do this if you want, you don't have to sit in,' Whitcombe offered insincerely.

'I think I should. Is the press briefing done?'

'Tarvey's still fielding questions. He's holding his own though. Doesn't help that the radio blew up earlier with people calling in about it. They extended Weston's show, it's still on.'

'Have you seen Aaron? I couldn't see him when I got here.'

'He had an emergency with his mum. He's had to pop over there.'

'Right, let's carry on then. Ready?' she asked, Whitcombe nodded, and she pressed play on the recording from exactly one year ago, the rape of Martha Akintola.

Chapter 58

I pull my phone out of my pocket and try to dial but there is no signal, I put my torch on instead and see that I am in a cellar. There are no windows and I run my fingers along the wall and feel the smooth metal, you've built a room that doubles as a Faraday cage. Clever boy. It's you, I know it is. I think I knew the moment I saw you on the doorstep, but then I think that about everyone. There is always that voice in the back of my mind that tells me to stop being paranoid, that it can't be you. You wouldn't be the first person I have suspected in the last three years. There are some screens built flush into the wall, but they are off. I shine my light on the ground and see plastic sheeting taped down. I wonder what you have planned for me. Nothing good. There is nothing else in this room, nothing to use as a weapon, nothing to hide behind, just a big metal box.

I don't know what I expected you to look like, but you look so normal, attractive even, not ugly. Sure, maybe there is something a little off about you, but there is something a little off about me. Whatever I am feeling right now, it isn't fear. In a strange way it's relief. We found each other again. Reunited. I'm not the woman I used to be; you saw to that. I sit on the ground and turn my torch off, preserving my battery. I watch the door and wait for you to open it. I am ready to meet my maker.

The cold hard floor is permeating through my jeans and into my buttocks. I can feel the hard edges of my bones against the floor, and I wish you would just get on with it. Let's do this. I wonder what you are doing up there, sharpening knives? Getting a noose ready? Maybe you aren't even up there at all, maybe you went out. I decide to go up the steps and see if I can see or hear anything. Footsteps pace up and down the hall outside the room. There is a slight mania to them, and I realise you're panicking. I've disrupted your pattern. I don't know if this is good news for me or not, but I know you haven't really planned this to the meticulous level you usually like to. Something has changed, you think you're about to be caught, maybe? Or maybe you want to get caught. I remember the fork in my boot, and I reach for it, sliding it instead into my sleeve and holding the head in the palm of my hand, comforted by the metal prongs that dig into my flesh. I pull out one of my laces and ball it in my pocket. I don't know why I need it yet, but I am all about contingency plans these days. It occurs to me that no one knows where I am, I have no friends, I haven't turned up to work for the last couple of days so I don't think they will report me missing. I'm all alone in the world, all alone in this room. This thought should scare me, but in reality it just makes me more resolved to defend myself. I have counted on people in the past and they let me down. Consistently and without fail I was abandoned by friends and family. My future starts with me, and I am getting out of here alive.

I hear the key in the lock and go back down the steps. I'm not going to cower or hide though, I'll just stand here. You'll find me soon enough anyway, let's get this over with.

You seem smaller than the monster I had envisaged in my mind, the friendly man who greeted me at the door is gone. I see you now, I see how broken you are behind the façade and how pathetic you are. I can't help myself. I burst out laughing.

'No wonder you covered our faces,' I say as I clutch my stomach, deliberately exaggerating my amusement. You rush down the steps clumsily, almost tripping. This isn't how you like to deal with women; I'm a little too awake for your liking. You charge towards me, but I am ready, I raise my arm and slam the fork into that pretty blue eye. You stagger backwards, your one good eye wide with amazement, shock even. You weren't expecting that.

'What the fuck did you do?' you burble, your voice high-pitched, scared, weak.

'Not as much fun when we're conscious, is it?'

The blood streams down your cheek and I rush up the stairs to the door before you have a chance to right yourself. I slam the door and lock it. I run towards the exit. I have every intention of leaving when that smell hits me again. It's like being back there in my lounge, on the floor, naked. I look at the landline and consider calling the police but then I remember what they have done for me in the past. Precisely nothing. You could pin this all on me, you could say I just randomly attacked you. There is no proof that you are the man I know you to be. You just look like my victim. You could get away with it, move to another town, start all over again. I have to stop you once and for all.

Chapter 59

Shona had watched three of the films so far. They weren't that long, which was the only blessing. No consolation for the victims, of course. He made no mistakes, knew how to position the camera so he couldn't be scrutinised. Shona knew what the next one would be; it would be Gail's, the rape she had all but accused her of making up. No point putting it off. She pressed play and then sat back in the chair and witnessed everything, from him standing over her body to him violating her. That's when something started to creep up on her. For a few moments she didn't even realise what it was she was noticing. There was something not right, something she couldn't place that she knew was wrong. It was the silliest thing, and nothing that would stand up in court, but it was his feet, the positioning of his feet to be precise. One of his feet turned inwards as he stood over her. A cold chill swept over her as she continued watching the film, with the knowledge that she now wished she didn't possess, looking for any indication that she might be wrong but every passing second of the film just confirmed her suspicions. If she hadn't known him as well as she knew herself, she wouldn't even have noticed it. It was Aaron Langford, her fiancé. It couldn't be. How could it be? She forwarded to the part where he was naked, this video much clearer than the others she had watched. He had positioned the camera a little wider so she could see more of him and as she did, she knew. It was him. Oh God, it was him. Nauseated by her own blindness, she stopped the tape and stood up.

'I need to speak to the DCI,' she said before rushing out of the room and to the DCI's office.

She went to her bag to get her phone to call Aaron, but her phone wasn't there. She tried to remember the last time she had it. She'd put it in her bag at home. He must have taken it. Fucking bastard.

'Did you see any of that? They fucking crucified me,' DCI Tarvey said, irate. 'Tell me you've got something.'

'I have, but you're not going to like it.'

'Well, that's just how today is going. Lay it on me.'

'I've been watching the videos we retrieved from one of the Sanctuary members and—'

'Do they confirm that Akintola and Reynolds were his victims?'

345

'They do, sir,' she said, taking a deep breath, unsure how to even say what she wanted to say next. Tarvey went to speak again but obviously thought better of it after seeing the look on her face.

'What is it?'

'I recognised him.'

'You can see his face?'

'No, his body.'

'How? What?' He was confused.

'It's Aaron. DS Aaron Langford,' she blurted out, still struggling to believe it. 'Come and see the video, you'll see what I mean.'

He followed her into the viewing room. Once she had seen it there was no way to unsee it. The way he held things, the way he walked, his hunch, his gait, everything about a person that makes them unique that you wouldn't notice unless you really knew what you were looking for.

How could it be Aaron? She searched her mind for any indication that it could be someone else, but she had seen his naked body enough times to know what it looked like. In the older videos with the shitty resolution, it was easier to hide, but not now with the ultra-high definition.

'You're sure that's him?' Tarvey said.

'More than sure. I would bet my life on it,' she said, which was actually what she was doing. If by some miracle it wasn't him, and she was sure it was, then how would he forgive her for an accusation like this? But none of that mattered because it was him, she knew it was him. God, what an idiot she had been. Pretty blue eyes and a perfect smile, that's all it took to blindside her. She tried to remember if there had been any indication of this. Of course there hadn't, if there had been she would have seen it. Wouldn't she? A thought crept up on her without notice. Was he only with her because he had heard what had happened with Post? Did that make her more attractive to him? It made her feel sick, his hands on her after what he had done to all those other women.

'Where is he now? Do you know?' Tarvey asked.

'He's taken my phone, I have no idea where he is. He might be at his mother's, Whitcombe said he had an emergency there. Presumably he knows nothing about the fact that we finally have these videos now, so I don't think he will be hiding. He may think he still has time. But then I guess he lies all the time so he could be anywhere. Please, sir, I'm begging you. Please don't sit me out of this one.'

'I'll get a team together and we'll head over there now. Are you OK? Do you need some time?'

'Oh no, I'm fine. Let's go get him.'

Chapter 60

You are trapped in your little room, and I am in your house. I consider burning it to the ground with you in it but although that's a terrible way to die, that just doesn't feel personal enough given our connection. I grab a knife from the kitchen, it's the biggest weapon I can find. I need to get back to you quickly before you manage to get on top of the shock you are probably in right now. I listen against the door. I can hear you moaning, you aren't near the door. I flick the switches outside the room, one of them must turn the light on. I want you to see me stick the knife in. I turn the key and push the handle, leaning against the heavy oak until I can see into the room. You're lying face down on the plastic-covered floor at the bottom. It feels a bit like poetic justice at this point. Walking slowly down the steps, I try to be as silent as possible although I know you know I am there, I sense a still-

348

ness in you. The knife is steady in my hands as I hold it out in front of me. I'm not afraid to use it, I'm not afraid to die here either. One way or another this twisted relationship ends. I need to silence you once and for all. You clamber to your feet. I almost laugh as you swipe out for the knife, but you obviously can't see properly as you miss by a clear foot. Only having one eye can fuck up your depth perception. You're grunting like a wounded animal and I can't help but chuckle. I don't know whether it's my lack of fear or the fact that I am awake that bothers you the most. You're so angry and it's making me happy to see you so out of control.

'You should see a doctor for that,' I say with fake sincerity.

'You fucking bitch.' You spit the words out like venom.

'It's weird, I thought you would be bigger, stronger somehow, but you're pathetic. I suppose that's why you had to drug us all to do it.'

'You got what you deserved. You all did.'

'Did your sister get what she deserved, too?' I say, knowing you don't think I know about that. I can feel the smile spreading across my face as a look of powerlessness passes over yours. I have talked to you so much over the last three years, it's strange to finally have you answering back. I've got to say you're kind of a disappointment. But I guess that's the point, isn't it?

'So what's your plan now? You going to teach me a lesson?'

'I'm going to kill you,' I say with more clarity and conviction than I have said anything in my life.

Watching as you launch yourself at me, I almost feel bad for how this story is going to end. I'll admit I wasn't expecting it and as you tackle me to the ground I can feel how weak you are. No longer this larger-than-life ominous faceless presence in my mind – now you're just a bloke with a fork in his eye. You look ridiculous. Laughing seems to be the most powerful weapon I have at the moment. I can see it's throwing you off your game. You thought you were special, strong maybe; I'm just proving that you're nothing. I can see that you don't know what to do with someone who fights back. You're really not used to this.

'So why me then? Why did you choose me?'

'I'm going to kill you.' You repeat my words back to me and I laugh again. If you could see the spit hanging from your lip as you hover over me then you would laugh, too.

Chapter 61

The last few years played through Shona's mind. She had always assumed that her lack of proper connection to Aaron was because of her inability to form proper connections. Did he see that in her? She was part of his mask. A young good-looking guy who didn't date or have a relationship was a little on the suspicious side and so he had brought Shona in to avoid any questions. Lucky for him she was happy with their relationship being unconventional and maybe even a bit cold. She thought back to the last time they had sex a few days ago. It was after Reynolds came into the station. Was that what got him going? Seeing his victim again made him excited and she was the sucker who obliged the impulses he had. She was the spare broken woman he kept for when he needed a fix. She wanted to throw up but now wasn't the time. All those reports she had read and all the videos she had seen about what he had done to the women. She tried to think if there was any way she could have known but there was nothing. Even now with hindsight she couldn't quite get her head around it, but she knew it was true. It was him. Her spectacularly poor judgement of character had really won the gold prize this time. Was any of it even real? Shona tried to remind herself that predators knew how to play people, that it wasn't her fault. That wasn't what people would say though, was it? They might even imply she had been helping him cover it up, especially when it came to how she had treated Gail Reynolds. No, she would have to put this right, she would have to stop him and bring him to justice not only to clear her name but to make him pay.

She put on her stab vest and went to find Aaron. She knew if she ran it past Tarvey he would tell her to stay away but she couldn't. This was beyond personal, and she would take any disciplinary action coming to her. Tarvey didn't need the headache of her involvement in the arrest, but she wasn't thinking straight. He must be feeling almost as stupid as she was. Aaron was one of his officers, someone he saw every single day. For all Shona's faults she had at least started an investigation into the 12th of June rapist. It was hard to reconcile that it was the man she had planned to spend the rest of her life with. Her heart thumped like a war drum as she pulled the seatbelt across her and the engine started. This was it.

Chapter 62

I should be afraid but I'm really not. Maybe I'm running on pure adrenaline but there's nothing you can do to me. I'll cut my own throat before I let you violate me again but, somehow, I don't think you can. I push you off me and clamber to my feet. I have lost the knife, it slid across the room in the fall.

'We both know you aren't capable of killing me. You're a coward. I know you better than anyone,' you sputter desperately.

'Fuck you.' I smirk as I watch you struggling to get to your feet, the fork still in your eye.

'You've assaulted a police officer. You are in so much trouble.'

I step backwards slowly, knowing that you are no match for me in your current state, the blood draining from you, dripping down your face. If only I had pushed that fork in a little deeper.

'There's no way out of this for you now. What are they going to say when they see your face? You can't explain that away as an accident. Unless you pretend you fell in the dishwasher or something.'

'I'll tell them you did it.'

'Then I'll tell them what you did,' I say with a smile.

'No one's going to believe a lying bitch like you.'

'But they'll look into you, and I bet they find something. The only reason you got away with it for so long before is because no one was looking, no one knew what to look for. Yeah, you were smart in one way, but I bet you weren't in others. It's different when they have a name. And look at this room. You can't tell me anyone is going to think this is normal?'

I can see I am getting to you. You're not giving up though, you rush forward yet again, almost falling. I'm a little embarrassed for you, if I am honest, I can see you're exhausted. I scan the room for the knife and see it at the same time as you. You throw yourself on top of it to stop me from getting there first and I jump on your back. I know if you get that knife then I am finished. Pure stubbornness is driving me on. You don't get to win this time. I punch you repeatedly in the back, the neck, the shoulders. I know if I just push your head into the ground, it will drive the fork into your brain but I don't think I can do it. Part of me isn't ready for this to be over. You seem to understand this at the same time as I do and reach up, pulling the

354

fork from your eye. I half expect it to come out with the eyeball attached but it doesn't. You're screaming again but so am I. I keep punching though I am not sure if it's even slowing you down. I just want to hurt you, I don't care if I hurt myself in the process.

I'm tiring and I don't know how much longer I can do this for. As you start to push yourself up, me still on your back, between my thighs again just like old times, except this time my hands are clawing at your throat, I remember the boot lace in my pocket and grab it. I'm thankful the end is sticking out. I manage to loop it around your head as you are pushing yourself up. I pull it tight and quickly slip it into a knot and knot it again as you buck against me, not the slow deliberate movements of the last time we met, but the urgency of someone clinging to life. It's tight enough that it's restricting your breathing on its own. We collapse to the ground together, like lovers after an epic night. I can hear you muttering, and your face is turning red. I scramble away from you on my elbows but before I know it, you're on top of me, your bloodied fingers around my throat, your face hovering above mine as you try to choke me. Everything is fading but so is your grip, the lace around your neck cutting into you now as you struggle to stay conscious. As I black out, I hear voices and from the corner of my eye I see boots as you're suddenly no longer on top of me. I feel weightless and all I want to do is sleep.

Chapter 63

Shona opened the door to her soon to be mother-in-law's house to hear a commotion coming from the understairs storage. She burst in with the other officers and there it was. There was no longer any need to question what she thought she saw. There was Aaron on the blood-smeared ground snarling like a rabid animal. She didn't have time to register what was going on before rushing forward and pulling him back.

'Call for an ambo,' she shouted to anyone who was listening, one of the uniforms would do it.

Gail Reynolds was lying on the ground, Shona quickly reached down to check her pulse. It was there. Thank God. Gail groaned and opened her eyes.

'You're OK, Gail, we're here,' Shona said, smoothing her hair out of her eyes.

'Is he dead?' Gail croaked.

Shona turned to look at the uniformed officers who

were with Aaron. He was cuffed and they had cut the lace around his neck.

'No, he's not. But he's going to prison for what he's done. We've got evidence, that's how we found you. How did he get you here?'

'I got a text from you saying you had something for me. It must have been him. He gave me this address. I'm so stupid.'

The paramedics rushed into the room and started to tend to Gail.

'No. You're amazing. Don't forget it,' Shona said as she moved out of the way.

'His sister, you need to find his sister, he did this to her, too.'

'Don't worry about all that now, just rest. We'll find all of his victims,' Shona said. She would interrogate him herself if she had to, if she was allowed to. Hard to shake the feeling of complicity in what he had done. How hadn't she known?

Shona couldn't even look at Aaron. Nothing had been real between them. She was nothing but a disguise for him, a way to fit in and hide in plain sight. Even thinking back now, there were no clues as to what kind of man he was. She walked out into the hallway and up the stairs. The bedroom door was locked. She opened it and saw his mother inside, one wrist tied to the bedstead. The smell of faeces and urine was over-whelming, medicine vials and pills stacked next to the bed and a needle sticking out of her arm. He had given her a fatal overdose, obviously feeling the noose closing in on him. Shona had only met his mother once and that had been a very strange experience. She kept telling Shona her son was evil. He had told her his mother had dementia, but now Shona wondered if it was something else, was she trying to warn her? This was all too much, and she felt like such a fool, trying to remind herself that she wasn't the only one who fell for his lies, who believed his mask.

This house had always been off limits to Shona, never spoken but heavily implied that it was a miserable place. There would be the inevitable debriefing and an endless stream of questions she would have to answer. One thing was for sure though, she couldn't keep working for the police. This would forever be a stain on her record, on her soul. She would be judged by Aaron's actions and by her lack of actions. Who would trust a detective who couldn't even detect a serial rapist living under her nose. It was decided, she would find something else to do, something where she could affect real change and help people like she always wanted instead of just keeping the peace inside the institution, letting scum like Graham Post get away with what he did just so that people wouldn't hate her. It was crystal clear now that she had to resign, and while that thought might have filled her with dread in the past, this time it made sense. She didn't want this anymore. She stepped out of the house into the sunlight and watched as the circus started. They would pull Aaron's life apart and God only knew what else they would find.

'You OK?' DCI Tarvey said, a pained expression on his face. Of course he knew she wasn't OK. Out of everyone, she imagined he might be the only person who might feel more responsible than she did.

'He's got a sister, someone needs to notify her, I would like it to be me if that's possible.'

'I don't know if that's a good idea. You're already in deep shit for being here at all.'

'I know, but we know each other, and I think it would be best if I let her know what's happened.'

'Take Whitcombe with you then. Then I think you need an extended break.'

'I'm going to resign, sir, I don't see any way back from this for me.'

'I understand,' he said, and she believed that he did. He stepped away and left her standing there. Her first instinct had been to look for Aaron for some comfort, just seconds before realising that he was gone. Not only was he gone but he was never really there. He had been a lie, everything about him a creation to hide the beast inside. How could she ever forgive herself for not seeing through him? How could she move past this?

Chapter 64

I can't keep my eyes off the clock. The second hand seems to move slower the closer I get to the morning. I'm in a hospital bed, aware that you're somewhere else in this hospital handcuffed to a bed instead of out raping someone. It's the very early hours of the 12th of June and I got to you before the police did in the end, like I said I would. Maybe you got to me, too. I wonder which woman out there is just sleeping peacefully and will continue to do so, completely unaware of what this night would have held for her if I hadn't intervened, if I hadn't pushed and pushed. I saved myself and I saved the women who would have been me in the future had he remained unchecked. Despite everything I feel like I have drawn a line under all of this. I have no more revenge or justice left in me. I have no more desire to do violence.

Well, maybe a little.

One summer. One stranger.
One killer . . .

A scorching standalone thriller.

Available in paperback, ebook and audiobook now.

Everything you think
you know is a lie...

The second Miles and Grey novel
from the Katerina Diamond.

Available in paperback, ebook and audiobook now.

Some things can't be forgiven . . .

No one can protect
you from your past . . .

The fourth in the deliciously
dark Miles and Grey series.

Available in paperback, ebook and audiobook now.

Their darkest secrets won't
stay buried forever. . .

The fifth explosive, twisty novel
in the Miles and Grey series.

Available in paperback, ebook and audiobook now.

I'm alive. But I can't be saved . . .

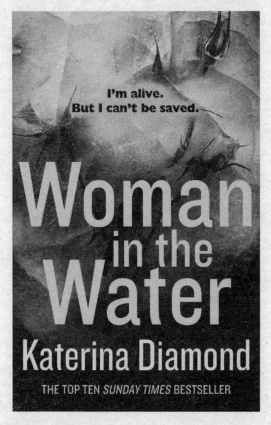

The sixth in the *Sunday Times*
bestselling Miles and Grey series.

Available in paperback, ebook and audiobook now.

Truth or lies?

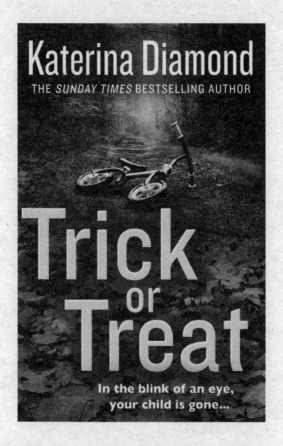

The seventh instalment in the completely addictive series.

Available in paperback, ebook and audiobook now.